TAKING THE REINS

This Large Print Book carries the
Seal of Approval of N.A.V.H.

TAKING THE REINS

CAROLYN MCSPARREN

THORNDIKE PRESS

A part of Gale, Cengage Learning

GALE
CENGAGE Learning·

Farmington Hills, Mich • San Francisco • New York • Waterville, Maine
Meriden, Conn • Mason, Ohio • Chicago

GALE
CENGAGE Learning®

LIBRARY OF CONGRESS CATALOGING-IN-PUBLICATION DATA

McSparren, Carolyn.
 Taking the reins / by Carolyn McSparren. — Large print edition.
  pages ; cm. — (Thorndike Press large print clean reads)
  ISBN 978-1-4104-7060-7 (hardcover) — ISBN 1-4104-7060-1 (hardcover)
  1. Widows—Fiction. 2. Veterans—Fiction. 3. Large type books. I. Title.
 PS3563.C84T35 2014
 813'.6—dc23   2014009552

Printed in Mexico
1 2 3 4 5 6 7 18 17 16 15 14

Taking the Reins is dedicated to Joanna Wilburn, Bob Martin and the wonderful clinicians who teach me to drive my big half-Shire mare, Zoe. Thanks to the Nashoba Carriage Driving Association, my local driving club, for their stories, and their comradeship. Thanks for Meredith Giere, who makes sure I do things right on my harness and carriage, and to Sam Garner, who taught me to drive in the first place. Thanks to Pam Gamble, who drives a big carriage in downtown Memphis and showed me how to run a stable for very large horses in a very small city space. Finally, thanks to Beverly Hollingsworth, who conned me into my first carriage ride behind a nasty little Welsh pony named Picadilly. I've been hooked ever since.

CHAPTER ONE

Charlotte Nicholson, known as Charlie, slewed the elderly pickup through the farm's front gate in a cloud of dust. She slammed on her brakes, slid to a stop five feet behind the Veterans Administration van, climbed out and ran to meet her class. She was late. Her father, the colonel, would kill her.

"Sorry, Daddy," she said as she raced up to him. "I had to wait while they loaded the oats into the truck, and then they could only find three of the big trace mineral blocks I need for the pasture."

Her father stood straight and tall, eyes on the van doors. "Charlotte Abigail, you are ten minutes late. You should learn to budget your time better, if you expect to teach this class."

"You *hired* me to run the farm. You *blackmailed* me into teaching. Anyway, I didn't miss anything. The van just got here."

7

"That's hardly the point. They were late. You should not have been." He didn't turn his head to look at her but continued to smile at the van doors as they soughed open. "I'm not blackmailing you. Call it other duties as assigned."

Right. Maybe not blackmail, but he'd implied that this class was her baptism by fire. If she could train this small group of wounded vets to drive the draft horses the farm bred, all the while managing the daily operation of the place, she'd prove she was competent to take over the draft horse operation on her own without her father's constant oversight.

He'd never cared about the farm, but it had always been her paradise. The place where her grandfather taught her to love horses.

Since the colonel owned the farm until his death, when it would pass to Charlie, she didn't have much choice but to follow his orders. She loved the colonel in spite of what he called their *issues,* but she'd have preferred to love him from afar after he moved to a luxury condominium in Outer Mongolia. Harder to micromanage her from there.

Teaching this group couldn't be tougher than teaching her seventh-grade English class at their last post. These veterans actually *wanted* to learn. Her seventh-graders definitely hadn't. Thank heaven, her daughter, Sarah, had been in the eighth grade. No teenager liked to be taught by her mother. Sarah would have died of embarrassment.

Except for the vacations Charlie had spent with Granddad, she'd never lived in a house that didn't belong to the United States Army. She swore she and Sarah would have a real home. Even if it killed her.

Her father hadn't expected his grant to teach wounded veterans to drive draft horses with an aim of future employment would be approved so soon. *I had planned to hire someone to teach while DeMarcus and Maurice continued to handle the barn and the horses,* he'd told her. *Now that you and Sarah are living here, it's the perfect opportunity for you to show me what you can do.*

Asking her father to provide a home for her and Sarah after Charlie's husband was killed had been the toughest thing she had ever done, but she had no money until Steve's death benefits kicked in. That might take a year. In the meantime, it was go home to daddy or live in her truck.

The colonel's invitation was gracious. Once she got his attention he was always gracious. He refused to admit, though, that so long as he controlled the purse strings, he controlled her.

Now that Steve was dead, any man who tried to control her was in for the fight of his life and that included dear old Dad. She intended to be her own boss from here on. No more men telling her what to do. Definitely no more warriors.

Being back with the horses was heaven. Living as a hired hand in the old home was not. She simply had to convince the colonel she could run it alone. This was her chance.

"Come on, Charlie girl, let's greet our guests," he said, taking her arm.

What little confidence she had fled, and if she didn't already have ulcers, she was about to develop them. But she had to continue to talk a good game. Otherwise, the vets would never trust her to train them.

What if she messed up? What if she made them worse? She shivered despite the ninety-five-degree temperature. "Remember, Charlie, Don't teach the disabilities. Teach the people." Her father waved to the van and whispered back, "Of course, if you don't think you can manage . . ."

Talk about fighting words. Shoot, yeah, she could do it. "There are times I hate you." She smiled as she said it, but he knew she was only half kidding.

"Most children hate their parents when they act like parents."

"Oh, is that what you're doing?"

"Absolutely." The colonel stepped forward with his hand outstretched. His worn jeans and red polo shirt couldn't conceal his military posture. His short hair might be gray, but his belly was still flat. He would always look like Colonel Sanders, the Kentucky Fried Chicken front man, as he had before he retired. Well, semiretired. Technically, he was a civilian psychologist volunteering at the VA hospital in Memphis. This whole project was his baby. He'd written the grant that paid for it.

He had as much an investment in the success of this program as she did. And it had been a long time since she'd made a success of anything. She squared her shoulders and pasted a smile on her face. She'd pull this off if it killed her.

"Welcome to Great Horse Farm. Come on down," the colonel said as the first figure appeared in the doorway. The woman inside didn't take the hand he offered but scrambled down the few steps, carrying a duffel bag almost as big as she was.

"Colonel Vining, *sir,*" she said. She was only about five foot two and weighed maybe a hundred and ten pounds. She wore huge wraparound sunglasses and kept her face turned to the right. Her voice was unexpectedly deep, and for a moment Charlie thought she might salute, but she caught herself. After all, none of them was officially in the military any longer.

"Welcome, Mary Anne," the colonel said. He didn't offer to shake her hand; nor did she offer it. Despite the August heat, she wore a long-sleeved plaid cotton shirt over tight jeans, and had tied a plain blue silk scarf over her ears and knotted it at the nape of her neck. A khaki leather glove covered her right hand.

"Mary Anne Howell, may I introduce my daughter, your instructor, Charlie Nicholson. Charlie, this is Mary Anne."

"Ma'am," Mary Anne said. No smile. No handshake. She picked up her duffel and stepped aside as a grizzled man with sun-roughened skin and close-cropped gray hair backed down the stairs.

"Come on, Major," he said, "time to get out. Bring your gear with you." He might have been coaxing a puppy out of a crate.

As he backed away, a tall, thin man stepped off the bus. Hatless, he blinked in the sunlight. His hair hadn't been cut in a while, and whoever had done it last hadn't so much barbered as butchered it. He might even have whacked at it himself. It must have been corn-gold when he was younger. Now the gray had muted it to pewter. His face bore the creases and wrinkles that came from living under a fierce sun.

"Afternoon, Colonel, ma'am," said the shorter man with a broad grin. "Retired Master Sergeant Sean O'Riley at your service. I won't shake hands if you don't mind." He lifted his right arm. "I don't have the hang of this danged mechanical gadget yet. I could crush your fingers."

At first glance the sergeant's prosthetic hand looked remarkably natural. The skin tone matched O'Riley's tan, but the skin itself was too perfect. Charlie thought a couple of freckles or liver spots would make it more lifelike.

O'Riley indicated the man beside him, who had neither moved nor spoken. "This is Major Jacob Thompson. Jake, come on over and meet these good folks."

The man took two steps forward, shook hands with the colonel and nodded to Charlie.

He then took two steps back and waited patiently.

As the daughter of an army psychologist, Charlie had grown up watching her father's patients come and go. She recognized at once that this man had hit the disconnect switch.

"Hey, get me down off this thing before I fall on my face!"

The tenor voice came from behind the van.

"Hang on," grumbled a baritone. "Or I'll shoot you off this lift and onto the road!"

Charlie heard a whir, and a moment later a young man — a very young man — barreled around the end of the bus in his wheelchair like an Indy racer. "Hey. I'm Mickey Peterson. Bet you didn't expect to have to teach *me* to drive a carriage, did you?"

The colonel smiled broadly. "Actually, Mickey, we have a carriage set up for your wheelchair."

"I'm not spending the rest of my life in this thing," Mickey said. "Soon as I get strong enough on my braces, I'll race you *and* your carriage." He pumped the air. "Hey, Hank," he called over his shoulder. "Bring me my gear, will ya?"

"You got it." The man in question walked up behind Mickey and dumped the duffel onto Mickey's lap.

"Hey, man, not so hard!"

"Why? You can't feel it."

"Wanna bet?" Mickey whispered, "Jerk."

"So you must be Hank," the colonel said.

"Second Lieutenant Hank Ames." He shook the colonel's hand and tossed a dazzling smile at Charlie. "Ma'am?"

"Charlotte Nicholson," she said. "Everyone calls me Charlie."

Hank's hand was rough and strong, like the rest of him, but his nails were manicured. He had the broad shoulders and slim hips of an athlete, and stood eye to eye with her own five-ten. He was also one of the handsomest men Charlie had ever seen outside a Ralph Lauren ad. His too-long mop of black curly hair had been razor cut and he boasted incredible chocolate eyes, and teeth that looked as though every one had been professionally capped and bleached. His Levi's were starched and pressed, and his plaid rodeo shirt had snaps down the front instead of buttons.

She glanced at his feet. Yep. The boot-cut jeans were too long and bunched at the ankle over cowboy boots, the way real cowboys wore them. Expensive boots, from the look of them. Ostrich, maybe.

"You're the rodeo rider," the colonel said.

Instantly the man's handsome face clouded. "Used to be. Need two feet in the stirrups to ride saddle broncs."

Major Jake Thompson considered climbing back in the van and returning to Memphis, but while he hesitated, the doors closed and the engine started.

He turned to follow the others and met the woman's eyes. Charlie?

She smiled at him. He surprised himself by smiling back, then felt his face flush. She wasn't beautiful, but her gray eyes were warm and her mouth was generous. He dropped his gaze, surprised that he had responded to her.

She was tall and straight and strong, the way he remembered his sisters being.

Don't think about your sisters.

Sean grabbed his arm and propelled him forward to join the group. "Come on, Jake, my bucko. You're going to love it here. You'll be better in no time."

He doubted that, but he didn't argue. He smelled the dry summer Bermuda grass, closed his eyes and heard the breeze whispering through the big oak trees. What would it feel like to lie in the grass again and stare at the stars the way he had as a kid? When everything seemed possible. When his family was still permitted to speak to him. Before he had all those lives on his conscience.

When he'd dreamed of all the places he'd go after he left the farm behind, he hadn't included Iraq and Afghanistan on his wish list.

"Man, smell that manure," Hank said. "I do love the smell of horse."

"Are you kidding me?" Mickey turned in his chair. "Manure? Really?"

"Really," Jake said, butting into the conversation. Better than the garbage Dumpsters in downtown Memphis. Better than the crowds and noise that never seemed to stop, even at four in the morning when he walked to escape the nightmares. When he saw all those faces. Even after the colonel took charge and rented him a room in a halfway house, he'd stayed only long enough for meals before he began those lone walks again.

Most of the men who hung out on the street and under the overpasses in the downtown badlands had problems with alcohol or drugs. Once they discovered he hardly carried any money, they didn't hassle him. Everyone left him alone. He was sober and clean, and he didn't beg.

In any case, even if he'd had the money to dull the pain, he wouldn't have been able to choose between all the various substances. Since the very, very bad early days after leaving the military, he hadn't been able to make a decision about anything.

His rational mind knew that wearing mismatched socks would not cause a meteor to fall on Tennessee. But the voice in his head whispered, *But if it did, it would be your fault.*

You give yourself too much power, the colonel had said in one of their sessions.

Okay, so I choose the wrong pair of socks and get some poor old lady hit by a truck because she's staring at my ankles. Same difference.

He knew it wasn't. Why did he keep feeling it was?

He might get better if he could go back in time and change some of the disastrous decisions he'd made. As it was, his safest course was not to make any more. How did he atone for disasters everyone else told him weren't his fault?

Sean dropped back a stride. "Keep up, Jake."

"Hey, look at the size of those suckers," Hank said and pointed toward the pasture, where a half-dozen giant horses lifted their heads and watched the newcomers before continuing to graze. "When do we get to drive 'em?"

"Soon enough," the colonel said. "Orientation and house rules first. Come on, everybody." He opened a door into the stable and waited while the group walked inside. "This is the common room. It's where you'll meet and eat while you're here. Mickey, will your chair fit through the entrance?"

"Yeah, if I aim right. Boy, this is some kind of plush for a stable."

"The living quarters are for visiting clinicians and people interested in the horses," the colonel said. "The bedrooms are through there."

"The nearest motel is ten miles away," Charlie added. "You would *not* want to stay there. This way, you're with the horses twenty-four/seven."

"We've got a room and bath set up on the first floor for you, Mickey," the colonel said, heading in that direction. The others took a quick look and drifted back to the common room, but Charlie stayed with her father and Mickey.

The pocket door to Mickey's room was extra wide to accommodate his wheelchair. Once inside, the colonel waved around the room. "Lift for the bed, shower and john set up for you. Dr. Steadman vetted it before he signed off to let you come out here. You and Mary Anne will be on the main floor. Sean, Jake and Hank all have rooms upstairs."

"May need some help with the lifts and stuff," Mickey said with a grimace. "Call me Tin Man. My braces don't take to showers real well." Charlie sensed how much he hated asking for assistance. He cocked an eyebrow at her and leered, "Want to help me?"

She laughed. "Good try. The colonel swears you can manage fine on your own."

"Oh, well, if I have to. Just keep Li'l Buckaroo Hank away from me. He thinks because he was an officer he's too good to help an enlisted man."

"He's not in the army any longer," Charlie said. "I'm the only one with rank in this organization."

"I thought the colonel was in charge here."

"I'm officially retired," her father said, "although this program is my idea." He leaned a hip against the corner of the wheelchair-height dresser and folded his arms. "Charlie is actually responsible for training you guys." He walked back into the hall. "When you've finished exploring, join us in the common room."

"Excellent," Mickey said, spinning his

chair and rolling over to Charlie. "I can plug my battery in beside the bed. I don't really need the hoist. I can make it from my chair to the bed and back without hydraulics. This should work."

"How often do you wear your braces?"

"Not often enough right now, but I'm getting stronger. I'm supposed to walk every day."

"Don't you?"

He shrugged. "The braces are a pain to put on and a pain to wear. Sometimes I let it slide, you know? You do have Wi-Fi, right?"

"Yes, Mickey, even here in the outer reaches of space we have Wi-Fi. See you in the common room in fifteen minutes." She shut his door behind her.

The other trainee room on the first floor had been given to Mary Anne Howell, since she was the only female. Charlie knocked on her door, which stood ajar.

"Settling in all right?" she asked.

Mary Ann turned away and pulled down the sleeve of her shirt to cover the edge of her glove. "Yes, ma'am. Thank you."

"It's Charlie, not ma'am, okay?" Charlie wanted to tell her that she didn't need to cover up, that nobody cared about her scars. Not quite true. Mary Anne cared. Charlie didn't know the extent of her disfigurement. The others might not, either.

Upstairs, Sean and Hank had rooms across the hall from one another. Charlie reminded them both about the meeting in the common room. "Short orientation, then lunch."

O'Riley followed her down the hall, caught her arm and said, "Ma'am, better let me bring the major."

By that time she'd reached Jake's room. The door stood wide open, and she could see him sitting on the edge of his bed, his hands loose in his lap, while he stared out the window. What was he seeing? The trees and fields, or something else?

"Hey, Jake, buddy, we've got to go downstairs for a meeting," O'Riley said. "You gotta be hungry."

Without a word, Jake stood. As he passed Charlie in the doorway, he flashed her a smile so sweet it took her breath away. Watching him walk down the hall and start down the steps, she noticed the limp. She pointed to Sean's room, followed him in and shut the door.

"Okay, what's with Major Thompson?"

"He's a good man."

"I'm sure he is."

"He took shrapnel in his knee. Knees

22

don't ever heal right, so he'll always limp."

"Sean, that's not all. I need to know, if I'm going to train him to drive a horse-drawn carriage and take care of draft horses."

Sean sank onto his bed. Charlie leaned against the wall.

"All I know, he was wounded in an ambush in Iraq. He got out with a bum knee. Nobody else did. Since then he can't make decisions." O'Riley shrugged. "Hard to hold a job."

"I'll bet."

"He was my roommate at our halfway house, so I've been kind of looking after him since I went there to learn to use my hand."

Great. So far, the kid in the wheelchair showed the most potential of the lot.

Sean could crush a carriage shaft with his prosthetic hand. Mary Ann wouldn't look straight ahead, take off her glove or wear a short-sleeved shirt in Memphis heat because of what must be burn scars on her arm. The handsome rodeo rider with one foot gave every impression of being both bad-tempered and bitter.

And finally, Jake Thompson wouldn't be able to take the reins on a carriage because he couldn't make a decision about which

23

way to go.

Lovely.

If she could train these people to drive well enough to land them jobs with carriage outfits after they finished the course, she deserved a medal — she just hoped it wouldn't be a Purple Heart.

CHAPTER TWO

The colonel leaned one arm along the rough wood mantel in the big common room while he waited for the others to find places to sit. He was always relaxed with patients and strangers. Not so much with his family. When he noticed them.

"Where's the major?" Charlie asked. "He came down just before us."

"I'll go find him," Sean said, and started for the door to the stable.

Charlie touched his arm. "You need to listen to this. I'll find him."

"But . . ."

She was already out the door. Maybe Major Thompson had decided he couldn't endure being so close to other people. Had he walked to the road to hitchhike back to Memphis?

According to Sean, he didn't have that much gumption.

Several of the horses that weren't out in

pasture were taking midmorning naps in their stalls. A couple snored. Over their snuffles she heard a soft male voice. As she stood listening, her cell phone rang. She snatched it out of her jeans and answered quietly.

"Charlie, it's DeMarcus. They there yet?"

"Half an hour ago," she told the farm-hand.

"You know I'm not happy the colonel gave me and Maurice two weeks' vacation, even if he is paying us. You gonna be able to do it all with just those folks to help?"

"I have to try."

DeMarcus snorted. "Huh. He's got no kinda idea how much work goes into keeping the pastures cut and the barn clean. You want us to come back? Give you a hand?"

"Give me a couple of days to see if I can manage. I may call you screaming for help."

"You know you got shavings coming first thing tomorrow morning."

"I've also got three trace mineral blocks and a dozen fifty-pound bags of oats in the back of the truck."

"Don't you unload 'em by yourself!"

"I promise I won't. Bye, DeMarcus. Have fun on your vacation." She sighed as she stuck her cell phone back into her jeans. Hank, Jake and Sean all looked capable of stacking bags of oats and shoveling shavings. She had argued and argued with her father about giving the regular grooms time off, but he wanted the students to learn to do everything themselves.

"They'll have to know the basics if they're going to work with horses," he had said.

Actually, it wasn't that big an operation. The new arrivals should be able to handle things with her to straw boss them. Jake was still talking. Sounded as though he was down by the double stall where the stallion Picard held court.

The nineteen-hand black shire was usually a good guy unless you tried to get between him and a mare in heat, but he was still a stallion, given to mood swings from loving to irascible. Always arrogant. For safety's sake, the rule was that nobody messed with him without backup.

Jake hadn't gotten the word. She found him inside the stall running a dandy brush over Picard's shining black pelt, while the big horse leaned into him and sighed in ecstasy. "Who's a good boy, then?" Jake crooned. "You're a fine old boy, aren't you?" His gentle voice warmed something deep inside her.

She held her breath so that she wouldn't spook either man or horse and waited for

Jake to notice her. It was like watching your child play in the gorilla cage at the zoo.

"Uh, Major? Jake?" Charlie whispered.

Jake's shoulders stiffened, and he dug the brush into Picard's shoulder so hard the stallion gave an annoyed "harrumph."

"We're late for the orientation meeting," she said, emphasizing the *we*. "I came to get you." She held her hand out to him. He opened the stall door and laid the brush on her outstretched palm.

"I broke the rules?" he asked.

Working alone with Picard was definitely against the rules, but nothing had happened. "We don't generally go into his stall without someone outside in case there's a mare in season he wants to get to. He can be a handful, but he obviously appreciates what you're doing."

"I like the big guys," Jake said. "I'd forgotten how good clean horse and fresh hay smell." He grinned. "Yeah, even manure. I'm sorry if I worried you." Picard leaned his head over his stall door and bopped Jake on the shoulder. Jake reached up and scratched between the stallion's eyes, then gave that angelic smile again. She didn't think she'd ever seen such a mix of joy and loss in one expression.

"Picard was obviously pleased, so don't

worry about it." She walked beside him back toward the common room. "The colonel mentioned you grew up on a farm. Did you drive draft horses?"

He looked away, the smile replaced by a rictus of pain. "I plowed my first furrow behind a Percheron when I was seven. By the time I left home, I could plow all day with a six-across team of Belgians."

Charlie blinked. The idea of driving six draft horses across a single line was mind-boggling. She laughed. "Maybe you should be teaching this course." She knew the minute the words left her mouth she'd said the wrong thing.

He froze. "No," he said, and walked ahead of her into the den.

Ms. Big Mouth, Charlie thought. He might not have driven any kind of equine for years, but driving draft horses was like riding a bicycle. Hadn't taken Charlie long to get her skills back after she and Sarah moved in.

He was probably a better driver than she was, and a better horseman, as well, considering Picard's reaction. He'd be a great second in command if she could convince him to come out of his shell.

How could she get through to him? She'd do anything to see that smile again and hear the gentle voice he used with Picard. She intended to know the officer he must have been, even if she had to drag him kicking out of the shadows.

Sean settled Jake in an empty seat on the banquette under the windows.

"Okay," the colonel said, "here's the deal. You five signed up to be test cases in a pilot program." He held up a hand. "Sounds better than guinea pigs, doesn't it? A similar program to train veterans to drive carriages has been a success in northern Virginia, and I think it can work down here. If you succeed, we already have jobs lined up for you."

"What kind of jobs?" Hank asked.

Mary Ann's hand went up. "How can we make a living driving horses? Who even does that anymore?"

"Can you say weddings, girl?" Mickey said. "Don't see how you can fit a wheelchair on one of those Cinderella carriages, though." He grinned at her. "Can't you just see me hauling the bride's train up to the church? Get that net stuff wound around my wheels and she'd wind up on her butt."

"Shut up, Mickey," Sean said without heat.

"We'll talk about the opportunities over the next few weeks as we figure out your particular skill set," the colonel continued. "Take the rest of the day to unpack, settle in and learn your way around. This wing of the stable contains your living, dining and cooking area."

Mickey raised a hand. "How come you have a dormitory in your barn?"

The colonel smiled. "My father ran training courses where people could learn to farm with draft horses. This is our first course since his death some years ago."

"We'll set up a roster of chores both for the living areas and the stable," Charlie said. "Or you can make your own. You're not simply going to be driving. You'll be mucking stalls, cleaning tack — maybe even a little farriery. Learning everything it takes to become a horseman. For the first few weeks, you will be the only people working with the horses. After that, our regular grooms come back."

"How about food?" Mickey asked. He had that perpetually famished teenage look. Charlie guessed that no matter how much he ate, he'd always be hungry and skinny.

"There'll be breakfast makings sent over from the main house every morning," the colonel said. "Cereal, juices, bagels, rolls. If you want to cook, there are eggs and bacon in the refrigerator." He gestured to the

31

doublewide steel refrigerator in the small but well-equipped kitchen area open to the main room. "Make your own coffee. Clean up after yourselves. There's a dishwasher. The lunch and dinner dishes will be sent over from the kitchen in my house on a trolley. They'll either be picked up after dinner, or one of you can take the trolley back. There's a bigger dishwasher at the house. Anything special you want, there's a whiteboard beside the refrigerator you can write on. We'll try to accommodate you as much as possible."

"Beer?" Hank asked.

"Within reason," the colonel said. "I don't recommend wine or liquor. And don't overdo it. Working in the hot sun long-lining a seventeen-hand Percheron while nursing a hangover will be plenty of punishment for getting drunk."

"So how do we get it?" Hank asked. "We're prisoners out here working our rear ends off to run your operation and all we get is room and board."

"Plus a small weekly stipend," the colonel said. "You all knew the rules going in. It's not much, but it'll give you spending money in town."

"Do we have to hitchhike?" Hank seemed intent on being belligerent, and Charlie wondered where his anger came from.

"There's a couple of pickup trucks for farm use," Charlie said. "I see no reason why we can't have a weekly pizza run. Maybe Chinese or sushi."

"Our cook, Vittorio, will provide lunch and dinner over here six nights a week," the colonel added. "Saturday night you're on your own. I'll join you for the occasional meal, but this is Charlie's baby, not mine. It is imperative that you all have lunch and dinner together. That's when you'll discuss the day's instruction, get assignments and handle problems. Now, there should be sandwiches for lunch today already in the refrigerator."

"We can set stuff out on the counter," Charlie said. "I'm starved." She turned to ask Mary Anne to help, then realized she had chosen her because she was a woman. "Hank, give me a hand, will you?"

"Sure." He flashed her a smile. Huh. So he argued with male authority figures and charmed the females. She could use that.

"Silverware's in that drawer, place mats in the one under it."

Hank was already pulling glasses and plates out of the cabinets above the sink. He was apparently over his pet for the moment. Maybe it was only the colonel who annoyed him. If he had a problem with authority figures — and many rodeo cowboys did — why did he join the military? And how on earth did he get to be an officer?

By now everyone was helping to set out lunch. Everyone except Jake. He sat with his hands loose in his lap and his face turned toward the window and the pasture beyond. It wasn't that he was avoiding the job. He simply didn't seem to be aware it needed doing.

When the food was ready, everybody sat down except Jake, who didn't look up. Charlie gave a slight shake of her head at Sean, who was about to call him over. "Let me," she whispered. Jake didn't react as her shadow fell across him. "Time to eat, Jake. Aren't you hungry?"

He made no move toward the table.

"Come on, join us," she said.

As the platters of sandwiches were passed around, he ignored them.

Charlie took a sandwich from each platter, put them on his plate, poured his diet soda into his glass and asked, "Would you like mayo and mustard?"

He didn't respond.

"Yeah. And pickles and potato chips." Sean took the plate. "I'll do it for him."

When Charlie raised her eyebrows, Sean added in a whisper, "He doesn't eat with people."

"I beg your pardon?"

"He'll go outside on the patio or up to his room, but he won't sit at the table with us."

"But he has to. It's one of the few hard and fast rules the colonel's set up for this group."

Sean added condiments to Jake's sandwiches and picked up a soda with his prosthetic hand. "Hey, look at that. I didn't crush the can. I'm actually getting the hang of this thing."

Charlie decided not to push Jake at this meal. She'd stand back and watch what he did. But he *would* have dinner with them.

Jake took the plate and drink from Sean, walked out onto the patio, sat in the swing and wolfed down his sandwiches.

Nothing wrong with his appetite. He'd *chosen* to groom the stallion, although he might not think of it as a choice. Maybe horses were the key to getting him to reconnect with the world.

Charlie would start by cajoling him into making small decisions with the horses. Could other animals help, as well? She'd try him out on the barn cats.

If he could actually touch one without getting himself raked to the bone, he was a true animal whisperer.

But even felines made allowances for damaged human beings. Usually. The big brindle tomcat regarded man as a lesser species created only to provide for his comfort. He wouldn't cut the *president* any slack.

Jake brought his empty plate and soda can back into the kitchen but didn't seem to know what to do with them.

"Put the can in the trash and the plate in the dishwasher," Sean said.

Charlie added, "We have brownies in the microwave for dessert. Jake, why don't you get them?"

That apparently counted as a command, because he took them from the microwave and carried them to the table, then looked uncertain where to put them. Charlie took the plate. "Thanks."

She was passing the brownies to Mary Anne when the door from the stable burst open and Sarah burst in, then came to an abrupt halt. "Oh!" she said. "They're here already. I didn't see the van." She turned to flee.

"Been and gone. Lunch was scheduled for noon," Charlie said with a glance at the clock on the mantelpiece. It read twelve thirty-five.

"You *could* have called me. Did you leave me anything to eat?"

"Sarah, we have guests."

She pivoted toward the table. From her vantage point, Charlie caught the precise moment her daughter spotted Mickey and Hank. "Uh, hi," she said, but her words, like her eyes, took in no one except the two young men.

"This is my daughter, Sarah," Charlie said. At fourteen, Sarah was already six feet, a tall colt of a girl. She'd cried for days when one of the boys she liked at school called her the Jolly Pink Giant.

When Charlie heard about that, she wanted to complain to the guidance counselor. Actually, she wanted to drop the boy down the nearest volcano, but Sarah begged her to let it go.

The vets would read Sarah's toss of her head and peremptory tone as arrogance, but Charlie knew it masked terminal shyness.

She put the last two sandwiches on a plate and handed them to her daughter. "Soda's in the fridge. What have you been up to all morning?"

Sarah bristled. "I've been answering my emails, okay? There's nothing to do around here."

"That's not what I —"

"Nothing to do?" Hank gaped and pointed out the window. "Girl, you got horses!"

"They're just driving horses," Sarah said. "You can't ride 'em or anything."

Hank laughed, showing every one of his perfect teeth. "If you can drive 'em, you can ride 'em."

"Mom was the only one who ever hung around the post stables." Sarah eyed Charlie. "But then there was tons of other stuff to do. Actual humans and the post exchange and a pool and stuff."

"You'll make new friends once school starts," Hank said. "Hey, you must be good at it, right? Army brats are."

"They'll hate me."

"Why would they hate a foxy chick like you?" Hank said.

Charlie cleared her throat and caught Hank's eye. This was *her daughter* he was calling a foxy chick. He had the grace to look away.

"Right. As if." Sarah picked up the sandwiches, added a couple of brownies to the pile, stuck a diet soda under her arm and headed for the door.

"Lay off the computer for the rest of the day," Charlie said.

"Mom!"

"Show us around this afternoon," Mickey

said, looking to Charlie to make sure that was okay. She nodded. "You can wheel the crip." His chair whirred as it backed away from the table.

Sarah's eyes widened. Apparently she hadn't realized he was in a wheelchair. She recovered instantly and flashed him a grin of her own, the first real smile Charlie had seen on her face in days. "I'm up for that, just not right now." She flipped her long, light-brown hair over her shoulder. "I suppose I'll go read an actual *b-o-o-k*. Is that all right with you, Mother dear?"

"Sarah —" Charlie began. Without waiting for an answer her daughter went out and shut the door firmly behind her.

"She hated having to move down here," Charlie explained. "She's lived on post since she was born. Out here she's lonely and bored." There was no reason to tell them that Sarah had lost her father less than a year ago. She might not act as though she was still grieving, but Charlie knew she was and ached for her. She wanted so much to help, but Sarah wasn't interested. She blamed her mother for her father's defection and death and didn't hesitate to tell her.

Nobody said anything. Men. They probably had no idea what to say.

"I haven't helped much," Charlie added. Big understatement. Why couldn't she simply tell Sarah she loved her and keep on telling her until she believed it? Charlie asked herself for the hundredth time. Heaven knew she wanted to, but she didn't know how.

One thing she'd learned from her father very early — don't show your heart to anybody, especially the people you love. You do, you get zapped.

"At her age she'd find fault with Paradise," Sean finally said. "I've got two daughters of my own. One's majoring in engineering in St. Louis and is relatively civilized. The other — not so much." After lunch, everyone went off to unpack, then reassembled to explore the farm. All except Sean and Jake, who was staring out his window again.

"Hey, Jake, how about I show you around?" Charlie said. Sean appeared grateful for the break. "Unless you're tired and want to unpack." She watched him weigh his choices and was prepared to choose for him if he couldn't or wouldn't. He needed an opportunity to make small decisions and build up to larger ones.

Sean started to speak, but Charlie wiggled her fingers behind her back to stop him.

She caught Jake's panicked glance at his friend.

"I'll introduce you to the other horses," she said. "Come on."

"Okay."

She heard Sean release his breath behind her.

She handed Jake a baseball cap off the rack in the corner. "Down here the sun is dangerous to your skin all year round."

He nodded. "Like Iraq."

He put on the cap. She plopped her battered khaki safari hat on her head and started out into the stable. As she passed Sean, he touched her arm and winked at her.

CHAPTER THREE

Jake mustn't think she was watching him. All the students had emotional as well as physical problems, but Charlie suspected Jake would be the most difficult to deal with.

She needed to figure out the hot buttons for the others, too. She heard Hank's boots click on the staircase and realized he also limped, though less than Jake.

Without the front half of his of his right foot, Hank would never be able to balance on a saddle bronc. He'd probably be able to ride bareback, but not on a bucking horse.

He could drive draft horses. No balance required.

And he obviously loved horses. Carriage driving didn't involve as much adrenaline as rodeo, but there were still moments of terror. Vic Piper, the farrier, said that carriage wrecks were less frequent than riding accidents, but were usually worse, especially when the horse in question was a big old

Belgian or shire.

She looked around and realized that Jake was no longer walking beside her.

"Jake?" she called.

"Down here," he answered.

In the hay-storage room the bales were stacked in stair steps all the way to the roof of the barn some twenty feet above.

Charlie found Jake sitting cross-legged on one of the lower bales. Two feet away stood big Mama Cat, twenty pounds of yellow tabby with orange eyes that could shoot fire. Her tail had swelled to twice normal size, and the tip flicked back and forth an inch in either direction.

Usually by this time she'd disappeared up to the top of one of the rafters or gone for the nearest jugular. Charlie was afraid to move. It was another one of those "child in the gorilla cage" moments.

She held her breath as he reached two fingers toward the big tabby. The world stopped while man and cat stared deep into each other's eyes.

Jake's eyes were the color of the Aegean Sea in high summer. She still remembered that blue from the vacation she and her parents took to Crete during one of her father's tours of duty. She'd felt that if she looked over the side of the little boat, the mermaids would pull her down. She felt the same drowning sensation now as she stared into Jake's eyes.

Good grief!

She'd sworn off men! Definitely no more soldiers. Celibacy was the order of the day. Men wanted to own you, to make you go where they wanted you to go, be what they wanted you to be. Military men, especially. And you better not make any changes in your life while they were off fighting the bad guys. Steve would have preferred she go into suspended animation while he was away.

She turned before Jake could catch sight of the blood suffusing her face. She suspected if he took her temperature, she'd blow the lid off the mercury.

This would not do. One did not get turned on by a student. And a soldier. And a loner with psychological problems. He could have a wife and sixteen kids for all she knew.

Why not react to Sean? He wasn't that much older, and his hand couldn't be called a handicap. Or even Hank, the gorgeous macho guy. But neither of them pushed her hot buttons. Actually, she was kind of surprised she still *had* hot buttons. She hadn't felt physically attracted to Steve since before his last tour, and he had definitely not been attracted to her.

Jake was holding something between his slim fingers. How long could he maintain his position with his arm extended that way? Would cat or man break first?

Then Mama took a single step, flattened her ears, stuck out her neck and snatched something — a bit of chicken saved from lunch? — from Jake's fingers. A moment later she was gone in a honey-colored blur.

"That cat is a killer," she said. "How did you do that?"

"You know she's pregnant?"

Charlie nodded. "We've tried every trick in the book to catch her so we can have her neutered. She's much smarter than we are. She showed up here a couple of years ago all skin and bones with more battle scars than Galactica. She's a Tennessee feral cat."

He unfolded himself from the bale of hay. "Man, is she ever!"

It seemed the most natural thing in the world to offer him her hand to pull him up.

Not so natural to stand closer than she'd intended. She caught her breath and heard his catch, as well. She looked away from those blue eyes, but not before they'd held hers a moment too long for comfort. Aware of her quickened breathing, she turned away and walked down the aisle. She heard him following her, the slight hitch in his step

45

already familiar.

"Tennessee feral cats are an actual breed," she babbled. "There's a stuffed one in the local museum. Probably descendants from the cats the Scots traders brought with them in the eighteen hundreds. I've no idea whether it's feasible for a domestic cat to interbreed with a bobcat, but I do know the few remaining representatives of the feral cat breed are all that big, all that beige yellow tabby color and all fierce fighters."

"Feral cats always regress to that beige tabby color within five generations in the wild."

"How would you know that?"

He shrugged. "I grew up on a farm where all the barn cats were feral. We never had a problem with field mice or even the pink-eared rats. Everybody worked on my family's farm, even the snakes."

"I beg your pardon?" This time she stopped to stare at him.

He grinned at her. "This place is bound to have a couple of resident king snakes to keep the poisonous snakes down."

"I'd rather not know, thank you."

"If you meet one, tip your cap, thank him for his good work, and send him on his way."

"How will I know the difference? What's more important, how do *you*?"

"You weren't born a country girl, were you?"

"No." She didn't offer him any further explanation.

"Hey, want company?" Hank, Sean and Mary Anne came down the aisle to join them.

"Where's Mickey?" Charlie asked.

"Said he was tired," Hank said. Charlie picked up the faintest trace of a sneer.

"He *was*," Mary Anne snapped. "You have any idea how hard it is trying to be upbeat and funny all the time you're driving a wheelchair?"

Hank held his hands up in front of him, palms out. "I didn't mean anything. I'm not used to him is all."

"Get used to this, too, why don't you?" She yanked off her scarf and glared at them.

Charlie managed not to gasp. The colonel had warned her that Mary Anne needed more reconstructive surgery, more skin grafts on the side of her face and her arms. Most of her scars would eventually be gone or less evident. She had to go through a period of healing both physically and emotionally before her next round of surgeries.

The doctors hadn't yet reconstructed her right ear. A patch of skin the size of two dollar bills ran red, puckered and hairless down her scalp and along the side of her jaw, disappearing beneath the collar of her shirt. "Get used to it, people. I did." She turned on her heel.

"Hey, Mary Anne," Hank called after her. "The horses don't care and neither do we."

"Yeah," Sean said. "Too hot for those long sleeves anyway. Come on back." He held out his right hand to her.

When she turned, Charlie could see she was fighting tears but she reached out to Sean with her left hand, hesitated, then held out her right, as well. The scars covered only the pinkie side. Without looking down, Sean took the injured hand gingerly in his latex-covered one.

For a moment, no one breathed, then Hank said, "Come on, girl. Time's awastin'. I want to get my hands on some horse."

Charlie's throat tightened. She caught Jake's eye, and knew he got it.

We're all damaged. Maybe together we can heal one another.

CHAPTER FOUR

They heard Mickey's whir before his wheel-chair whipped out the door to the common room and down the aisle toward them. "Hey! Yous guys taking a trip without me?"

"You snooze, you lose," Hank said. He stopped at the first stall. "Would you look at the size of him? That's not a horse, that's a hippopotamus."

"Hippos are short," Sean said. "That's more moose size. Y'all got mooses in Wyo-ming, don't you?"

Mary Anne pulled away from him and backed across the aisle.

"Hey, did I grab you too tight?" Sean called.

Mary Anne shook her head, her dark eyes the size of eight balls. "I . . . I didn't think they'd be so big."

The gray Percheron gelding poked his head over the top of his stall gate, delighted by the attention. He looked straight at Mary

Anne and snorted — a big, wet, huffy snort.

She yelped.

"He's a real sweetie," Charlie said, and scratched his nose.

"Don't you have anything smaller?" Mary Anne asked. "Like maybe a pony?"

"Our newborn foals are bigger than the average pony," Charlie said.

Mary Anne turned paler.

"Are you all right?"

"I knew I shouldn't have said I'd do this." Mary Anne dropped her face into her hands. "But I wanted to get out of that place so bad. . . ." She stared around at all of them. "I lied on the forms. I'm so sorry . . . I'm terrified of horses."

"And that pretty much put an end to the Great Horse tour," Charlie said.

She slipped off her paddock boots and propped her stocking feet on the coffee table in her father's study. He handed her a cold can of diet soda from the small refrigerator under the wet bar in the corner. She rolled it against her forehead, popped the top and drank half of it in one pull before continuing.

"I turned the tour over to Hank, since he knows the most about horses and stables. Meanwhile, Mary Anne flew back to the dorm with me at her heels, and locked herself in her room. I knocked and tried to reassure her, but she sounded as though she was throwing stuff around, probably packing. She told me to go away."

"You carry a master key."

"I didn't sign on to be a prison warden." She scowled at her father. "I only met them a few hours ago. You're the big psychologist. What should I have done?"

"What *did* you do?"

She set her soda onto the end table beside her. "Daddy, sometimes this answering a question with a question is pretty annoying. I spoke to her the way I'd speak to a spooked horse. Gentle, quiet. I kept reassuring her that we'd deal with it, that we'd all help her, that of course we wanted her to stay. . . ."

"Successful?"

"If *I'd* kept trying to talk to her through the door, she'd have sneaked out the window and hitchhiked to town by now." She sighed. "No, Jake did it. I already knew he had a thing with animals. Seems people like him, too."

"People are animals."

Charlie struck her forehead. "Wow! What a concept! Why didn't *I* think of that?" She tossed her soda can into the big wastebasket

51

beside her father's desk. "Three points."

Jamming her hands into the pockets of her jeans, she started to pace. "The others were pretty upset about Mary Anne. Were we going to toss her out on her rear? If we did that, they'd all leave. . . . I had to do some fine tap dancing. Then, she and Jake came walking down the aisle like nothing had happened. She'd obviously been crying, but she hadn't tied that scarf back around her head or rolled her sleeves down." She braced herself against the edge of her father's desk. "She was trembling, she was so scared, but she faced us all down. She's got guts. I like her."

"What did Jake say to her in there?"

"No idea. Maybe he just witched her through the closed door." She chuckled. "You should have seen him feeding Mama Cat chicken. It's like he gave up part of what he was when he gave up making decisions, but maybe he got something else in return."

"No matter how hard he tries not to, my dear Charlie, he's forced to make decisions. If he starts with small ones and nothing bad happens, maybe he'll learn to make larger ones."

"You've worked with all of them. . . ."

He shrugged. "Some more than others."

"But all you'll give me is name, age and rank. What's Jake's story?"

He shook his finger at her. "I can only give you the bare outline without contravening the Privacy Act. I can't, for instance, show you Jake's file — or any of their files."

"So Jake made a decision that caused havoc. Are we talking a full-blown case of PTSD here? I am not competent to deal with that."

"He has a bad case of survivor guilt, Charlie. He feels that his decisions resulted in suffering for other people and left him unscathed."

"Did they?"

"Not in the sense he means. It's a form of magical thinking. Not much different from 'step on a crack, break your mother's back.' Except in degree, of course."

Can you at least tell me what he did in the army before he was wounded?"

"He was G-2."

"Intelligence. A spook."

The colonel nodded.

"What about his family?"

"Never been married."

"Can you at least tell me whether or not he's gay?"

"From what I can gather, he had an extremely healthy heterosexual sex life."

She blew out her breath. "Not that it matters."

"Of course not." The colonel smiled the infuriating "I see all" smile that drove her crazy. "I'll be down at the hospital at least four days a week, but I suggest we talk every night after dinner. Completely up to you."

"Uh-huh." As if. She was surprised he hadn't asked her to write him case notes.

"If you have time, you might prepare case notes to jog your memory."

She threw back her head and roared with laughter.

"What?"

"No case notes. I am not one of your worshipful acolytes."

"This class is a huge responsibility for someone with your limited experience."

"Then why the heck did you stick me with it?" She didn't wait for his answer, but grabbed her paddock boots and started out of the library in her stocking feet.

"Charlie girl, I'm selfish enough to want to keep you and Sarah around. The way to do that is to keep you interested, involved and employed. Is it wrong to want to get to know my adult daughter and my grandchild? Besides, you must see that I can't simply turn this place over to you without any supervision. You have no prior experience running an operation this size."

"Granddad taught me more in my vacations here than he ever taught you, and I've been working my tail off to learn everything I can since we came back. I'm thinking of all those classes and clinics I should be taking instead of teaching these people to drive."

"Dad was aware I would never be a farmer or a horseman," the colonel said. "As a matter of fact, until I came home to look after him when he got so sick, he didn't believe I'd ever live here after I left for college. He expected me to hire a manager to handle the place after he died until Steve retired and you two came back here to take over." He shrugged. "I thought then he was living a fantasy. You would never have been able to convince Steve to retire from the army and move to a horse farm. He was an adrenaline junkie, Charlie. They don't change."

"We don't have to worry about that any longer, do we?" She padded out of the library, shut the door and fought back tears. He was doing the same thing he'd always done when she was growing up. The absentee father shows up, issues orders for her own good and then leaves again. The gospel according to Colonel Vining. Most of the time she disobeyed just to prove she could. She must have driven her mother nuts.

If he hadn't made her leave her horse when she was thirteen, her whole life might have been different. If her mother hadn't died and left her without a buffer, if her father hadn't forbidden her to see Steve, she'd never have run away and married him. The colonel always tried to control her and she always fought him, even when he was right.

Especially when he was right.

Carrying her boots, she took the stairs to the bedrooms two at a time. As she reached the top she heard Sarah clicking away on their shared computer.

Time to close down so they could go help Vittorio with dinner. She stopped with her hand on the doorknob. Wasn't she trying to control Sarah the way the colonel tried to control her? She wanted Sarah to be happy, but her idea of what constituted happiness might not mesh with Sarah's any more than the colonel's had meshed with hers.

Should she let Sarah have her head a little bit? She was a good kid who was lonely and grieving. She'd never betrayed Charlie's trust. She ought to be able to make her own mistakes.

And wind up pregnant and married? No

way. If that meant controlling her, then so be it. Wasn't that what the colonel said? Kids at this age hate their parents when they act like parents. Tough.

For all practical purposes Charlie had been a single parent most of Sarah's fourteen years, but while he was home between deployments, Steve was always better with their daughter than she was. He was the good guy, Charlie was the ogre. No wonder Sarah missed him so much. No wonder when she had to blame someone for his death, Charlie was elected.

Why am I so uptight? Why don't I just go in there and hug her? Because if she went stiff and backed away, I'd cry.

One of the four bedrooms on the second floor of the main house had been fitted out with Sarah's shabby furniture brought from their base housing, and another had been given over to a home office that she was supposed to share with Charlie. In reality, however, Sarah spread out like kudzu vine, overrunning every flat surface in her own room and threatening to engulf the office.

The computer keys kept popping like soggy popcorn. Sarah couldn't touch-type yet. She planned to take typing in the fall at her new private school. She could, however, race the wind with her two-finger technique.

And texting? Did anyone over twenty have thumbs that small or nimble?

Charlie walked by the computer room and went into her own bedroom instead. She longed to lie down for a few minutes before she plunged back into her job, but she didn't dare. She'd fall asleep and not get up until tomorrow.

Every piece of furniture in the room was new. Most of the things in their army quarters, except for Sarah's bed and dresser, belonged to the quartermaster and had to be returned to stores every time they moved. Each new post meant another requisition of boring quartermaster offerings. The cheap furniture she and Steve had accumulated during their fifteen years of marriage had grown shabbier with every move. After he died, she'd sold everything except the photo albums, keepsakes, personal papers and Sarah's furniture in a garage sale. Sarah had wanted her own bedroom furniture and other familiar objects around her, so she could have the illusion of home wherever the family landed. Charlie, on the other hand, wanted to slam the door on her life with Steve. Two years ago, she wouldn't have felt that way, but that was before Steve came home from his second tour in Afghanistan and asked for a divorce.

Even combat widows were not welcome in post housing for very long. She'd had to beg to keep her quarters until school let out in mid-May. So here she was with the colonel. His house, his rules.

She stood under the shower for five minutes to wash the dust and sweat off, washed her hair for the second time that day, then redid her makeup and put on a clean polo shirt and jeans. Her mother had always taken an afternoon shower and changed into fresh clothes. She said it was a carryover from the days before air-conditioning. Charlie had picked up the habit from her. "Sarah?" Charlie opened the office door and stood in the doorway with her hand on the knob. Sarah jumped and hit the escape key in one motion. Whoever she was on line with disappeared.

"Mother! You scared me spitless." She wheeled in her chair and glared at Charlie. "You ooze around like a fungus."

"Green and soggy, that's me. Thought you were cutting down on the social networking."

Sarah avoided her eyes and did that flouncy, hair-swinging thing. "I am trying to help you. I looked up all those people on Google and Facebook. Don't you want to know what all I found out?"

"I would love to know what you found out," Charlie said. "Thank you. But you ought to be outside, not sitting in here over a hot keyboard."

"What else is there to do out here? Go to the mall or the movies with my BFFs? Last time I checked they were in Kansas."

"Once school starts you'll make plenty of friends."

Sarah rolled her eyes. "Oh, right. Most of them have been together since kindergarten. They're going to fall over to welcome the outsider. We should have stayed in Kansas."

"Ah, Kansas, the center for sophistication in the known universe."

Sarah opened her mouth to make another snappy comeback, then giggled. "Good one, Mom."

Charlie pulled her up from her chair and Sarah hugged her. Charlie felt a surge of joy. She lived for these moments. She hugged Sarah back hard. Then she whispered, "I love you."

The moment passed in a flash as Sarah slipped past her and down the stairs. Charlie followed more slowly. At least she'd said the words.

An hour later, Charlie helped the students set the food dishes on the table in the common room, and watched everyone find seats. All except Jake.

"Sean, where's Jake?" she asked.

"I'll take him a plate."

"No, you won't. He needs to join us at the table. That's the rule. I thought he obeyed rules. No decisions necessary."

"Charlie, he'll starve before he comes down here. Don't ask me why. I just know it."

"Oh, for Pete's sake!" She took a deep breath. "I'm not going to get into a battle tonight I will probably lose, but Sean, would you talk to him? Convince him that sitting at the table with you all is not going to cause the end of Western civilization as we know it?"

Sean shrugged. "I'll sure try, but I'm not guaranteeing it'll do any good."

They'd already worked out an informal seating arrangement. Jake at the far end, then Sean, Mary Anne. Mickey's wheelchair at the other end, then Hank.

"I'm not joining you for dinner tonight anyway," Charlie said. "Give you a chance to talk things over, get to know one another without either the colonel or me eavesdropping."

"No bugs in the light fixtures?" Mickey said.

"Nope. Not yet, at any rate. If you'd load

the serving dishes onto the trolley, Vittorio or I will come get it and put everything into the dishwasher in the house. Anybody need something or just want to talk to me or the colonel, push the button on the intercom and leave a message. I suggest you get to bed early. Tomorrow morning I'll be rousting you all out at six o'clock."

"No way!" Mickey groaned.

"You need help getting to bed?" Charlie asked.

"I'm not helpless."

"If you do, push the button beside your bed."

"Or holler," Sean said.

Mickey rolled his eyes. "I can stand. I just can't walk far yet."

"Yeah, and when you fall, you flop around like a turtle on its back," Hank said.

"Flopping around on your back in the dirt ought to be a real familiar sensation for you," Mickey said. "At least I can stay on my feet for more than eight seconds."

Hank flushed and opened his mouth to retort. Charlie was about to lambaste him when Mary Anne snapped, "Stop it! What is the *matter* with you, Hank?" She turned to Mickey. "You're no better. Knock it off."

"It's a miracle, Hank," Charlie said. "You're missing half a foot and still manage to stuff a whole one into your mouth. Mary Anne's right. Both of you, knock it off."

Jake might have a point in not wanting to join the group for dinner.

"Sean, so you will take Jake a plate?" Charlie asked.

"Yes, ma'am. Sure better than at the halfway house."

"Or the hospital," Mary Anne said. "I love gazpacho."

"The tomatoes and corn on the cob are from the farmer's market in Collierville," Charlie said. "The corn's Silver Queen." Her stomach rumbled. That sandwich at lunch had been years ago.

"Have one," Sean said. "There's plenty."

"Thanks, but the colonel expects me for dinner." She could see the lights of the big kitchen in the main house across the patio. Vittorio would be furious if she came in late. Charlie had come close to snatching an ear from the students' platter, but managed to quiet the rumblings of her stomach. That sandwich at lunch seemed a long ago memory. The heat of the day was finally beginning to diminish as much as it ever did between Memorial Day and the end of September. It wouldn't get cool enough to manage without air-conditioning even in the middle of the night, of course, but it was still cooler than daytime.

The heat flat wore everybody out and increased appetites at dinnertime. The colonel demanded the family sit down together and was adamant that the students do the same thing. Even after her mother died, he kept up the custom, although he and Charlie sometimes didn't speak to each other from entrée through dessert. Of course, when he wasn't around, which was often, Charlie could con whoever was looking after her into letting her grab a sandwich and leave.

For Sarah, used to running in and out between sport practices or hanging out with BFFs, the formality of evening dinner was a new experience. She endured it because she was eating Vittorio's cooking and not Charlie's. And at the moment she had nothing better to do than fool with the computer in the evenings.

Charlie's mind hovered at the other dining table tonight and she only half listened to Sarah and her father bicker. As soon as she could, she escaped to check on her students.

She worried about Mickey. He might give Hank as good as he got, but Hank didn't tease — he went for the jugular. Seeing Mickey must be a constant reminder of how close he had come to losing his ability to walk as well as ride.

In any case, it wasn't acceptable.

Her father had explained to her her that Mickey wasn't actually paralyzed, although the nerve damage to his back and hips was extensive. He had rods and pins in his legs where the bones had been fragmented, as well. Still, if Mickey kept at his strength training, he might eventually be able to dispense with the wheelchair and use braces and a cane full-time. Maybe giving Hank the task of getting Mickey on his feet would provide him with a vested interest in Mickey's success.

According to the colonel, once he took his leg braces off, Mickey could pull himself up, stand and swing around to get into bed. He could handle bathroom chores and dress himself. But could he actually walk unaided for any distance *with* his braces? Charlie knew what his enrolment forms said, but then, Mary Anne had sworn she'd ridden horses, so who knew?

Charlie found the students' dishes neatly stacked on the rolling cart in the common room, the kitchen clean and the table scoured. She rolled the cart back to the kitchen, where Vittorio and Sarah were loading the dishes from the colonel's table into the dishwasher.

Vittorio, who seldom spoke even when he was happy, merely rolled his eyes at her, sighed deeply and began to unload the trolley.

"I'm sorry," Charlie said. "We'll work something out so you don't have to stay late to clean up this mess."

"Good," he said. "Go." Sarah started to strip off her apron. Vittorio pointed a stubby index finger at her. "Not you. You eat, you clean."

"Mom . . ."

"Hey, it's his kitchen. Thanks, Vittorio. Leave the sweet rolls out. I'll heat them up tomorrow morning for the students."

"Huh." He turned away with an empty platter in his hands. "These people — they eat. Even that skinny girl with the scars." Eating his food was the biggest compliment anyone could give Vittorio.

"Wait until I start teaching them. Then they'll eat us out of house and home."

She walked back to the stable, knocked on Mickey's door and found him tucked up in bed with a graphic novel. "You manage okay?" she asked, then immediately regretted her words. "I mean . . ."

"I managed," he said with a grin. "Don't worry about me. I won't break my neck."

"What's with you and Hank?"

He didn't answer for a long moment. She had started to turn away, when he said, "The colonel says he's jealous. I may be messed up, but at least I'm physically whole."

"So he undercuts you and tries to make you fail?" Charlie said.

"Hey, Charlie, it's his problem. Don't sweat it, okay? I can take care of myself."

After she said good-night to Mickey, she stopped by Mary Anne's door, heard her moving around, but didn't disturb her.

She figured Sean would check on Jake. She really didn't want to tackle Hank at the moment. But she would soon. He needed an attitude adjustment bad.

She walked back to the house. Man, she was tired. She really hadn't worked that hard physically today. Starting tomorrow, when she had to teach her students, she'd be totally exhausted by lunch.

So why did she feel as if she'd been dragged backward through a knothole?

Because emotional labor was harder than physical labor. Because she already cared about these people as people, not just students. Especially Jake. Now where had that come from?

She was too keyed up to sleep, no matter

how badly she wanted to. She needed some quiet time without anybody asking her for decisions or direction. She wanted to think about her students.

One of them, at any rate.

She walked out onto the dark patio behind the den and sank onto the glider. She stretched her legs in front of her and rested her head on the back. If she weren't careful, she'd fall asleep out here and wake up unable to straighten her spine.

F. Scott Fitzgerald was right — nights like this couldn't be called anything except tender. A cool zephyr toyed with the hair at the nape of her neck and played across the skin of her throat and arms as gently as a lover's caress.

She closed her eyes and listened to the soft sounds of the evening. In mid-August such breezes were an unusual blessing. Normally, the temperature wouldn't drop more than five degrees after the sun went down. The nights were steamy, the air a mosquito-laden miasma that wouldn't relent until late September.

But on a clear night like tonight, so many stars shimmered in the Milky Way that they tumbled like celestial milk poured from a pitcher. Charlie sighed deeply, and let the beauty seep into her bones.

Unable to decide whether to slip silently back into the common room or speak to her, Jake stood in the small stand of oaks and maples behind the patio and watched Charlie. He'd come out to see if he could recapture that peace he'd felt gazing at the stars at home when he was a kid. Instead, he was troubled by the same memories of those that hadn't survived.

He hadn't expected to see anyone else.

He could either melt back into the trees or say something to Charlie. If he didn't choose one or the other, he might stand here until morning when Sean found him.

The colonel kept reminding him that he couldn't avoid choice, and that he should make small ones that didn't matter. He wasn't crazy enough to believe that if he killed a butterfly in Mexico, he could trigger a tsunami in Samoa, but something warned him that where Charlie was concerned, his smallest decision might cause a personal earthquake for both of them. His decisions hurt people and left him alone. She had enough on her plate without adding him to the mix.

She straightened and looked into the dark.

"Is somebody there?"

She'd made his decision for him. "Just Jake," he said. He came out and walked up to the patio. When she motioned to the glider, he sat down beside her. The roses around the patio smelled sweet, but the scent of pure woman was headier by far.

Where his thigh lay along hers he felt his skin tingle. How long had it been since he'd reacted to the nearness of an attractive woman? After the attack, his body had shut down along with his mind. The doctors told him it was his way to heal faster by pulling whatever energy he had into his core. He didn't believe them.

He was used to being numb, but if he allowed himself to feel, could he control the intensity of his emotions? Or would they wake hungry for sensation like a newly wakened grizzly starved for blackberries?

Charlie had caught her breath when he sat beside her, and her shoulders tensed. Even though she'd invited him to sit with her, she might be afraid of him. That would be funny if it weren't so disturbing.

Her hand lay on her thigh. He could reach over and take it. If he chose. She wouldn't make *that* decision for him.

She'd probably slap his hand away and bolt for the house. He wouldn't be able to stay here if that happened, and he admitted he wanted to stay. A small choice but a choice all the same. This woman, this place, were already beginning to smooth out his soul.

When she realized he didn't intend to touch her, she relaxed and asked, "Where did you learn to drive draft horses?"

"In Missouri. On my father's farm." Simple question, simple answer. "Where did you?"

"Here. On my grandfather's farm." She waved a hand. "I spent every moment I could here — vacations, school holidays. I spent a whole year on the farm while my parents were stationed in Belgium. I wanted to graduate here, but the colonel said I had to join them after they came home."

"You don't sound happy about that."

"Try furious. Granddad fought to keep me, but nobody fights the colonel and wins. Oh, he thought he was doing the best thing for all of us. He always does." She clapped her hand over her mouth. "I can't believe I said that." She touched his hand. "The colonel really is an excellent psychologist. I mustn't undermine him in your eyes."

She removed her hand, but he could feel the lingering warmth of her fingers. "Not so expert with his own family?" He'd assumed the colonel was a genius with everyone, not just his patients. Thanks to him, Jake could at least acknowledge that most of his problem with decisions arose from his survivor guilt.

Actually, to discover the colonel had feet of good Tennessee clay was somehow reassuring. "Haven't you heard that old cliché that psychologists and psychiatrists raise bratty kids?" Charlie said. "You've plowed with horses, so you know the difference between telling a horse to 'gee' or 'haw,' don't you?"

He nodded although she couldn't see him. "Go right or left."

"When I was twelve, I hung out at the post stables in Maryland after school nearly every day. I didn't own my own horse, but there was a big half Percheron that I rode whenever I could. Daddy hated that I didn't go in for golf or tennis or some team sport that would — and I quote — serve me in later life. When we moved, I wanted to buy Doyle and bring him down to Granddad's, but Daddy wouldn't let me. Mom, as usual, backed him up. He said I already had horses to ride during my vacations, and we certainly couldn't ship a horse to the District of Columbia and pay expensive board. He just didn't get it. Leaving Doyle for the next kid to ride nearly killed me."

He felt his heart go out to her. When he left home, he'd missed the horses almost as much as he missed his family, even though leaving them behind had been his choice. "I'm sorry."

"He still doesn't think he did anything wrong." She spread her arms wide. "What was the big deal? I could ride when I came down here. After Mom got sick, I didn't have time for extracurricular activities anyway. We declared a truce for her sake, but I've never forgotten."

She turned to him, and even in the dark he could see the glint of tears in her eyes. "After she died, when he said gee, I went haw."

He longed to take her in his arms, but she might mistake his comfort for something else. Besides, if the colonel walked out to the patio, he might deck Jake. How could the man be so empathetic toward his patients and so blind to his daughter? "He does miraculous things as a psychologist," she said. "I'm sure he'll help you. I can't believe you let me run my mouth like that."

"I'm honored you told me."

He expected she'd bolt, but she stayed quiet and moved the glider with her toe.

Maybe he could lighten the atmosphere

between them. In the distance the sound of a bullfrog filled the silence. Jake took that as his cue. "Well, Mr. Bullfrog, I hope the lady you're courting appreciates your fine bass baritone."

Charlie sighed and relaxed. "I wonder what he did to shut down his rivals."

An answering chorus settled that question.

"They sound like one of those Russian army choruses," Jake said. "No tenors need apply."

"The peepers have their own choir," Charlie said. "And then there are the cicadas — they remind me of fingernails on a blackboard."

"Not this late in the summer."

Sitting beside him, Charlie felt grateful that he'd directed the subject away from her and her life. It was so easy to open up to Jake. Was that what Mary Anne had sensed? What had she told him when she was locked in her room? He might not trust himself, but Mary Anne trusted him. So did Charlie.

And boy, was that dangerous. "We'd both better get to bed," she said, stopping the movement of the glider and standing up. "Tomorrow's going to be a tough day."

She left him sitting alone and fled up the

stairs to her room. Did cold showers work for females? She washed off her makeup, brushed her teeth, pulled on the T-shirt she slept in and crawled into the big Lincoln bed, sure that she'd sleep. But her mind kept churning.

Jake was a stranger, a student and a soldier. Triple threat.

After Steve died, she vowed never to allow anyone remotely military into her life again. No more warriors. No more dragging around the world after them and making a new home each time, the way her mother had done for her father. No more sudden deployments to Nowheresville or the other side of the world. No more shaking with terror every time the doorbell rang for fear it was the bad one — the notification that her husband was dead. Once was enough. She and Sarah had never been enough for Steve. Oh, he'd tried, but in the final analysis the pleasure of being with his wife and daughter couldn't compete with his need to be back in the action. Between deployments, he loathed being a garrison soldier. He was addicted to danger and eventually, like most addictions, it killed him.

Warriors were great to have around when Genghis Khan and Attila the Hun were just over the horizon and coming fast. Not so great when they weren't.

Sitting next to Jake, she could feel her resolution to avoid warriors weakening. Bad. Bad and stupid. Jake might seem gentle, he might be an *ex*-soldier, but she could still sense the testosterone.

She'd fallen for Steve on sight. In the fourteen years they'd been married, she'd never looked at another man, even though that meant months of celibacy while he was on temporary duty or deployed somewhere she and Sarah couldn't follow.

He'd really had to work to kill her love for him, but he'd finally managed.

No matter how attracted she was to Jake, he was her student. Not acceptable. He also had psychological problems that she couldn't possibly inflict on Sarah.

CHAPTER FIVE

"Okay, you tenderfoots — tenderfeet — time to take your breakfast dishes into the house, pick up your hats and gloves, and learn the fine art of stall mucking." Charlie realized what she'd said after the words left her mouth. She gave a quick glance at Hank, but he seemed not to have caught her incredible gaffe. Calling him a tenderfoot! How could she?

She caught Jake's eye and felt herself blushing. He'd made the connection, all right. He gave a tiny nod as though to assure her that he absolved her. For a man who ignored his own lunch, he was too aware of the nuances of other people's behavior.

"I did you a big favor this morning," she continued. "I've already fed and watered the horses. From here on you'll do that before breakfast. Then we muck stalls. I did *not* do that for you."

"I'm exempt from mucking stalls," Mickey said cheerfully. "I don't swing a pitchfork too good from a wheelchair."

"Put on your doggone leg braces," Hank snapped. "Aren't you supposed to practice standing and walking?"

"He can't pick up a pitchfork full of horse manure yet," Sean said, and turned to Mickey. "Good try, kid. I didn't get my sergeant stripes putting up with slackers. I will personally find some nasty chore you can do sitting down."

"You're retired, Sarge," Mickey said with a grin. "You ain't the boss o' me any longer."

"But I am," Charlie said, and slapped the back of the wheelchair cheerfully. "While the rest of us are learning to muck horse manure out of stalls, I'll set you up in the tack room with saddle soap and harness polish. I'll bet you know how to put a spit shine on leather, am I right?"

Mickey groaned. "When do I get to try out that handicapped carriage the colonel was talking about yesterday?"

"After you've learned how to handle the reins and been approved by an instructor. Me. And you won't be driving alone for a while."

She glanced around the table. "Since our regular grooms are on vacation, you'll be doing their work as well as learning to drive. You can get used to handling reins by practicing on a rein board that emulates what it feels like to drive a horse. We have three in the tack room. We'll rotate, since I imagine some of you need more practice than others." She smiled at Jake, who had joined them after breakfast. She hadn't bothered to try to get him to eat breakfast with them. Lunch was another matter.

She was grateful that he acted as though nothing had happened between them last night.

"Our grooms, Maurice and DeMarcus, feed and water at seven every morning." She slid into one of the remaining chairs around the common room table. "Then they muck stalls and help harness and put to the horses."

"Put to what?" Sean asked.

"That's what you call harnessing a horse," Charlie said. "And a horse that is harnessed to a cart or carriage is called being 'in draft.' There are a lot of peculiar terms and traditions about carriage driving because it's been around such a long time. Any of you ever see the big parades from England with the fancy golden carriages and all the white horses?"

Several heads nodded. Jake's didn't move.

"The carriages are fancier than ours, but we do the same things. The horses are already well broke and used to being in draft, but there's not a horse in the world that won't spook in certain circumstances." Charlie glanced at Mary Anne and saw her twist her hands in her lap. "It's not like driving a truck or a motorcycle. Remember, the horse wants to survive, too. The motorcycle doesn't give a darn."

Charlie decided to see if she could borrow a small pony and cart from one of her carriage-driving friends for Mary Anne to try. She might be less frightened behind a pony. She could progress to a horse. If they were lucky.

"Now, you're also going to learn what it takes to run a farm like this. Yesterday I picked up twenty bags of rolled oats from the feed store, and some trace mineral blocks. They need to be unloaded from my truck. Then later, a load of bagged wood shavings is being delivered from a sawmill in Mississippi."

"Mary Anne can't pick up fifty-pound feed bags," Hank said.

"I can pick up anything you can," Mary Anne snapped.

"Sure you can," Hank snickered.

"This is not a contest," Charlie said. She

noted that Hank's snide remark had brought Jake's gaze up, but he said nothing. Jake's fuse might be long, but she suspected it would burn hot once somebody lit it. If he hadn't had some propensity for violence, why would he have joined the army?

She continued. "The horses that are not actually on the driving roster are in pasture. That includes four Percheron mares, two of whom have foals at foot. We'll take a look at them after lunch. One shire mare is pregnant with a late foal, the other is barren this year. So, with luck, you'll get to see a baby born sometime soon. If we can catch her having it, that is."

"Can't you tell when it's coming?" Mary Anne asked.

"Theoretically. But mares are sneaky. We'll bring her into the foaling stall when she starts showing signs she's close to labor, but she'll probably wait until the darkest, stormiest night of the year when everybody's back is turned before she drops her foal." She nodded. "Okay, people, let's get to it."

Mary Anne stacked fifty-pound bags of feed right along with Charlie and the men. Every time she passed Hank, she tossed her head at him. He grinned and shrugged.

Midmorning a rusty three-quarter-ton

truck with square bags of shavings loaded precariously on its bed pulled up outside the aisle door.

"Hey, Charlie, you got room to stack these shavings in the same place?" The middle-aged man who stuck his head out of the truck wore a straw Stetson over a face that looked as tough as if it had been professionally tanned but not stretched afterward.

"Man has more wrinkles than a Shar-Pei," Sean whispered.

"Hush," Charlie whispered back. Then she said in a normal voice, "Drive on down the aisle to the end as usual, Bobby."

"We got any help? Where's Maurice and DeMarcus?"

"On vacation. Jake and Sean here will help unload. Guys, this is Bobby Holzer. He owns the sawmill down in Slayden that bags our shavings."

Bobby nodded and pointed to the figure beside him in the shadows. "I brung some help just in case. This here's one of my summer helpers." He put the truck in gear, drove down the stable aisle to the far end and parked by the storage area where the few remaining bales sat waiting for the new load to be added.

The white-blond hair of the kid who climbed from the passenger seat was partially covered by a St. Louis Cardinals baseball cap. Unlike Bobby, who wore baggy bib overalls over a plaid shirt with the sleeves rolled up, the boy had on distressed jeans stretched tight over thigh muscles the size of hawsers on an aircraft carrier, while his arms and torso strained the stitching on his green polo shirt. He stood at six-six or six-seven and probably weighed well over three hundred pounds. None of it was fat. "Aidan, this is Miss Charlie Nicholson, owner and manager." The giant nodded.

"Whoa!" Sean whispered.

Bobby smiled and winked at him. "Aidan's starting at tackle for Mississippi State this fall. Coach sends 'em to me for the summer. Tells 'em working in the sawmill builds muscles."

"He's got enough already," Sean said.

Charlie introduced Sean and Jake. Bobby shook hands. Aidan didn't.

He looked sulky at the prospect of unloading and stacking an entire truckload of sixty-pound bales, but he hopped up on the back of the truck and worked his way to the front without comment.

"Give them a hand, please," Charlie said to Sean and Jake. "I'm off to the tack room to teach Mickey and Mary Anne how to use the rein board."

Jake climbed up on the tailgate and waited for the first bale.

The moment Charlie turned her back, Aidan swung it at Jake's chest so hard he would have knocked him off the back of the truck if Sean hadn't balanced him from the ground. His grin said he'd done it on purpose.

"Knock that off, Aidan," Bobby said equably. "Sorry, Jake. He gets above himself sometimes. Likes to show off how strong he is."

Aidan shrugged and lobbed the next bale high and easy. Jake fielded it and passed it down to Sean.

After that Aidan settled down, and the three men established an easy rhythm from Aidan to Jake to Sean to the shavings shed. After all the bales were off the truck, Bobby directed Aidan to finish stacking them.

As he passed Sean, Aidan asked, "Hey, man, that some kind of phony hand?"

"Nope. It's real plastic," Sean answered cheerfully. "A gift from the United States Army."

By the time the stacks were complete, all three men were soaked with sweat and Aidan's designer jeans were filthy. Bobby rose from the front step of the truck and joined them. "Hot work."

Sean's glance at Jake said "none of which *he* did."

"Y'all got any cold sodas?" Bobby asked. "I'm flat parched."

Aidan slouched past him toward the front of the truck. "Aw, come on, Bobby, let's go get some lunch."

Wiping her face with her scarf, Mary Anne came out of the tack room and strode toward them. She wore a sleeveless muscle shirt that revealed the puckered skin that ran from the side of her head to her glove. The sheen of sweat made the scars look red and raw.

She noticed Bobby and Aidan a minute before they noticed her, and wheeled back toward the tack room.

"Ooo-eee," whispered Aidan as he watched her retreating rear in its tight jeans. "Hellooo, mama."

She froze in midstride, turned and strode back toward them.

Jake heard Bobby catch his breath.

Aidan gaped and looked away. "No way. I don't mess with ugly chicks."

Jake saw Mary Anne stiffen and heard Sean groan.

"Jake — leave it," Sean cautioned. "Jake!"

Jake ignored him and moved into Aidan.

A moment later, the big man lay flat on

his back.

"Here now," Bobby said. "Both of y'all take it easy."

Aidan was big, but he was fast. He came off the ground in a lineman's crouch, prepared to tear Jake in two.

"Back off, fool." Sean stepped between the two men. Aidan brushed him out of the way.

Jake felt Sean's hand on his arm and shook him off. He blocked the fist Aidan swung at his jaw, twisted, bent and thrust. A moment later Aidan was back on the ground, looking surprised.

"Stay down!" Sean snarled at him.

Aidan gasped. "What'd I do?"

"Apologize to the lady," Jake whispered.

Aidan struggled to his feet. That a man twenty years older and a hundred pounds lighter could toss him around like a football seemed to hit him square in his manhood. "Listen, old man." He lowered his voice. "Y'all gotta know that's a freak." A moment later, he was back on the ground with Bobby standing over him.

"Aidan, you idiot, stay down," Bobby said. "You ain't got the brains of a goose. Stop running your mouth before you get your teeth handed to you."

"I warned you to stay down, goober,"

Sean said pleasantly. "Now do what the man says and apologize to the little lady before he tears your arm off and feeds it to you."

Jake glanced back at Mary Anne, who was glaring at Aidan. Sean grasped her hand with his right one and pulled her forward. As if his touch inflated her, she squared her shoulders, lifted her chin and snapped, "Yeah, jerk. Apologize to the ugly lady."

From the ground, Aidan had to look up at her, but he couldn't hold her gaze. "I'm sorry, okay? I didn't mean nothing. Bobby says I got a big mouth."

"Ya think?" she said, and kept her hand in Sean's.

"You can get up, now," Jake said. "I assume you were recruited for your size and not your GPA. Come on, Sean, we have horses to groom." He strode off toward the wash rack.

Charlie passed him at a trot. "Bobby, what's going on?"

"Aidan here," Sean said, "slipped and fell." He grinned.

"Three times," Bobby said. "A man that big, sometimes he's real clumsy, aren't you, Aidan." He gave his helper a hand up, then a gentle shove toward the truck. "Here's the bill, Charlie. Me 'n Aidan are gonna go get some lunch."

"Good girl," Sean said to Mary Anne under his breath. He turned to Aidan. "You have just had a narrow escape. The major can take off the top of a man's head with the flat of his hand."

Bobby laughed as Aidan climbed into the truck, put it in gear and waved to them through the driver's window as they drove away.

The moment the truck cleared the stable aisle, Mary Anne caught her breath in a sob and ran past Charlie to the common room.

"Sean?" Charlie asked.

"Ask Jake." He followed Mary Anne.

Charlie trotted after him. "Where is he?"

"Mary Anne . . ."

"Leave her to me," Charlie said. "You go find Jake."

Sean hesitated, then nodded.

The common room was empty. Mary Anne's bedroom door was locked again. When she pressed her ear against it, Charlie heard what sounded like sobbing. "Mary Anne? It's Charlie. Please let me in."

"Go 'way."

"Not this time. I'm not Jake, but I can sit in the hall and wait as long as he did."

She thought she might have to, but after a moment she heard the lock click. By the time she opened the door, Mary Anne lay facedown on her bed with her arms locked over her head. "I want to go back to the hospital."

Charlie sat on the bed but didn't touch her. "You'll get over being afraid of the horses."

Mary Anne rolled over and sat up. "Jake nearly got himself killed because that jock said I was ugly. I *am* ugly! I'm so ugly people want to vomit when they look at me."

"That's not true."

Mary Anne got off the bed and began to pace the small room. "Don't lie, Charlie. I saw that kid's face. I saw all your faces when I took off my scarf. The first time my husband — sorry, my *ex*-husband — saw me in the hospital without my bandages, he ran into the bathroom and threw up."

What could Charlie say to that? "I'm sure it was just the initial shock. Soldiers know what happens in a war zone."

Mary Anne leaned her forehead against her window. "Charlie, he's a civilian. An accountant, would you believe. I'd already enlisted when I met him. Bad enough I was a mechanic. Bad enough I deployed six months after we got married, but with the internet we stayed connected. We were in love! We had all these plans for when my enlistment was over. Then this happened."

"Of course, he was devastated for you," Charlie said. "But he didn't stop loving you."

Mary Anne leaned a hip against the windowsill. "He really tried. He took a part-time job close to the hospital to be with me. But the first time one of the nurses tried to teach him to change my dressings, he ran. When they let me out on a twenty-four-hour pass to be with him, he couldn't touch me. We sat up all night crying. The next week I filed for divorce. It wasn't his fault, Charlie, and it definitely wasn't mine."

"So you want to go back to the hospital to start more operations right now? I thought you wanted to take a break."

Mary Anne flopped back down on the bed. "I did. I do. But nobody looks at me twice in the hospital."

Charlie wrapped her arm around Mary Anne. "We won't let you quit. And when you do have more operations, we'll learn to change your dressings and you'll come back here to recuperate."

"You can't promise that!"

"The heck I can't. Now wash your face and let's go groom horses."

While Charlie talked to Mary Anne, Jake leaned against the trunk of the big oak at the edge of the stallion's paddock and fought to get his breathing back to normal.

"Jake, you okay?" Sean said.

"I might have killed that kid," Jake said. His voice shook.

"Huh. Good thing you didn't. Would have caused Charlie no end of trouble." Sean squatted in the grass at Jake's feet.

Jake slid down with his back to the trunk. "You see why I don't trust myself? A stupid kid makes a hurtful remark and I go for him."

"Most likely he'd tear your head off," Sean said.

"You and I are trained in hand-to-hand combat. That was like pairing a Golden Gloves semifinalist against Sugar Ray Leonard."

"He insulted Mary Anne. I'd have done worse if you hadn't gotten to him first. But you backed off, Jake. That was a choice. The right choice. Come on, we got horses to tend."

"In a minute. Soon as my hands stop shaking."

Jake had felt certain he'd tamed his rage. But he'd been wrong. Going after Aidan was crazy. But when the boy insulted Mary Anne, Jake had responded automatically.

He shouldn't have.

What if he had actually hurt Aidan? What if Aidan sued Charlie and brought the whole program down? It would have been his fault.

Another decision, another disaster.

The old tape began to play in his head. He held his head between his palms to make it stop, but that never worked.

The army had absolved him of blame. Why couldn't he absolve himself? He hadn't trusted the order that sent them in, but he'd led his team anyway, because you didn't disobey a direct order. Then he drove off and lived, while they had died.

He'd been unconscious all the way to Ramstein hospital in Germany, and he'd spent two months in rehab before he could walk without a cane. Without intravenous antibiotics, superb surgery and aftercare, he'd have lost his leg above the knee. His limp was a small price to pay for a whole leg.

He'd hated the insurgents who'd suckered them, but they were soldiers, too, doing what they thought to be their duty.

The colonel who'd ordered them in, on the other hand, delivered the command from an air-conditioned office behind a concrete perimeter. The men he moved around weren't men to him at all, but numbers on his fitness report.

Jake went over to the outdoor spigot beside the water trough at the edge of the pasture, leaned down and turned on the water. He stuck his head under it and gasped as the icy stream struck the back of his neck. Bracing one hand on the fence post, he felt his pulse slow.

The brass had rotated his so-called superior officer back home at Mach ten. His career was over. He'd never make brigadier. The man deserved more punishment than that, but the months of surgery and rehab had scoured Jake clean of the will for revenge. By the time the hospital declared him cured — right — he couldn't make up his mind what he wanted for breakfast. He couldn't choose to search and destroy an ant on the sidewalk.

He turned off the hose and shook his hair back. Grooming horses had always calmed him. He headed back into the barn and found Sean waiting for him.

Twenty minutes and two geldings later, Charlie appeared in the door to the common room. "Jake, may I speak to you a minute?"

He sighed and followed her into the room. Charlie was going to toss him out. He'd be back on the streets of Memphis before dinnertime.

The realization that he wanted to stay in the program stunned him. Then came the equally shocking revelation that the reason he wanted to stay was because of Charlie.

"Where's Mary Anne? Is she all right?" he asked.

She nodded. "In her room cleaning up. Sit."

He sat on the couch with his head bowed, ready for the blow.

"Sean and Mary Anne told me what happened out there. What's your version?"

"That young man made a foul comment about Mary Anne loud enough for her to hear."

"So you attacked him? That rhinoceros? He could have killed you."

"I asked him to apologize. Forcefully."

She pulled off her baseball cap and ran her hand through her short hair. He'd thought from the first that she had great hair. Shining and sleek as an otter's pelt. At the moment, her fine gray eyes were as chilly as the Bering Sea. He'd disappointed her. He hated that.

"Charlie, I'm sorry, I got annoyed."

She lifted her hand to shut him up.

He could tell she didn't quite know how to react. She teetered on the edge between exasperation and what?

"*Forcefully?* Annoyed?" She dropped onto the sofa beside him. "Oh, Jake, heaven preserve us all if you ever get pushed past annoyed."

She was right. He'd dropped his guard for a moment, and look what had happened.

"I would probably have driven the truck over him," Charlie admitted.

"You're not angry at me?"

"I'm furious at you. Officially. Unofficially, good for you." She took his hand and pulled him up.

He surged off the couch with more force than he'd intended and almost fell into her. His body reacted instantly.

Their eyes met and held for much too long. He felt as though he'd been hit with a Taser and electricity flowed through them both, welding them together. "Charlie . . ." His hand slid to the nape of her neck as she lifted her chin. Then he ran his fingers along her cheek and across her soft lips. The hunger he felt to taste them was unbearable. He bent his head . . .

"Mom? Get the door."

They jumped apart like a pair of teenagers caught necking.

Charlie opened the door to the breezeway for Sarah.

"I've got the cold cuts and I'm about to drop the platter. Help!"

Jake swooped the plate out of Sarah's arms and carried it to the kitchen counter.

"Thanks." Sarah narrowed her eyes at him, then sat on the sofa and folded her arms like a teenage duenna.

"Don't you have some other stuff to bring over for lunch?" Charlie asked.

"It won't be ready for a couple of minutes."

"That'll give you just enough time to help Vittorio organize everything. Unless you'd prefer to help teach Mary Anne not to be afraid of horses."

"I'll go help Vittorio."

"You are having lunch with us, aren't you?"

"I guess."

Charlie nodded. "Good." She leaned down and kissed the top of Sarah's head. The girl flinched.

Mary Anne joined the group in the stable ten minutes later. The big red mare was cross tied on the wash rack while Hank lounged against the wall and Sean hovered. Mary Anne wasn't precisely shaking, but her arms were wrapped around her body protectively. At the door of the tack room Mickey sat in his wheelchair with a grin on

96

his impish face.

"Her name's Annie, like yours," Charlie said.

Mary Anne made a sound that was half bleat, half whimper. "She's humongous."

Charlie fished in the pocket of her jeans, pulled out a sugar cube and handed it to Mary Anne. "Put it flat on the palm of your hand like this." The mare reached her lips forward and scarfed up the sugar cube. The instant Mary Anne felt the horse's touch, she snatched her hand away.

"See, she didn't bite you." Charlie said. "Try again. She'd be happy to stand here and let you feed her sugar cubes all day."

Mary Anne hunched her shoulders. This time she stretched her hand out without Charlie's grip on her wrist, but she still pulled away the instant Annie vacuumed up the cube.

Sean gave Charlie a thumbs-up sign. "We'll work on her," he said.

Charlie left them to it and went across to the house. She heard Sarah talking to Vittorio in the kitchen, took the stairs two at a time and threw herself on her bed. Today, Jake had revealed he still reacted like a soldier. No thought, no decision. Action. What if it happened again? How could she head him off? She was glad Sarah hadn't been there.

In the meantime . . . she pulled her cell phone out of her pocket and dialed a familiar number.

Time to find a pony and cart for Mary Anne.

CHAPTER SIX

Lunch went much smoother than yesterday. Jake selected a sandwich and put his own mustard and mayo on the dark rye without asking Sean first.

"Jake, come join us at the table," Charlie said.

"No, thank you," he said, and went outside to eat in the glider on the patio.

"Let him be, Charlie," Sean said. "I'm working on him. You fight him every meal, he'll starve and we'll all have ulcers."

Or pitch a fit. She'd tackle him alone later.

Outside Jake must have attacked the sandwich ravenously, because he quickly reappeared and chose another from the platter. He brought his dishes in and stacked them on the trolley, then sat by the window and stared out over the back pasture.

"Okay, break time," Charlie said. "Go take a siesta or read a book where it's cool. I'll see you at three."

She was dragging, and she was used to the work. Everyone else must be exhausted. She barely made it upstairs to her room before she collapsed on her bed.

This afternoon, however, she couldn't turn her mind off. She hadn't expected to react physically when she felt Jake against her. Steve hadn't been dead a year yet, though their marriage had been dead much longer.

Until this morning, Jake had seemed so gentle, so calm.

He could have done much more damage to that big jerk. She knew from her years growing up among soldiers and being married to a soldier that their reactions had to be completely automatic to be effective. They were trained to kill.

Few of them were natural-born killers, though. Most couldn't wait to get home to their families.

Get a bunch of the guys together at the club, and like as not they'd keep everyone in stitches with all the stories about funny things that happened while they were deployed.

Then you caught the glances between them and realized how much you would never know of what they had endured.

Most settled back into the real world

happy never to have to go to war again. But so many of them were on their fourth or fifth tours in Iraq or Afghanistan. Each time changed them a little more.

Then there were a few, like Steve, who only felt alive when he was experiencing the excitement, the danger of living on the edge. He'd always been a fear junky. Drag racing on the streets, racing motorcycles. He'd done it all and survived. He'd never taken drugs and, until he came home the last time, seldom drank. Nothing to dull that exhilaration of cheating death one more time.

Falling for Steve had been the ultimate rebellion against her father after her mother died. Her father had tried to talk her out of marrying him. He might have succeeded eventually, if she hadn't gotten pregnant with Sarah.

To Steve's credit, he'd asked her to marry him the minute she told him about the baby. He adored his child long after he stopped loving his wife.

What chance did they have to build a successful marriage when he was away from home more often than he was there? A backyard barbecue couldn't compete with a night patrol.

Steve had been gone most of two years

the last time he came home. He'd expected things to have remained exactly the same as when he left.

But Sarah had changed. And Charlie, too. Without Steve, she'd been forced to grow up, and found she liked it.

She'd grown accustomed to making all the decisions, including the ones about automobile maintenance, cleaning the gutters, paying the bills, filing the income tax, unclogging the toilet. . . .

She replaced the belt on the riding lawn mower and drove it without killing herself or someone else, managed a teaching job, mastered technology that Steve didn't understand and denigrated because he didn't. He'd left a young wife who deferred to him for every decision. He came home to a grown woman who handled the logistics of life quite well without him.

Steve hated that. Pretty soon he hated her.

She was no longer in awe of him, but she grew afraid of him. He never hit her, but he came close in a couple of his rages. And close to hitting Sarah.

Even Sarah got to the point where she avoided him.

At the end, he hadn't even tried to make the marriage work. He told her to divorce him, because he was volunteering to go back in-country ASAP. Being a garrison soldier was a bore and so was she.

Two months later he was dead.

And she was left to grieve the man she married. She didn't even know the man who died.

Chapter Seven

Charlie was surprised to find Sarah and Mary Anne sitting on the worn leather couch in the common room. Sarah was sucking down some kind of purple smoothie. Mary Anne was finishing a diet soda. Sarah gave her a glance when Charlie went to get herself one from the small kitchen but spoke to Mary Anne, not to her mother.

"Does your face still hurt, Mary Anne?"

Charlie cringed. "Sarah!"

"It's okay, Charlie," Mary Anne said over her shoulder. "No more freak-outs. Besides, she wants information, right, Sarah?"

Sarah gave her mother a look that said, *See?*

Mary Anne turned to Sarah. "The colonel says I should talk about it, distance it. Sometimes it works, sometimes it doesn't. Right after it happened, they kept me doped up, but they couldn't keep doing that forever without turning me into a drug addict. Skin grafts are the worst. They have to break up the scar tissue with healthy skin or it'll get so tight I won't be able to flex my arm."

Sarah's eyes grew wide.

Mary Anne shook her head. "You do not want to know the details. It's really going to be fun when they sew on my new ear in a couple of months."

"Ew," Sarah said. "I'd be scared stiff."

Mary Anne went to the refrigerator and came back with another can of diet soda. "I needed a break. That's why I lied to everybody about how much I like horses."

She curled up on the sofa alongside Sarah again, popped the top and took a hefty swallow. "Can't believe I'm still thirsty. It's a whole lot hotter in the desert. I'm actually a truck mechanic. Diesel engines don't bite."

Charlie thought, *No, they explode and burn you alive.*

Mary Anne laughed when she saw the surprise in Sarah's eyes. "You don't have to be that big to handle an impact wrench, and I can climb into places under the hood that the moose-size guys can't reach."

"You can actually do stuff like that?"

"Show me a truck or a tractor that needs fixing, give me the tools, and I'll lay you odds I can fix it." Her face clouded. "Or I could when I had two good arms."

Charlie stood at the kitchen counter and watched the two sitting side by side on the scratched leather sofa. There couldn't be that much difference in their ages, and Sarah was already five inches taller than Mary Anne.

She'd be eighteen in four short years. Eligible to enlist without anyone's permission. Her baby! Charlie shuddered. Please God, she'd go to college. Please God, there wouldn't be any wars after she graduated.

Please God, she'd never see her child wounded. So much worse than being in pain herself.

"Did you get bombed?" Sarah asked.

"You could say that," Mary Anne said. She stared out the window. Her right arm lay along the back of the sofa, and Charlie saw her scarred fingers flex.

She wondered if she should interrupt but couldn't bring herself to intrude. Instead, she stood quietly behind the kitchen counter, afraid to breathe.

"I was driving back to base in an APC — that's an Armored Personnel Carrier. It had busted a belt, and I'd gone out to change it and volunteered to ride back with the driver in case it didn't hold."

"First rule," Sarah said. "Never volunteer. My daddy taught me that."

"Yeah. Your daddy was right. We triggered a roadside bomb. I got blown out the right side. You go deaf, you know? I just had the breath knocked out of me, but the truck was listing to the right and smoking. The driver was stuck."

"Was he a friend of yours?" Sarah asked.

Mary Anne shook her head. "Never met him. I thought I had time to get him out before the cab caught or the gas tank blew, so I ran around the rear end and managed to pull his door open. I didn't even know I was hurt. All that adrenaline, you know?"

"Did you get him out?" Sarah whispered.

Mary Anne looked into the distance. "Yeah, I actually did. He lost a leg, but his face is okay. Sometimes I'd be willing to swap."

"Can they fix you?"

"Most of me. Eventually. My new ear will probably look like they stole it from a goat."

"What are you gonna do in the meantime?"

Mary Anne shrugged. "Unless I'm among friends like now, long sleeves and scarves. What else?"

Sarah shook her head. "Uh-uh. When we were stationed in Tacoma a couple of years ago, my BFF Keira got alopecia. You know what that is?"

"Not a clue."

"It's genetic. Her sister has it, too. You lose all your hair — I mean *all.* Eyebrows, eyelashes, even the down on her arms."

"Must have been tough for a teenager."

"At first, she covered up and hid out. But she had to go to school, and she was an acolyte at the Episcopal Church. Her mother bought her a couple of cheap wigs that looked like they belonged on a yak. Then she decided to go commando. Came to school bald as a billiard ball. After a couple of hours, nobody even noticed, much less said anything. Like you, today."

"Oh, I think people notice me."

"The thing is, Keira's learned to do a super job with makeup, and her mother finally bought her two really nice real hair wigs she wears for church and parties and stuff."

"Not exactly like my case."

"Sure it is," Sarah said.

"I beg your pardon?"

"I mean, like I could help you." Sarah swung around and pulled her legs up under her so that she was kneeling on the sofa.

This was the first time Charlie had seen Sarah enthusiastic since she'd told her they were moving down to Tennessee. Sarah wanted to help someone else. If she hadn't been afraid to break the spell, Charlie would have hugged her.

"I'm really good with makeup, and you could get a nice wig that curls around your face."

"It's a great idea, but good wigs cost a fortune."

"I'll bet the army would pay. I can check the net for bargains."

"Slow down, honey," Charlie said. The light went out of Sarah's eyes when she looked at her mother. "It's up to Mary Anne."

"I was just trying to help." Sarah flung herself off the sofa and started for the door.

"Sarah, I know you want to help. . . ." More guilt. *You, too, can rain on your daughter's parade.*

"Yeah, Sarah, come on back," Mary Anne said. "She's not pushing me, Charlie. Let me think about it."

"Great!" Sarah said. "How about you come up to my room after dinner and we can fool around with some stuff." She wrinkled her nose at her mother in a "so there" expression.

"Sure, why not?"

"My room's kind of a mess, but I've

stashed plenty of samples from the mall in Kansas, and I'll bet I can find great stuff on the net. See you after dinner." She ran out and let the door slam behind her.

She actually sounded happy!

But Charlie felt she had to offer Mary Anne an out. "You don't have to do this if you don't want to."

"I want to. Could a wig work? Without looking phony? Maybe I should just shave my head." She chuckled. "Go commando like Sarah's friend."

"If you're serious, we can drive the truck into town tomorrow afternoon and try on a couple." Charlie grinned. "Preferably not made to fit a yak. And I'll ask the colonel if the army will pay. If not, we'll work something out."

"I don't want to take you away from the rest of the class," Mary Anne said.

"Are you nuts? We're talking actual shopping here."

Late in the afternoon the temperature hadn't gone down much, but the sun was no longer scalding.

"Okay, people, time for your first carriage ride," Charlie said. "Come on, Sean, Jake. You two can bring out the marathon carriage. Mickey, you can go with them and

110

check out the disabled carriage." She led the three men through the exit at the far end of the barn and into another building that looked like a warehouse. "This is our carriage storage area. Back there is the shed where we keep the tractors and the farm equipment." She pulled the wide doors open and tripped the light switch. "Voilà."

"Ah, right!" Mickey said.

"That one on the left is set up for your wheelchair," she said. "We roll it up the ramp, lock it down to the floor of the carriage, raise the ramp, and you're good to go."

"Yeah, but I can't do it alone," he said.

"That, Mickey, me bucko, is what grooms are for. Right, Charlie?" Sean said.

"Until Maurice and DeMarcus get back, that means the rest of you. Now, here's the carriage we're going to use most of the time. It can be driven single or to a pair, but you'll be limited to a single horse for a while."

Jake had wandered down to the far end.

"Hey, earth to Jake. We need you to pull one of the shafts," Charlie said.

"When can we drive the victoria?" he asked.

Charlie turned on the overhead fluorescent lights.

"Hey, man, that's a beast!" Mickey said,

and powered off down the aisle. At the far end sat an elegant carriage that looked as though it had been transported from the mid-nineteenth century. It was painted black with yellow striping on the tires and had bright yellow leather seats facing each other. The tall box where the driver sat was edged with gold bullion fringe, as was the canopy that could be raised in a rainstorm to cover the passengers.

"It's actually a vis-à-vis," Charlie said. "The passengers sit facing one another while the coachman drives high up in front." She pointed to another carriage, this one painted bright red. "*That's* a victoria."

"Where's the pumpkin coach for Cinderella?" Mickey asked.

"We don't have one," Charlie said. "I think they're tacky."

"Aw, where's the romance in your soul?" he asked with a big grin.

"Try dragging one of those things into a big horse van to transport to a wedding, and then talk to me about romance."

"I'm excused from the dragging part," Mickey said. "No can do, remember?"

"Yet," Jake said. He'd been staring so quietly at the vis-à-vis that the others had supposed he wasn't listening.

"Huh?" Mickey asked.

Jake turned. Charlie had been expecting a sweet smile. Instead, he gave Mickey a stern look as he came toward them. "I said, you are not walking *yet.*"

"Heck, yeah, I'm walking, if you count three steps and then fall on my face."

"You will be," Jake said, and grabbed the end of one of the shafts on the carriage.

Sean raised an eyebrow at Charlie and grabbed the other shaft. "Comin' through. Out of the way, kid."

Charlie spent an hour instructing her students on the way to put the harness on the Percheron. It was heavy and complicated from the big horse collar to the steel hames, to the bridle, back to the crupper that buckled under his tail.

"Make sure you keep the tail hairs out of the crupper," Charlie continued. "It's like having your own hair pulled. Horses don't like it and can kick the stew out of you. Sean and Jake, raise the shafts high over the horse's when you bring the carriage up. Horses take exception to being poked in the butt by the ends of carriage shafts."

"How come he's got those flat leather pieces that stick out beside his eyes?" Mickey asked.

"They're blinders," Jake said. "The horses don't like seeing the carriage behind them.

They can feel it's there, but if they can see it, some of them react as though it's chasing them and try to get away from it."

"And you know this how?" Hank said with narrowed eyes.

"I read a lot."

"Jake has driven before," Charlie said. "But not for a long time, right, Jake?"

"Do I have to get up there?" Mary Anne asked Charlie, pointing to the tall seats in the front. She was leaning against Sean, who had dropped a protective arm across her shoulders.

"I'll be in front in the driver's seat," Charlie said. "The really high one on the right. Hank will sit beside me for the first drive, then you can swap places. The rear seats are for the navigator and groom. You can step up on that low step, slide in, sit down and hang on to the metal struts. When we stop, Sean or Jake will help you down. I promise I'll put you down before we trot. You and Mickey can watch us."

"What about me?" Mickey said. "How come *he* gets to go first?" He nodded at Hank.

"If we have time and energy after this, we'll get out your carriage. We may have to wait until tomorrow morning to actually put a horse to it. You all right with that?"

"I guess." Mickey glared at Hank, who smirked back.

"Everybody stop in the tack room, find a hard hat that fits, put it on and fasten the chin strap," Charlie said. "I don't expect anyone to fall off, but if you should bump your head it's nice to have a big hunk of fiberglass and padding between your skull and the dirt."

By the time they came back in their hats, Charlie had put on hers and donned her brown leather driving gloves. "Jake, can you take the ties off and head the horse?" Charlie asked.

"Head the horse?" Sean repeated.

"Never leave a horse loose when it's attached to a carriage," Charlie said. "You stand at its head and hold the bridle until the driver is seated and in control of the reins."

Hank had started to climb aboard when Charlie stopped him. "Hey, cowboy! Never, ever mount before the driver is up and gives you permission."

"Yes, ma'am," Hank said.

"Okay, everybody climb aboard," Charlie said. "Pindar, stand." Charlie felt the carriage shift slightly as Jake and Sean stepped on, then Mary Anne. Hank put his good foot on the front step and climbed into the seat beside Charlie.

"Everybody settled?" she asked. "Pindar, walk on."

The late afternoon still shimmered with heat, but a breeze from the northwest presaged cooler temperatures for the evening with maybe a late shower. The leaves moved listlessly, but they did move. The only sounds were the clop of Pindar's giant feet, the steel-rimmed carriage tires swooshing on the grass and the rhythmic creak of the carriage itself. In the driver's seat, Charlie always felt as though she were sitting in the clouds.

"How you doin' back there?" she called over her shoulder.

"Fine," said Sean.

"All right," said Mary Anne, and expelled the breath she'd obviously been holding.

This was the way to see the farm. Her grandfather had laid out his pastures with broad avenues between the fences so that two big carriages could pass one another. Beyond the fenced pastures, the rest of the acreage was planted in hay and grass. Pindar snorted. Mary Anne squeaked.

"That's his signal he's completely re-laxed," Charlie said. "That is a happy horse."

"Oh, look," Mary Anne said, as they

rounded the corner by the mares' pasture. The mares and foals spotted them and came trotting up, hoping for treats. "Ooh, the babies are adorable. But so big!"

The foals began to buck and kick and run circles around their mothers, who ignored them and went back to grazing on the lush grass. At the end of the avenue, Charlie turned the carriage around and walked Pindar back to the stable. Mickey waited for them under the overhang.

"Mary Anne, how'd you like your first carriage drive?" Charlie asked. "Pindar, stand."

Mary Anne climbed down, came around to the front and smiled up at Charlie. "Actually, after I relaxed, it wasn't that bad." She walked over to Mickey and settled on the bench beside his wheelchair.

Everybody laughed.

"Okay, you guys, ready for a little trot?" Charlie asked. She swung Pindar in another big circle and headed for the long drive to the road in front of the farm. "Pindar, trot."

He moved off in an easy rhythm. After a while she said, "Pindar, working trot."

The big horse seemed to shift gears in one stride, and a few minutes later when she said, "Pindar, trot on," he opened up into a ground-covering gait that brought them to the road in no time.

"Pindar's getting pretty warm, but we've got a few minutes left before we need to cool him out. Anybody game for a canter?"

"Yeah, man!" Hank said.

"Oh, Lord," whispered Sean.

Jake said nothing.

"Pindar, can-ter," Charlie said. And they were off. For a big horse, he was amazingly agile and seemed to enjoy himself immensely as he wove between the pastures.

"Pindar, walk," she said after only a couple of minutes. Instantly Pindar resumed his contented amble. "Now, let's cool him out and settle him for the night."

The consensus was that they should bring Mickey's carriage out of storage, but not try to put to another horse this late in the hot afternoon.

"Sure is a lot more work than tossing a saddle and bridle on a horse and riding off into the sunset," Hank said, after they were done unbuckling the harness and cleaning horse and carriage. "Man, could I use a beer right now."

"I think that can be arranged," said the colonel from the door to the common room. "I picked up a couple of cases this afternoon when I was in town."

"Lead me to it," Sean said.

"Me first," Mickey said.

"No, ladies first," Mary Anne said. She retrieved the beer from the fridge and handed the cold long-necked bottles around to the men.

Charlie shook her head. "No thanks, I'll stick to diet soda." So the colonel was checking up on her. Between Jake's fight and Mary Anne's meltdown, she hadn't done too well. Time to switch to teacher mode.

"I'm staying in the air-conditioning," Mickey said. The others agreed and found seats in the common room.

"We have a while until dinner, people," Charlie said. "Time for questions."

"How can anybody figure out where all that harness goes on the horse?" Sean asked. "It's like a nest of pythons."

"You'll learn to recognize the bits and pieces and learn where they go. Never leave a horse in draft unattended. There's nothing scarier than a loose horse with nobody behind him holding the reins."

"I really needed to hear that," Mary Anne said.

"If you pay attention to the other first rule — never drive alone — you won't have to worry about it."

"So what kind of jobs can we get?" Sean asked the colonel.

"I don't think either Mary Anne or Mickey would fit into logging with draft horses and mules, although horse loggers make an excellent living. They're also ecofriendly. Say a farmer has some big trees among the smaller ones in his forest that he wants to cut and sell without cutting roads or clear-cutting, he'll bring in the draft horse loggers. We have a couple of groups in this area who are booked months in advance."

"I've seen those guys on a couple of the TV shows about loggers," Hank said. "I'm tough, but I'm not sure I'm *that* tough."

"Wimp," Sean said amiably. "I put myself through junior college logging in Washington State." He flexed his right hand. "Set this bionic do-jigger up right, and I sure won't drop an ax. Not so sure about a chain saw."

"You've seen those movies where the hero loses an arm or a leg and attaches a fifty-caliber machine gun directly to the stump and massacres the bad guys?" Mickey said, warming to his subject. "I can see you now, Sarge, running through the woods slicing and dicing. You'd be a logging fool."

"Hey, kid, you might have something there."

"Don't worry, Sean, the horses are a sight smarter than you are," the colonel said.

"The Campbell brothers are going to let us go to one of the sites they're working to see what they do," Charlie said. "Then we'll practice ground driving here on the property. We have a couple of old-growth trees ready for you guys to take on."

Hank rolled his eyes. "Don't you have anything cleaner? Like maybe driving one of those fancy tourist carriages around downtown Memphis? Maybe in a top hat and tails?"

"Just like you to be picking up women," Mary Anne said. She spread her arms to unroll an imaginary banner. "How about a sign on the carriage that reads, I Flirt for Tips?"

"Flirt?" Mickey said. "You gonna stop at flirting, Hank?"

"Okay," Charlie said. "Let's move on."

"How about me?" Mickey grumbled. "I don't see me climbing on and off one of those vis-à-vis things loading and unloading tourists on Beale Street."

"You could do the driving with a groom for the up-and-down part," Mary Anne said.

"More and more funerals are using horse-drawn hearses," the colonel interjected. "Especially in the military cemeteries."

"Perfect," Hank said. "Your passenger sure won't ask you to open the back door for *him.*"

Mickey flushed. "And how great it would be for his family to see the crip in the wheelchair driving their son to his grave. I don't think so." He wheeled down the hall. A few moments later the door of his bedroom slammed.

"What did I say?" Hank asked, his expression innocent.

"You *know* what you said," Mary Anne snapped. "You total jerk!" She smacked him hard across his shoulder. "I'm gonna take a shower before dinner."

"Well, *excuse* me," Hank said, and stomped off up the stairs. Charlie noticed he'd changed the cowboy boots for a pair of sneakers, and today's jeans didn't pool around his ankles. He'd either dropped the rodeo persona or had put it on hold while he actually did some work.

"Come on, Jake," Sean said. "Let's go upstairs. Party's over. See you at dinner," he said to Charlie and the colonel. "I hate prima donnas."

Since Saturday night was Vittorio's night off, the colonel grilled steaks on the patio. He hadn't mentioned Jake's confrontation with Aidan, but Charlie would bet he knew.

Both he and Sarah joined the others in

the common room to eat the steaks and potatoes. Jake relented enough to sit in the window seat on the far side of the room with his back to them. Charlie regarded that as a small victory. Only a few strides from the table itself.

Afterward Sarah and Mary Anne went upstairs in the main house to work on Mary Anne's possible transformation.

After dinner, Charlie walked through the barn checking that the water buckets were full and the horses happy before she slipped out onto the patio to sit down on the glider.

Would Jake materialize out of the darkness as he had the night before or had she scared him off? She and Steve had been estranged for two years before his last tour, and set on divorce before he left for the one from which he never returned. Not too soon to be attracted to another man, but Jake? She'd met unattached men who were better looking, more charming — even rich. Definitely healthier mentally.

Her vow to stay celibate had been easy to keep before Jake climbed down from that bus.

He was physically attractive enough . . . all right, he was extremely physically attractive with his strong jaw and his bright blue eyes and his muscles. Kind of a combination of Alan Alda and Gary Cooper.

He'd shown this morning with Aidan that underneath the laconic aw-shucks attitude the warrior was still alive and kicking. She had sworn she would never, ever have anything to do with a warrior again.

She'd also seen the gentle side of him, the way he touched the horses, talked to Mary Anne, won over Mama Cat. Heck, he touched *her* emotionally. She absolutely hated, loathed and despised the thought that she wanted him to touch her physically, too.

My world is complicated enough without falling for an incredibly damaged man who won't even eat at the same table as other people. I want this farm and a home for my daughter. I do not either want or need a man in my life.

Even though she was alert, listening, she wasn't aware that he had joined her until he sank onto the glider next to her. Neither of them spoke. For what seemed an incredibly long time but was probably no more than a couple of minutes, they swung without speaking.

"From the relative quiet, I'd say our bullfrog buddy won his ladylove," Jake said at last. "He's out there in the lake right now making millions of pollywogs."

"Most of which will be devoured by the

snapping turtles." And wasn't that a romantic image?

"Ever find a gator in your pond?"

"Good grief, no! I hope I never do."

"Mama Cat is close to having her kittens," he said. "Where does she go where the tomcat can't kill them?"

"I've never discovered," Charlie said. "If you can manage to catch her, I'll have her spayed after the kittens are born."

She felt his shoulder stiffen. She should have known better than to make a direct request of him. "Sarah's wanted a kitten forever, but we couldn't have one in quarters. She'll be delighted to socialize them. She needs a job. She's bored and lonely and misses her daddy and her friends. I haven't been much help."

"You've been busy making a home for her."

"Not good enough. She blames me because Steve went back and got himself killed. I can't tell her he's the one who demanded a divorce."

"I'll try to find Mama Cat before she delivers. For Sarah."

She was so startled at his offer that she squeezed his knee. His *bad* knee. She couldn't just snatch her hand away, so she left it there. He didn't move. Then she felt

125

his long fingers interlace with hers. She wanted him to turn her face and kiss her, but he'd never get up the nerve to make that decision.

No way would she kiss him first. Time to make polite conversation. "Did you learn to drive draft horses at home in Missouri?"

He took his hand away instantly. She removed hers, as well. Now he'd bolt.

Instead, he sighed and sat up straighter. "I grew up in an extremely strict Amish community."

"Really? Amish? I thought they were all in Pennsylvania."

He chuckled. "Look at a census of Indiana, or Ohio, or any Midwestern state sometime and see how many Zooks and Yoders you find. Have to be the census, because most of them don't have phones, so they're not listed in the telephone book."

"How did a Thompson sneak in there?"

"Somewhere along the line, either what the Amish call an English slipped into the clan, or an immigration agent at Ellis Island couldn't figure out the German name my ancestor was born with and gave him what he considered an American one. The name embarrassed my father, who was called Amos Micah Thompson. My family named me Jacob Zedediah. How'd you like to go through public school with a name like that?"

"Oh, dear. But how on earth did you wind up in the army with that kind of background?"

This time he did stand up. "Long story." Instead of the anger she'd expected at her intrusion, he sounded worn-out. She felt his long fingers stroke her cheek, "Good night, dear Charlie," he said, and was gone.

Jake had to drag his right leg with its bum knee up the stairs to his room. He could still feel the touch of Charlie's gentle fingers.

He'd worked his leg hard today, and it hurt like blazes. He refused to take drugs for the pain, but he'd use a heat wrap. With luck he'd be able to sleep, and it would be better by morning. Today's work and the confrontation with Aidan had taken more out of him than he'd realized.

He'd forgotten that the best view in the world was from the driver's box, watching the undulating rump of a big draft horse moving in front of him. It had always been that way at home. When he itched to run away, the horses kept him grounded.

Until they weren't enough any longer.

This afternoon his soul seemed to smooth out while Charlie drove Pindar around the farm. Or maybe it was sitting beside Charlie. Her grin told him she felt the same way.

"Jake? You okay, buddy?"

Sean.

"Fine."

"You couldn't sleep, either?" Sean walked into Jake's room with him and sat down on the chair at the little student desk, his stocking feet propped on the top.

"My knee's giving me fits."

"After the day you had I do not doubt that. I was thinking about that draft horse logging. You think we could handle that?"

Jake sat on the edge of the bed and massaged his knee. "I can handle one end of a two-man pull saw, and I know how to use a peavey hook to stack logs, but I haven't had your experience as an ax man, and I've never worked a big power saw. At home we didn't use power tools."

"The job I had in Washington State, we used chain saws and flatbeds, not horses. You think I could learn to drive horses well enough?"

"Sure."

"I'm thinking I'd like to learn. Whatever I wind up doing, I'm going to be my own boss. No more brass giving me orders they're too dumb to carry out."

Jake propped himself on his pillows.

"Maybe I can work for *you.* I want a boss who'll make all the decisions and send me home at night too tired to have nightmares."

After Sean left, he lay in bed waiting for the pain in his knee to subside.

He'd been rude to walk away from Charlie so abruptly. She had no idea she was on sensitive ground.

Since he ran away from home and joined the army he'd never met a woman he could visualize living with for the rest of his life. Now he was supremely glad of that. Fine husband he'd make.

Since he'd been on the colonel's farm he thought more often of home and what it would be like to see his family again after all these years. It wasn't easy to keep up with them when no one in the community was supposed to speak to him or open his letters. He gleaned updates occasionally from old friends who were more flexible.

In the beginning he'd felt sure his mother and his sisters would never cut him off, whatever his father did. But they had. Finally, after years of returned notes and ignored messages, he'd given up.

He didn't regret leaving the community and joining the army. He couldn't stay. It was sneaking off in the middle of the night he regretted. The first time he'd truly hurt people he cared about.

His father would have stopped him if he'd known he was going. Micah Thompson always believed that sooner or later Jake would settle down, accept the boundaries of his narrow world, inherit his father's farm and his father's life and be happy. Jake's departure broke his heart.

Jake mustn't hurt Charlie. He'd been touched by her when he'd climbed off that bus and seen the sun glinting off her summer ermine hair.

He liked her broad forehead, those quirky eyebrows and her eyes, which changed from gray to blue to lavender. He liked her strong jaw and her wide mouth. He liked her laughter and her toughness.

The people he cared for weren't safe. For her sake he didn't dare allow himself to fall any harder. But he didn't seem to have the willpower to stay away.

Chapter Eight

Sunday was another miserably hot day.

"This sucker weighs a ton," Hank said. "Can't we rig an electric winch to haul you and your doggone wheelchair up the ramp into the carriage?"

"Stop complaining," Mickey said over his shoulder. "Problem is you rodeo types don't develop upper-body strength."

"Bull."

Charlie told Hank to push Mickey's wheelchair into the driver's side of the handicapped carriage. She was afraid that if Mickey drove it up, he'd run off the edge.

Hank griped with each shove. Even at nine in the morning the temperature was in the high eighties and would undoubtedly near a hundred before the day was out. The colonel's land might be shady, the ponds overhung with old-growth water oaks, but any driving would have to be done before noon.

Hank gave one last effort and shoved

Mickey into place. "There you are, hotshot. Safe and sound. Put on your brakes. I'm not catching you if you slide back down."

"Thank you, Hank," Charlie said, climbing into the left-hand seat. "Now lift the ramp behind us and fasten it up to the back."

Hank grumbled.

"Jake, give him a hand. Thanks." Charlie turned to Mickey. "Ready?"

"Yeah, gimme the reins."

"Not yet."

"I practiced on that rein board thingie this morning like the colonel showed me. This drivin' stuff's a piece o' cake."

Charlie took the reins. "Annie, walk on."

"Oh, man," Mickey said as the mare walked out of the stable. "I flat love this! It's almost like I got legs."

"You do have legs. Can I trust you to do exactly what I say if I let you handle the reins?"

"Like, yeah."

"Mickey, no shenanigans. No trotting, and don't even think about cantering. You want to learn to use the reins gently to guide and direct her. We'll work on using the whip to bend her after you've mastered the reins."

"I'm not about to hit her!"

Charlie laughed. "The whip is not to hit

her with. If you smacked her hard, I suspect she'd kick the stew out of the dashboard. When you ride in a saddle, you use the pressure of your legs to tell her how to bend and when to turn. In a carriage, you don't have your legs —"

"Got that right."

"— so you kind of tickle her with the whip on her belly to bend her one side of the other. Turn left. Easy! Tighten up a hair on the left rein and give a hair with the right."

Mickey shifted in his chair and pulled both hands off to the right.

"Keep both hands in front of you. You see where the reins attach to her bit, and go through the steel circles on her collar and back to the ones on her saddle?"

"Yeah, the terrets."

"Right. You do remember something. Once the reins go back through the terrets, she can't tell whether your hands are out to the left or the right. Slightly tighter on the left, more give on the right. Yes. That's it. Walk a nice wide circle."

By the time they had worked for thirty minutes, both the humans and the horse were dripping. "Annie's had enough for today," Charlie said. "She needs to be washed down and put out to pasture."

"She's not the only one," Mickey said.

"Man, this doesn't look like hard work, but I'm sweatin' bullets here."

"And the day's barely started." Charlie laughed. "Drive Annie into the barn. Jake can head her while Hank and Sean help you back down your ramp. Did you have fun?"

"Fun! Man, I'd live up here if you'd let me."

"So when are you going to walk up the ramp and climb into your seat?" Jake asked, coming up to them.

"Aw, man, he'll never do that," Hank said.

Mickey twisted in his chair. "Watch me, clown."

Hank winced at that "clown" remark.

Once the ramp was in place, Sean helped Mickey back his chair down. "Good job," he said, and clapped Mickey on the shoulder. "Who's next?"

"You," said the colonel, pointing to Mary Anne as he walked down the aisle toward them. "Let's get Annie rinsed off and back in the pasture, then we'll get Pindar."

"Me?" Mary Anne's voice quavered. "Rinse her off?"

"Jake," Charlie said, "give her a hand, will you?"

He blinked. Charlie tried again. "You handle the hose, Jake. You know how to wash down a horse, so you instruct Mary Anne."

She turned to her father. "Good morning, Colonel. All present and correct, sir. Checking up on me again?"

"It's Sunday, so I don't have to go into the hospital. I thought I might cut the far pasture."

"You'll have heat stroke."

"I can drive the tractor, sir," Mary Anne said eagerly.

"I'm sure you can, but you need to rinse off that horse."

Her face fell. "Yessir."

"Since you're here, Colonel," Charlie said, "I'm off to run an errand. I'll be back in an hour or so." Five minutes later she pulled the big farm truck and trailer out of the driveway.

"Where's she going?" asked Hank.

"I didn't ask and she didn't tell," the colonel said. "Come on, Sean, we have work to do. Hank, you go practice on the rein board. Mickey, rinse off the harness and help Mary Anne and Jake to wash down Annie."

As she drove toward her friend Catherine Brinkley's Welsh pony breeding farm, Charlie worried whether or not she was doing the right thing for Mary Anne. The entire operation could backfire. Mary Anne might be just as frightened of a Welsh pony as she was of a Percheron or Belgian. Charlie planned to borrow Catherine's old campaigner Holy Terror, as kind a pony as ever drew breath, for each of the students' first solo drive. Mickey could even be lifted into the right seat and belted in. Mary Anne would feel less as though she'd been singled out, and the disaster quotient was less.

Charlie could teach Mary Anne to drive to the small cart and Holy Terror. Small horse for a small person. It should work. If not, she'd have to find a plan B. She intended to train Mary Anne to drive and get her a job doing it.

Funny how much she'd initially resented her father's demand that she teach these people to drive. They had become *her* people in just a couple of days. She no longer thought in terms of her own success, but *theirs.* And not simply their success at driving, but also in conquering their demons.

Especially Jake.

After a fast round trip, she pulled back into the farm, dropped the tailgate of her horse trailer and backed Holy Terror, all fourteen hands of his little gray hide, down the ramp in front of the stable. "Here, Mary Anne, take this line and lead him into the barn. Put him in the first stall opposite the stallion. I've already put hay and water in for him."

"Me?"

"Absolutely. You can handle him. Guys, come get this carriage out and pull it into the barn aisle for me. Isn't it almost time for lunch?" She watched Sean move in on the other side of Holy Terror to give Mary Anne silent support. Mary Anne drew in a couple of deep breaths, took the line and marched into the barn at the pony's shoulder the way she'd watched the others lead the draft horses.

After lunch, when everyone took it for granted that there would be a couple of hours of free time before the afternoon sessions, Sarah dragged Mary Anne upstairs to her lair. They were snickering and whispering. More wig and makeup sessions, Charlie figured.

"What's that all about?" Sean asked.

"I'd guess the good ol' social network," he continued. "The next step in evolution — human hands will be nothing but a big, fat pair of thumbs to text with."

"Actually," Jake said, "won't they be long, narrow thumbs to fit those tiny keys?"

"Yeah, you get the idea. I'm off for my siesta."

"Me, too," Mickey said. Sean followed him, leaving Charlie and Jake alone in the common room.

"You're not tired?" Charlie asked.

"Not really. I didn't drive this morning. I'm going to try to find Mama Cat's lair, maybe walk out to the pasture and watch the foals."

Another choice. Progress. "May I come with you?" He'd have to say yes or no.

He smiled down at her and offered her his hand. She took it and let him pull her up. This time they kept their distance, but Charlie's hand burned where his fingers had enclosed it.

They searched for half an hour. Although they found evidence that at least one of the cats was a good ratter, they saw no sign of Mama Cat.

"You're limping," Charlie said. "Jake, I'm sorry. Your knee . . . I should have realized . . ."

"I'll be fine if I can sit for a few minutes." He sank onto the nearest hay bale and Charlie sat beside him. He began to massage his knee. "So, how come you got a nickname like Charlie?" he asked.

"If you can have a long story, so can I."

"Tell me. Take my mind off the heat."

She leaned back against the stall. "It's not nearly so interesting as how you came to be landed with Jacob Zedediah."

"Tell me anyway."

She sat down beside him and plucked a couple of strands of hay out from under her. "My maternal grandfather was a cavalry brigadier . . ."

"So your mother was also an army brat."

"Yep." She chewed on the ends of the hay and leaned back against the bale behind her. "Mom was preprogrammed to traipse after her man like an old-time camp follower. Not that she ever complained. I did all the complaining."

"Still do?"

She smacked him lightly on the shoulder. "Only when appropriate. Mother was a menopause baby. Grandmother was embarrassed." She chortled. "But my grandfather was so delighted he wanted to name Mother after Ulysses S. Grant. Grandmother flipped out. She finally convinced him to call her Abigail Baker. Then when I came along, Daddy was conned into naming me Charlotte Abigail. Therefore . . . ?" She held her hands palms up.

"Able Baker Charlie."

"The good old army alphabet." She

dropped the blades of hay and stood. "I don't know how far down the alphabet he would have gone if Mother had produced more children, but . . ."

"Your brother would have been called Dog."

"Followed by Echo — good for either a girl or a boy." She went over to the wash rack, picked up a set of reins and began coiling them. She avoided Jake's eyes. She didn't want Jake to see the tears welling there when she thought of the year her mother died. "Mom died when I was fifteen. That's why we moved to Washington — so she could be treated at Walter Reed. That's why the colonel wouldn't buy me a horse. I just wish he'd told me at the time. I had to figure it out for myself later."

"I'm sorry."

"Daddy was a huge catch for any woman, but nobody ever sealed the deal. Instead, he kept on working until Granddaddy got sick. Then he retired officially and moved down here to look after him and manage the farm after he died. He'd prefer to have a condominium downtown on the Mississippi. So would I."

"You want a condo on the river?"

"No, I want him to move to the river and let me manage this place without his looking over my shoulder."

"He's not retired," Jake said.

Charlie waggled a hand. "Semi. Officially he's considered a consultant. His grant has been in the works for nearly a year." She shrugged. "When Steve was killed, Sarah and I had to move out of quarters. We didn't have any other place to go."

"He seems happy to have you."

She hung up the reins and began to organize the grooming brushes. This was getting too close to the bone for her comfort, but something about Jake made him easy to talk to. "Makes up for all the soccer games and horse shows he missed when I was growing up. We'd better be getting back. I want some time in the air-conditioned common room with at least one cool drink before we put to again." He joined her and they walked there together but not quite touching.

"So you plan to stay here?" Jake asked.

Charlie stopped and stared at him. "Of course I do. It's my farm."

Charlie waited in the darkness of the patio for over an hour after dinner, but Jake didn't come. She felt as though she'd been stood up by her prom date. She'd thought they were connecting, that he liked her the way she liked him. Guess not. For a man like Jake, sharing even as much as he had would make him draw back instinctively. Too much information, obviously. Got him right in the comfort zone.

He probably couldn't make up his mind whether to stay upstairs or come down without asking Sean.

Finally, she sighed and went into the house. She heard Mary Anne and Sarah hooting with laughter from the computer room, and she knocked.

"Come on in," Mary Anne said. "Join the party."

The pair hunkered in front of the monitor with soft drinks in their hands and a bag of corn chips on the floor beside the computer table. "Don't worry, Charlie, we won't spill anything on the keyboard," Mary Anne said. She turned around and grinned. "Ta-da."

"My Lord."

"Yeah, I know it's too much, but you have to start somewhere."

"You do know your face is green."

"Green grays red," Sarah said. "That's the first thing you learn in art class like in the second grade. When we get the real foundation on over it, it will barely show."

"This is actually lipstick," Mary Anne said. "Sarah didn't have any real green foundation."

"We can get some when we're in town," Sarah said.

"I hesitate to ask why you have green lipstick," Charlie said.

"Don't. And we have to buy some better fake eyelashes that aren't too heavy to keep Mary Anne from opening her eyes."

"The ones you have are impressive," Charlie said with a gulp. "Where did they come from?"

"We had a heck of a time getting them on straight," Mary Anne snickered. "One of them kept crawling up into my eyebrow like a woolly bear."

"They're from last Halloween. So's the lipstick."

Looking at Mary Anne's eager face, Charlie nearly burst into tears. "Tomorrow after lunch we forgo siesta and drive into town to try on wigs."

"And get some real green cover foundation," Sarah said.

"Have you given any thought to what style of wig you want?" Charlie asked.

"Come help me try some on," Mary Anne said, and twisted the desk chair around to face the computer screen. "Okay, this is me. See, you paste my picture on the screen, size it, then superimpose different types of wigs to see how they'll look." She cut her eyes at Sarah. "Want to show her our favorite?"

"Totally."

Charlie almost choked. The wig that appeared to frame Mary Anne's face was platinum-blond and had obviously been styled by someone who believed deeply in the immediate return of disco sung by country music stars from the sixties. It towered on top and fell down the sides in long ringlets. "Uh . . ."

Both girls cracked up. "That's not really the one we like, Charlie," Mary Anne said. "How about this?" The platinum tower was replaced by a medium-brown, short, layered wig that framed Mary Anne's face and covered most of her scars and her missing ear.

"Now, that's more like it," Charlie said.

"You like it?" Sarah asked.

"Absolutely. Where do we get it?"

"We could order it," Mary Anne said, "but I really need to try it on with the net cap you wear underneath it."

"There's a shop in the Carriage Mall that advertises a full line of wigs," Sarah said. "So, can we go look? Puhlease?"

"Of course we can."

"You don't have to come. Mary Anne can drive."

"I wouldn't miss it for the world. Now, I suggest you get rid of the woolly bears and the green guck and go to bed. Tomorrow starts early." Charlie leaned over and kissed Sarah's forehead. She nearly kissed Mary Anne's, as well, but caught herself in time. She was feeling very maternal toward her. She prayed that the transformation would work out.

CHAPTER NINE

By dawn the cool front that had been inching down from Montana slipped through West Tennessee accompanied by gusts of wind, followed by rain. Not the sort of storm that sparked tornadoes, but the gentle soaking rain that West Tennessee so desperately needed and seldom got in late August.

"No sense in getting us and the horses drenched," Charlie said over the remains of breakfast with the others. "Get the horses fed and the stalls cleaned, sweep the aisle, then practice your reinsmanship on the rein boards, clean and polish carriages and horses. This afternoon I have another errand to run in town."

Jake wandered out to the mare's paddock and fed treats to the foals in the rain. Hank found a rerun of last year's Professional Rodeo Cowboys' finals from Las Vegas and plopped himself down in front of the television to make snide remarks about the finalists, most of whom he knew. Charlie clipped the horses' bridle paths with the electric clippers.

On her way to wash up for lunch, Charlie heard the clomp and swish of heavy footsteps from Mickey's room. He'd been missing most of the morning. He must be practicing walking with his braces. Charlie had no doubt he would climb up the ramp to his carriage eventually if only to prove to Hank that he could.

After lunch, Charlie knocked on Mary Anne's door. "Ready for the big expedition?"

Mary Anne had pulled on a long-sleeved shirt and tied one of her silk kerchiefs over her hair. "Charlie, I've been thinking."

Uh-oh. Cold feet. Not surprising.

"I'll have to wear one of those net caps under my wig, right?"

Charlie nodded.

"I was watching you trim the horses before lunch. I think you should shave my head."

"I beg your pardon?"

Mary Anne pulled off her kerchief. The hair that remained on the left side of her scalp sprouted among her scars like weeds in a fallow field. She shrugged. "People will think I'm having chemo."

"Are you sure?"

"No, but if I hate it, what hair I have will grow back."

"Your hair, your call. I've got a small pair of electric clippers in the tack room. I'll go get them."

When Charlie returned with the clippers, she had Sarah with her. Mary Anne sat at the student desk, facing away from the mirror, and Sarah held her hand while the clippers whirred.

"Okay, you can look now," Charlie said, and swiveled the chair around.

Mary Anne opened her eyes. "I love it."

"You look like Nefertiti," Sarah said.

"Half Nefertiti," Mary Anne corrected. "Now let's go take care of the rest."

Charlie had already talked to the colonel about paying for the wig. "The army will pay or I will," he said.

Charlie dropped the two women . . . scary thought, but there it was — Sarah was a woman too — at the beauty-and-wig store.

Sarah should do some shopping, too, with school starting in a couple of weeks, but Charlie dreaded the thought. At Sarah's age, the wrong clothes with the wrong labels meant social disaster.

She felt a sudden panic that she didn't know what her child liked any longer — not her music, not her books, not her friends. She had been so caught up with her own problems that she'd ignored Sarah the way the colonel ignored *her* when she was Sarah's age, except to issue commands as to what she should do without ever asking what Charlie wanted.

I refuse to turn into my father!

As soon as she walked into the wig shop, Sarah called to her. "Mother, come look."

When Mary Anne came out of the area in the back of the store where the makeup was done and wigs were fitted, Charlie gasped.

Mary Anne dropped her eyes and gave a little smile.

The wig lady stood back. "Doesn't she look beautiful?"

Of course the scars were still there, but the green foundation had taken the red out so that the puffiness was barely noticeable, and, of course, the wig covered her missing ear. "I love it," Charlie said.

The wig was short and cut in feathery layers.

"It's natural hair," Sarah said.

"No yak hair?" Charlie asked.

"I beg your pardon," the stylist said.

"Private joke," Charlie assured her. "The hair looks as though it grew on her head. How do we take care of it?"

"Don't worry about it, Mother," Sarah said. "We know what we're doing, don't we, Mary Anne?"

The closer the three got to the farm, however, the quieter Mary Anne became. When they pulled in, Sarah jumped out and ran to the barn. Mary Anne dawdled with her hand on the door handle.

"Scared, huh?" Charlie said.

"Petrified. What if they laugh?"

"They won't."

"Why should I even imagine I could look normal? I was never beautiful before."

"You're beautiful now. Besides," Charlie added, "if anybody laughs, I'll run 'em through with a pitchfork."

CHAPTER TEN

The vets laughed all right, but it was happy laughter. Then they applauded. Sean, Hank and Mickey surrounded Mary Anne. Sean spun her in a waltz. Hank grabbed Sarah and twirled her.

Charlie smiled at them all from the door to the common room.

Jake laid a hand on her shoulder and she jumped. "I like *your* hair, too."

"Mine?"

"Did anyone ever tell you it's the color of summer ermine?"

"White with black spots?"

"That's *winter* ermine."

She could feel his breath on the nape of her neck and shivered where his hand still lay on her shoulder.

"In the summer it's a tawny dark gold with red in it that glows when the light catches it. Like yours."

"Hey, Charlie, how about we drive into

town for pizza or sushi or something?" Mickey asked as he whipped his chair around to face the door.

"Right," Sean said. "Wouldn't do to waste this beautiful woman on just us."

"Come on, guys, don't be silly," Mary Anne said.

"Take a vote," Charlie said. "Who wants what?"

"Sushi," Hank shouted. "We can make pizza here another time."

"Let me see if Vittorio can save tonight's dinner or freeze it. If he can, then sushi it is," Charlie said, and went to the kitchen.

The cook grumbled but admitted he'd planned big chef's salads with French bread for dinner. "Too hot for anything heavy," he said. "I haven't washed the lettuce yet, so go eat your sushi and I'll go home early."

When she went back to give them the news, Sarah asked, "Can I go too?"

Mary Anne said, "You have to come. Charlie'll be there."

"Actually, I'm exhausted," Charlie said, and suddenly she was. "Y'all go have fun."

"But you have to come," Sarah wailed.

"Go on with them. It's okay. They'll take good care of you. They know if they don't, they won't survive, right, guys?"

"Yes, ma'am," Sean said with a salute. He

offered Mary Anne his arm. "Come on, fair lady, let's go find us some sushi."

Not to be outdone, Hank offered his arm to Sarah. "Jake, you coming?" he called over his shoulder.

"Sure."

Charlie looked away as they scampered out to her truck like happy puppies. The keys were in it. They always were on the farm. The group fit into the big crew cab and Mickey's wheelchair slid easily into the bed. Sean drove.

For a few moments, she relished the sudden silence as she watched moisture drip from the trees by the patio. The rain had stopped, the air had cooled and the evening would be spectacular. The rain had already soaked into the parched fields, leaving only the occasional puddle . . .

It was too silent without them. She should have gone along. She considered taking the other truck and following them into town, but Sarah needed this time on her own. They'd look after her. *Please, please, let her make nice friends at school. Please make her happy here. Please let her know how much I love her when all I do is snap at her.*

She became aware of hoof falls in the aisle, and then the jingle of harness.

The colonel must have decided to drive.

He almost never did. He, too, must need some quiet time in the sudden cool of the evening.

She walked out to the barn aisle to join him.

Jake stood by Pindar's left shoulder with the reins of the two-wheel gig in his hand.

"You went to town." Charlie said. "I saw you go with the others."

"I changed my mind before I got in the truck," Jake said. "How about that? I made a real decision."

Uh-huh. If he'd gone, he'd have had to sit at the same table they did, so he'd stayed behind. Not a real decision, just a continuation of an old habit.

"It was definitely a decision to put Pindar to," she said. "Were you planning to drive alone? You know you're not supposed to do that, right?"

He shook his head. "As you should be aware by now, sometimes rules and I don't mix — not when there are horses involved. In this case, I knew you were in the common room, and I figured I could con you into joining me. I was even prepared to let you drive."

"Oh, you were, were you?" One look at his innocent face and she burst out laughing. "If I hadn't come out and found you, how were you going to come get me without leaving Pindar? Did you intend to bring him into the common room with you?"

"Pindar has big feet. He makes a lot of noise and the harness jingles. I knew you'd come out."

"You're aware the ground's still sopping from the rain."

"So? You melt?"

"We'll have to wash everything down afterward."

"Worth it. Climb aboard," Jake said, and mounted on the right side. "I've decided I'm driving."

Another decision. "Are you, now?"

She saw the set of his jaw. It must have cost him dearly to stay home when the others left. Making the decision to put to must have cost even more, but somewhere he'd found the strength. He *was* getting better. She climbed into the left seat.

They drove out with the purple and peach glow of a spectacular sunset in front of them, and the oversize disk of the full moon an eyelash above the horizon behind them.

Pindar clopped contentedly forward. Jake's hands were light on the reins.

The man was a born driver. Charlie's hands were still not that soft and quiet on the reins, probably never would be. The

155

two-wheeled gig trundled through puddles and over wet grass with barely a whisper. Late-afternoon mockingbirds serenaded their mates and pranced across the grass, occasionally stabbing at the ground and coming up with a dangling earthworm. The meadow daisies, so recently dusty and droopy, stretched and nodded in the twilight.

I could drive like this forever, Charlie thought. Their shoulders touched, and she felt a wave of pleasure. *Maybe he stayed back to be with me.*

Remember, he's still a warrior even if his smile and his hands are gentle at the moment.

Whatever terrible event broke him, he showed signs that with time he might heal. The colonel wouldn't have included him in the group if he hadn't believed Jake could be healthy eventually.

Who knew what he would become once he pushed himself?

He was used to being alone, used to moving to the ends of the earth at a moment's notice, just like Steve.

Were they so different, Jake and Steve?

Yes, she answered, here, in this carriage in this twilight, they were different. How deep that went, she had no way of knowing. Yet.

But she intended to find out.

"Why did you join the army?" she asked. "We have time for a long story right now. It seems an odd choice for an Amish boy."

He clucked to Pindar, who sped up to a faster walk. "The librarian at the school we kids all went to. She hooked me on reading and made me hungry for an education and travel. The army was the only avenue I could think of to get it."

"Weren't your grades good enough to win a scholarship?"

His laughter was without mirth. "I did win a partial scholarship to the University of Missouri, but it wasn't enough without help from my family. Never gonna happen. I was Micah Thompson's only son. I would inherit the farm. My job was to stay home and produce the next generation to inherit." He picked up the reins. "Pindar, easy, boy. That stream shallow?"

"Usually."

"Pindar, trot."

"It's been raining!"

The horse gave a little hop, the gig gave a bounce and into the stream they trotted.

"Ew!" Charlie yelped. Muddy creek water sprayed up over Pindar's back and down their faces and chests. A moment later they were trotting on dry land again.

Jake pulled up the carriage. They looked

at each other and broke into laughter.

"I know I said muddy, but seriously?" Charlie chuckled. "By the time we get back to the barn, we'll be so dry we'll crack."

"Sorry." He brushed a streak of mud off Charlie's cheek with his thumb.

"You don't sound sorry, mister."

"Is there another way back?"

"There's a little bridge way down there." She pointed.

"Okay. Pindar, walk on."

Once they were across the bridge, she asked, "You didn't like being a farmer?"

"I loved working with the animals. Farming crops is miserable, backbreaking and often heartbreaking. I'd look over those acres of grain stretching to the horizon and see prison bars. I wanted to see the world. Since I couldn't take the scholarship, the army was the next best thing."

"Even if that meant fighting in wars?"

"I didn't fully understand that most wars don't take place on the Champs-Élysées. I managed to get my bachelor's degree during my first few years, and my scores got me tapped for Officer's Candidate School. I hadn't intended to become an officer, but I certainly didn't turn down the chance."

"Did you make up with your family?"

He stiffened. "The letters I sent through

non-Amish friends were never answered."

"I'm so sorry. That must be terrible. Do you know what's happened to them?"

"My three sisters are married to Amish men and have a number of children between them. From what I glean occasionally, they're doing well."

"Your parents?"

"My father died some years ago. My mother's still alive."

"And you haven't tried to see her?"

"You don't understand. She can't see me — neither can any of the others. They can't even acknowledge I exist."

"That's barbaric! What was your father like?"

"He was stern, but he never raised a hand to me. Never raised his voice, for that matter. He was a tough taskmaster but a good teacher. He felt certain that if he kept me working with him, I'd learn to appreciate what he was leaving me. Graduation was the final straw."

"I thought Amish children left school in the eighth grade."

"My mother fought for me. She knew how much school meant to me, and she was a lot younger than my father, so she could get round him most of the time. He did it grudgingly, but he agreed to let me graduate. I graduated a year early, but he still wouldn't let me take up the scholarship. In high school I couldn't play sports. No extracurricular activities. Definitely no dating English girls. Then he told me I couldn't take part in the graduation ceremony."

"What's wrong with that?"

"It's not plain to wear robes and a mortarboard and stand out. I had my diploma sent to me."

"It meant so much to you, how could he?"

"For him it was the proper thing to do." He shook his head. "He thought he was doing what was best for me."

The colonel thought he was doing what was best for Charlie by not giving her the farm to run on her own. Charlie wanted what was best for Sarah. Did all parents get it wrong?

"I made arrangements with a friend from school to pick me up after midnight on the night after graduation. I had fake ID that said I was eighteen and didn't need my parents' permission to enlist, but the army really didn't care so long as I was healthy. I climbed out my bedroom window and met my buddy on the road. I left a letter for Pappa and Mama, but my father probably threw it away without opening it. Nobody ever came looking for me. The next meeting

160

they had, I was shunned. I never expected they'd go that far."

"Would they have taken you back?"

"I didn't want to go back."

"Does your family know what happened to you? That you were wounded?"

"They haven't tried to get in touch with me. They wouldn't want me to corrupt the children or members of the community with my dreams. I certainly would have, given the chance."

"So if you hate the country life, what are you doing here?"

She felt him stiffen beside her. When he didn't speak, she realized she'd pushed too hard again. He wasn't relaxed any longer.

"The colonel and Sean kidnapped me."

"You're kidding, right?" Did any of the others want to be here, either, or had the colonel pressured them all?

"I'm glad they did." He took his reins in one hand and held hers with his other.

"What changed your mind?"

"I've seen the world, and it's not all it's cracked up to be." He turned in his seat to smile at her.

She caught her breath. "I hope I can do a good job teaching you." Dumb, dumb, dumb. Back to student-teacher relationship.

The light went out of his eyes and he

tweaked the reins.

She wanted to grab them from him, throw herself at him and kiss him. He might have wanted to kiss her, too, but she'd screwed it up. As usual. No wonder Steve said she was boring.

After a while, she cleared her throat and asked, "Do you ever question your choice?"

"Not that one. Pindar, trot on."

"We'd better take Pindar back. If we get caught, the teacher could be accused of favoritism."

"I'll take a touch of favoritism. Pindar, trot."

CHAPTER ELEVEN

The farm truck rolled in from Collierville at nine-thirty that night, and everyone tumbled out. Hank grumbled less than usual when he hauled Mickey's chair out of the back and set it up.

"Thank you, my man," Mickey said with a formal British accent. "That will be all for this evening."

"Too right it will," Hank said in a broad Australian drawl.

"Let me push," Sarah said. "Come on, Mickey." Shoving Mickey's chair ahead of her, she took off toward the barn at a gallop.

"Hey! Girl! You'll have us both in the mud!" But he was laughing.

The others ran after them. A moment later the windows in the common room lit up, then, the lights came on behind the windows of Sean and Mickey's rooms.

Charlie watched from her own bedroom

until Sarah was safely inside the house. That was the most upbeat Sarah had sounded since before her father died. She'd worshipped Steve, possibly because he was so seldom there that she cherished the few memorable times they'd shared.

Across the way, Charlie saw the curtains at Jake's window twitch as though he, too, were watching. Did he regret not having gone with them?

She heard Sarah clatter up the stairs and hopped into bed so that Sarah wouldn't think she had been spying on her. She picked up her book and opened it across her lap, then realized it was upside down. "Sarah?" she called. "You have a good time?"

Sarah bounded into Charlie's room and sat cross-legged on the foot of her bed. She hadn't done that in a very long time.

"It was brilliant! The sushi was great and they treated me like I was one of them." She took a deep breath and blurted, "I met somebody from my school."

"Oh? What's her name?"

"Not a girl, Mother, a boy!" Sarah wriggled against the footboard. "His name is Robbie and he'll be a senior. He's gorgeous!"

"How'd you meet him?"

"He's waiting tables this summer at the sushi place. They don't do uniforms, so he was wearing a Marchwood T-shirt. He smiled at me, I smiled back and when he came over to our table Mickey asked him about the T-shirt. When I said I was going to be a lowly sophomore this fall, he acted like it didn't matter."

"What's his last name? Where does he live?" In her head, she heard her mother's voice, "Who are his *people*?" Charlie could remember rolling her eyes in exasperation whenever her mother asked her that. No matter how nice a boy this Robbie might be, his family could hold up gas stations or cook crystal meth in their kitchen.

Not that students from Marchwood were likely to do either, but some of the worst juvenile delinquents she'd ever known had been scions of the rich and privileged.

"Who cares? He said he's seen our horses when he drove by and he wants to come meet them sometime." She sighed. "He has his own truck. He got it when he turned sixteen."

"A pickup? Not a car?"

"Mother, everybody down here drives pick-ups, except the really rich kids who drive Porsches and Jaguars. This truck is so cute! Bright red with chrome running boards.

"Tell me you didn't follow him to the parking lot."

"He pointed it out through the window. There are some end-of-summer parties coming up, and he's going to try to get me invited."

Uh-oh. Charlie would face that one when it happened. Were all mothers condemned to rain on their daughters' parades? "You do know you can't date for another year?"

"Nobody dates anymore. Like tonight everybody was just hanging out, you know? Besides, you think some gorgeous senior is going to ask me for a date? But maybe they're not all cyclopses at Matchwood if he goes there."

"Cyclopses?"

"You know — one eye right in the middle of their foreheads — like dueling banjos." She played air banjo as she spun out of Charlie's room and slammed the door without saying good-night.

Charlie dropped her book on her nightstand, turned off her bedside lamp and stretched out under the thin cotton blanket. Even with the air-conditioning, that was sufficient cover during the night. She wanted desperately to sleep, but she could feel her heart racing and her stomach churning.

So it begins, she thought. At fourteen Sarah looked at least seventeen, and not because she overdid her makeup. She wasn't as beautiful as she'd be at twenty-five, but she was lovely enough to keep Charlie in a state of mild alarm when they met young males. It would be nice if she could connect with some of her classmates before school started, but let them be female and fourteen, not a male soon-to-be senior.

"Incoming, Major."

Jake whipped around at the sound of Sean's voice.

Bobby Holzer's battered and bruised flatbed clattered down the gravel road toward the barn. The truck bed was empty, so he obviously wasn't delivering anything.

Except payback. Jake sighed. That's what happened every time he took decisive action. Aidan had returned, possibly with reinforcements, loaded for bear and out to get his manhood back.

"That pair of rednecks looking for round two?" Hank said. He dropped the currycomb he was using on Pindar's shoulder and came to stand by Jake. "Think they're armed?"

"Of course they're armed," Sean said.

"Didn't you see the gun rack behind the seat? Damned arsenal. Maybe you were too far away."

"Probably a couple of handguns in the center console as well," Jake added. "They won't shoot up the place. Charlie's a customer."

Sean said, "Hank, go warn Charlie we may have trouble and head Mary Anne off. She doesn't need to hear any more nasty comments."

"They go for us, I'll lay you eight to five Mary Anne goes for them," Hank said.

"Last thing Charlie needs is a range war," Jake said.

"I'm stickin' with you two," Hank confirmed. "Uh-oh. Too late to head her off anyway. Mornin', Mary Anne."

The truck stopped at the front door of the barn, and both doors opened. Bobby climbed out of the driver's seat and Aidan climbed down and joined him. The two men were as big as steers, but both were freshly shaved and the shirts and jeans they wore looked freshly ironed.

"Not here for trouble," Bobby said, holding his hands out in front of him. His eyes took in the three men and landed on Mary Anne. "We're here to see Miss Mary Anne."

"I came to apologize," Aidan said, dropping his eyes. "*Really* apologize."

"I beg your pardon?" Mary Anne said.

"Yes'm. Bobby and me went down to the VFW after work. They already heard about us having a spot of trouble the other day. . . ." He looked sideways at Jake as though expecting him to erupt. "My uncle Travis — he was airborne in 'Nam — liked to have tanned my hide when he heard what I said."

"He could still do it, too, even if he is older than dirt," Bobby said. "Anyway, he called Aidan here a blockhead. Said no gentleman would say something like that to a lady."

"I didn't know y'all were heroes," Aidan added.

"Heroes?" Hank sputtered. "Us? More like fools in the wrong place at the wrong time."

"Anyway, Miss Mary Anne," Aidan said, "Uncle Travis said I ought to come apologize for real. So I do."

"Apology accepted," she said, then turned on her heel and walked down to the harness room. She had to slip by Mickey, who had wheeled himself into the aisle in solidarity with the others.

"Well, we got to get on the road," Bobby said.

"Good morning, Bobby," Charlie said from Picard's stall. "We'll see you next month with our shavings, as usual."

"Yes'm."

Charlie took in Jake, Sean and Hank standing shoulder to shoulder across the aisle as Bobby started his truck and drove out. "You look like fugitives from the O.K. Corral," she said.

"I figured they were here to go after the major," Hank said. "What just happened?"

"Uncle Travis happened," Sean said.

Ten minutes later, Charlie climbed into the marathon cart beside Hank. She planned to do some probing along with teaching. She either had to understand what made him grumpy or dump him from the class. Pindar was accommodating, as usual, but after ten minutes Charlie could see that Hank reacted too hard and too quickly to correct the horse.

"He's going to take exception to your hauling him around like that," Charlie said.

She heard Hank's sharp intake of breath and saw his hands tighten.

"I know how to steer a horse," he said.

"Maybe one-handed cutting horses, you do," Charlie said. "If Pindar got really annoyed at you, there isn't much you could do to stop him this side of Collierville. So, lighten up on the reins."

She thought Hank was going to snap at her. Instead, he took a deep breath and loosened his fingers. "Yeah, okay."

"Why did you join this class?" Charlie asked. "You obviously aren't happy here."

"Because I pick on Mickey? He gets my goat is all. What the heck has *he* lost?"

"I beg your pardon?"

"He's a computer geek. One chair is the same as any other. He keeps working at it, he's gonna walk. Maybe not run marathons, but he'll be able to go back to doing what he did in the army, go to college — he can use his hands and his brain to run his equipment as well as he ever did."

"Hank, you've lost half a foot. You barely limp."

"I started rodeoing in high school. I've lost everything."

"Bull!" She reached over and took the reins. "Pindar, stand." She turned him to face her. "You planned to rodeo until you were what — sixty, seventy?"

"Heck, no. I expected to have enough money to buy my own spread by the time I turned thirty. Raise Santa Gertrudis cattle and bucking horses."

"Then why on earth did you join the army?"

"I joined the National Guard, not the army. One weekend a month and a couple of weeks in the summer. I needed the money to tide me over when I wasn't winning. I sure as shootin' never expected to wind up in the desert with people trying to kill me."

"You should have expected it. Every day I read about some National Guard unit that's deploying for the fourth time in six years." She caught her breath. "You didn't actually do something goofy like shoot yourself in the foot to get to come home, did you?"

"What? Heck no! Whatever I am, I'm no coward. I love my country."

"Okay, can't you ride bareback broncs? You wouldn't need any stirrups, just balance and guts. Or how about this? Ride bulls."

Hank began to laugh. There was an edge of hysteria in it, but it was real laughter. The first Charlie had heard from him since he arrived. "I'm crazy, but I am not that crazy. My daddy warned me never to ride bulls. See, a bucking horse will devote his entire energy to keep you from staying on him for eight seconds. If he tosses you off, he'll go bucking across the arena. But a bull — never try to ride a critter that will spend eight seconds trying to kill you, then when he gets you off his back, turns around and tries to kill you all over again. No, ma'am. Bulls are out."

"Answer my question. Why are you here? Pindar, walk on." She handed Hank the reins.

"Pindar, stand," Hank said. He swiveled to look Charlie in the eye. "I needed me some horse, and this seemed the only way available to get some."

Charlie realized his eyes were full of tears. For the first time, she'd *got* him. All those years she'd given up horses entirely to work full-time and look after Sarah and Steve, she'd felt she "needed her some horse." The vacations at the farm came seldom then. No money, no time. Not nearly enough horse.

"I thought if I can't ride, maybe I can drive a carriage in some city. Better than nothing."

"How good a rider *are* you?"

"Oh, lady, before this I was one heck of a rider."

"When we get back to the barn, we're going to find out how good you still are. Pindar, walk on."

Charlie dug out her old dressage saddle and bridle, and led Aries, the Friesian gelding, out to the driving arena.

"You know what you're doing?" Jake slipped out of the stallion's stall and came to join Charlie.

"Not a clue," she replied. "I have to do something about Hank. Maybe if he sees he doesn't need his anger, he'll let it go."

"And make all our lives easier," Sean said as he came out of the common room.

"Where are Mary Anne and Mickey?"

"She was helping him walk," Sean said. He shook his head. "It's slow going and he looks like RoboCop when he gets in those leg braces, but the little sucker is game, I'll give him that. He says it doesn't hurt to walk. You believe that, I got some bridge stock in Brooklyn just aching for investors."

"Don't want him standing around making fun of me," Hank said as he walked back in the barn.

"After lunch we'll set Mary Anne up for her first lesson with Terror and the pony cart," Charlie said. "Jake, you and Sean can bring up the pony cart while I work with Hank."

"In the meantime, go away and don't watch me," Hank said. He came out of the tack room shoving a black hard hat on his dark curls.

Aries stood well over sixteen hands, much

taller than the average cow pony or bucking bronc, and considerably broader. Coal-black, his mane hung down below his shoulders, and all four fetlocks wore the heavy feathers standard to the breed. Charlie tacked him up in the dressage saddle and bridle while Hank made friends with him and gave him a few treats. Then he led him out to the indoor arena.

"Don't try any of that jumping-on-the-back-of-your-horse thing," Charlie said.

"Cowboys only try that on a short horse," Hank grinned. "And with both feet." He climbed the stairs of the mounting block and waited for Charlie to bring Aries up beside him.

He seemed relaxed. Then she noticed his hands were shaking.

"Good thing you're missing part of your right foot, not your left. You only need to swing your right leg over the saddle."

"And keep it in the stirrup afterward." Hank gathered the reins and swung aboard.

Charlie walked around to the right side of the horse, checked for stirrup length and said, "Stick your foot in."

Hank felt around without success. "I can't feel where it is."

Charlie guided his foot into the stirrup. "Okay now?" she asked.

"If feeling nothing is okay, then yeah. Saddle feels weird. No horn."

"There's a bucking strap across the pommel," Charlie pointed it out to him. "But you won't need it." She glanced behind Aries's broad rump and saw Sean, Jake, Mary Anne, Mickey and Sarah all peeking in the door to the arena, out of Hank's line of sight. She made shooing motions. They ignored her.

"What are you waiting for?" she asked. "You need your prosthesis in the stirrup for balance, but you know where it is. Keep your heels down. You can feel your calves and thighs on the horse. Walk on."

He took both reins in his right hand.

"Didn't you ever ride an English saddle?" Charlie asked.

"No need. Why?"

"Let me show you how to hold the reins. And dressage horses don't neck-rein."

Aries took a couple of steps. Hank grabbed the bucking strap and slipped to his right. "Whoa!"

"Push yourself left."

"I can't shove when I can't feel." He started to swing his right leg over the saddle to jump off.

Charlie grabbed his right ankle. "Stop that. I know you're not supposed to shove your foot all the way into the stirrup, but do it. Past the point where you feel your own foot."

"Puts me off balance."

"May I make a suggestion?"

Both Charlie and Hank jumped. Hank turned in his saddle and glared at Jake. "I told you not to watch."

"As Mickey noted previously, you are not the boss of me." But he said it with a grin. He pulled a piece of orange hay string out of his pocket, walked around to Hank's right side and bent to his stirrup. "The only difficulty with this is that if you fall off, your foot may stay behind you." He wrapped the hay string around Hank's ankle, foot and the stirrup, so that the ball of Hank's prosthesis was held securely in place. "So don't fall off. Now, stand in your stirrups to get your balance. You can use your leg to move the horse, but you need to keep the ball of your foot in your stirrup and your heel down."

Grumbling, Hank stood.

And slid off into the dirt.

"Hellfire!" He grabbed for the bucking strap, but he was well past the point of no return, so he let go and fell hard on his back.

"Hank!" Charlie said.

"I'm okay," he gasped, and lay still a moment. "I do hate that feeling like you'll never take a breath again."

"I'm sorry," Jake said, dropping on his good knee. "I thought . . . I shouldn't have tried . . ." He stood, reached down a hand and pulled Hank up. Then he turned and walked away from them toward the back pasture. "I know better."

"Hey, man, it's okay!" Hank called after him. Jake didn't break stride. "Shoot, I've fallen harder than that off the pasture fence."

The others had joined them by now, even Mickey. He was still wearing his braces in his wheelchair.

"I'll go after him," Sean said, and shook his head. "Too bad. He actually tried to help. He'll see it as just another screwup. I'd be surprised if this didn't set him back part of the distance he's come."

"We can't let it," Charlie said.

"You come up with an idea, you let me know." Sean broke into a jog and went after Jake.

Charlie took Aries's rein to walk him back to the wash rack, but Hank stopped her. "Did I say I was finished? Let's try that again." He went to the mounting block and climbed back onto the horse's back.

"All right, cowboy, let's make a dressage

rider out of you," Charlie said. Her insides were clenched. She wanted to follow Jake, to tell him what he'd done was fine. Instead, she concentrated on Hank.

"I think Jake was right about tying you on, but I think he should have started with your ankle rather than your foot," Charlie said. "Let me give it a shot."

A moment later with the string newly wrapped, she said, "Okay, Hank, get on with it. Show me what you can do."

"I haven't been on a horse in over a year, since I got hit."

"Excuses, excuses." She held her breath and crossed her fingers. He must not fall again. She had to show Jake that his idea was a good one.

She walked close beside Hank, not quite touching Aries, not quite touching Hank's thigh. Until he moved Aries away from her. A moment later the pair were executing a slow trot across the arena. Most cowboys knew how to post a trot. Hank certainly did. He might not be good with driving reins, but he was a natural horseman.

"Don't you dare canter!" she called to him.

"Aw, teach," he said as he trotted up to her. His body slid in the saddle when he stopped, but the tether on his stirrup gave him the purchase to right himself.

This was the third of her students to show her that happy smile. She couldn't exactly chalk Mary Anne's up to the horses. She was Sarah's success. But Jake and Hank had smiled because of the horses. Only three to go — four, if she included Sarah. But Sarah might never be attracted to horseflesh.

Hank was dripping sweat, but his face glowed.

"Walk Aries out a couple of minutes, then we'll get you down from there."

"Do I have to?"

She grinned. "Don't whine. You now have two assignments. Learn to drive and relearn how to ride."

"Deal."

CHAPTER TWELVE

After a nearly silent dinner with the colonel and Sarah, Sarah departed for the computer supposedly to play video games, and the colonel went to his study to work on an article.

Charlie, with a fluttering heart that she didn't appreciate, covered herself with mosquito repellant and sat in the swing in the darkness on the patio. She could see lights in both Sean's and Jake's bedrooms and wondered if Hank were upstairs with them. The television was on in the common room, and she could hear Mickey talking to Mary Anne.

Apparently the mosquito repellant repelled Jake, too. She swung and waited for him, feeling more and more foolish. She remembered all those times she'd sweated bullets waiting for some man to call her — usually Steve. She was no longer a teenager. The heck with Jake.

She noticed that the light was still on in her father's study, so she tapped on the French door, stepped in and regretted her impulse at once.

"Charlie, what a nice surprise. Come in, sit down. Would you like a soda?"

She considered running through the room, out the hall door and up to her bedroom. He always knew when she had a problem. But that would be childish. Couldn't hurt just to talk. She sank onto the big wing chair beside his desk — the one that had spent twenty years in his office, the one his patients sat in to pour their guts out to him.

"No thanks. I hate to admit this. You were right. I'm in over my head."

The colonel swung his feet off his desk and sat forward. "Horses not cooperating?"

"People not cooperating. The horses are fine." She ran her hands through her hair. "Hank is grumpy because he'd rather ride saddle broncs than drive and knows he can't, so he takes it out on Mickey. Mickey says Hank thinks he's too good to help Mickey because he's an officer and Mickey isn't. I don't think that's necessarily true. Sean is so busy looking after everybody else he's not keeping up with his own work. Mary Anne is scared of horses and brandishing her scars like a weapon. Then there's

Jake . . ."

"Ah, yes. Jake."

"What's that supposed to mean?"

"His situation is complicated."

"*He's* complicated," she said. "I need to know what happened to him in Afghanistan. If you can't show me the files, tell me. Call it professional courtesy. If that won't work, make it one father to one daughter. Whatever, but for pity's sake, please explain what made him the way he is."

He leaned back, sucked in a deep breath and regarded her steadily. "No one knows the details but Jake, and I am not certain how much he remembers."

She started to stand. "So you won't tell me. I should have known."

"Whoa, Charlie. Sit down. I *will* tell you what I can, and if you ever tell anyone I did, I'll swear you're lying. How's that for one father to one daughter?"

She nodded. "I won't tell a soul, cross my heart."

He grinned. "That's what you used to say when we kept things from your mother. Okay. His refusal to make decisions is not that unusual a reaction to the kind of trauma he experienced."

"PTSD?"

"Not precisely. He has a deep-seated case

183

of survivor guilt. He was already set up for something of the sort from his childhood. He's never said what. Since he is not actually brain damaged, that refusal to talk about it is a choice in and of itself. He believes that every decision he makes is catastrophic to people he cares about. Solution, don't choose."

"I got that part."

"Since no human being can guarantee that any choice is correct, no matter how insignificant, his only solution is total avoidance."

"But he makes small choices all the time."

The colonel nodded. "Ah, you caught that. Smart girl. Part of that is that he is actually getting better. Partly, he doesn't realize or admit he's deciding. If, however, he were forced to make a major decision to save something or someone he cared about, I believe he'd make it. I believe his training as a leader would override his fear of choosing wrong."

"And if it *was* wrong?"

The colonel shrugged. "He might shut down completely."

"Lovely. So if I push him and he messes up, he could wind up sitting in a corner sucking this thumb?"

He shook his head. "More likely he'd

184

regress to square one and wear mismatched socks again."

"So it's up to me to make him choose right? How do I do that?"

"The same way you let Sarah choose the clothes she wears to school. Make certain the choices are innocuous, and that either decision is acceptable."

She flopped back in her chair and brushed her hair off her forehead. "Something awful must have happened on deployment. What?"

"Here's what I know and what I surmise. I told you he was G-2, intelligence. Whatever the movies say, that generally entails sitting in an office reading reports and looking at maps. He was stationed in what was supposed to be a pacified zone. Then his hotshot new commanding officer met some village headman at a conference on rebuilding infrastructure and promised him medical supplies. Standard operating procedure. One step above handing out chocolate bars to the children. Jake wanted to delay the mission to gather better intelligence. The hotshot was certain Jake was just dragging his feet, so he ordered Jake and his team to take a couple of trucks out to the village to deliver the supplies and do some PR."

"Jake was right," Charlie said quietly.

The colonel nodded. "An hour after he

and his team drove out of the compound, fresh intelligence supporting Jake came across the colonel's desk. To his credit, the CO sent a couple of armored personnel carriers after them."

"They were too late."

"Jake's group was ambushed. One truck was blown up. Jake was hit in the leg, but wrestled a wounded man into the remaining truck and drove it out of the village. They met the APC down the hill and eventually were air-evacced out."

"The other man survived, too?"

The colonel shook his head. "Died on the flight to Germany. Jake was the only survivor."

"What happened to the officer who gave the original order?"

"Returned to the States. Retired immediately. Jake was absolved of any blame, but he doesn't absolve himself. To him it's the last in a long line of personal screwups."

"What would have happened to Jake if he had disobeyed the order?"

"He'd probably have been court-martialed and another officer would have led the team on the mission."

"The same thing would have happened whatever Jake did."

"That's about it."

Charlie leaned forward, braced her elbows on her knees and dangled her hands. "If it's a long line of screwups, where did it start?"

"I have no idea. Suffice it to say he's much improved since he's been here."

"Okay, that's Jake. What about the others?"

"I'll reschedule my appointments at the hospital for the next week and observe the group. I may not like to drive, but I'm perfectly capable of teaching Mickey and Mary Anne. I take it they are your problem drivers."

She went to the hall door and stopped with her hand on the knob. "You're not giving me even one *I told you so*?"

"Not one."

"Thanks."

After she left his office, the colonel returned his feet to his desk and tented his fingers in front of his face. He'd been too caught up in his own grief at Abigail's death to notice when Charlie went off the rails with Steve. He'd had no idea how bad the marriage was, because Charlie hid it from him.

She was much too interested in Jake. He liked Jake, but Charlie needed a man with a healthy mind. A man she could rely on. One day that might be Jake. Not yet.

■ ■ ■ ■

On the patio Charlie took a cold soda and went back to the glider. She needed to "process" what her father had told her about Jake. As she finished the soda, she heard the merest rustle in the leaves and the man in question slipped out of the darkness. She patted the seat beside her, but he shook his head.

"We have a problem," he said.

"You and me?" She had enough problems. "People or horses?"

"Neither. Two cats. At least when I left it was two cats. I suspect it's more by now."

"What are you talking about?"

"Come with me." He took her arm none too gently, half dragging her through the common room and up the stairs into his bedroom. "Keep quiet."

She laughed. "If this is your idea of seduction, Jake, you're bungling it."

"What?" He looked confused, then grinned at her and pointed. "At the moment, my bed is otherwise occupied. Look."

How could she have talked about seduction? Her whole body went hot with embarrassment as she dropped her eyes to his bed. "Oh! That was a very nice candlewick bedspread," Charlie whispered. "It'll never come clean again."

"You could boil it," Jake said. "That's what my mother did." He sank onto his heels beside the bed. "Three and a half already, and she doesn't look much thinner." He motioned Charlie over. "She's too preoccupied to realize we're here."

Mama Cat had pulled and scratched herself a nest in the center of Jake's bed, then settled down to deliver her litter. As they watched, the fourth and fifth kittens popped out. Mama cleaned up after them, then shoved all five close to her belly for their first milk. They didn't crawl so much as swim until their tiny paws found purchase on the mother cat's stomach, then a nipple. Finally they latched on and began the instinctive rhythmic pushing that was a kitten version of milking a cow.

Charlie sank onto the floor beside Jake. "I've never watched a cat have kittens."

"I have. Frequently." He stroked the space between Mama's ears with his index finger.

His caress was so gentle. Charlie longed to feel his long fingers against her skin. She took a deep breath. That would never do. Keep it practical, Charlie. "How on earth did she get in here?"

"I cracked open my window to smell the roses."

"She's purring," Charlie said.

"It must hurt to have kittens, but that never keeps them from purring."

"I did not purr when I had Sarah. I yelled and called Steve every name in every language I knew and some I made up."

Why on earth should this feral cat, whose dens were so well hidden that no one had an inkling where they were, have chosen the center of Jake's bed to birth her kittens?

She trusted him. As the stallion trusted him. Everybody seemed to trust Jake but Jake.

"She must know that's all of them the way she dragged them around to suckle."

"A competent lioness," Jake said.

"Knows her job much better than I ever did with Sarah. If the tom smells them, he'll kill them."

"I already shut the window. She's safe for the moment, but if we bother her she'll find a way to move them out and hide them. She'll have to stay here."

"Not on that bedspread. We'll make her a nest in your bathroom. Can you handle that?"

He looked at her as though he couldn't believe she had to ask. "Certainly."

Ha. Another decision. In the next twenty minutes they made a nest, set up litter, food and water, and moved cat and kittens to the corner of Jake's bathroom.

The others must have heard them running up and down stairs, in and out of Jake's bedroom. She expected them to open their doors and ask what was happening, but nobody did, not even Sean.

Surely they didn't think . . . she and Jake . . . Were the others being discreet and giving them privacy?

She considered banging on everyone's door to explain that she and Jake were being midwives, period. Teachers weren't supposed to fall for students. But then students weren't supposed to have such gentle hands, blue eyes that seemed to see into her soul. . . .

Bad enough he'd opted out of the sushi party and they had driven alone. Thank heaven the others didn't know about their patio trysts.

Was it possible to have a tryst when one of the two didn't realize what it was? To Jake they were pleasant interludes, but Charlie could hardly wait to clean up after dinner before she sat in the patio swing in hopes Jake would join her. When he did, she glowed. When he didn't, she felt so let down she wanted to cry.

This was bad and getting worse, especially since Jake probably had no idea he was anything to her except another student. She couldn't tell him. Couldn't tell anybody the way she felt. She must concentrate on acting as though Jake was no different from the other students. *Good luck.*

The newly dry kittens were all yellow-and-gray tabbies that scrabbled blindly with their tiny paws and carried their short, triangular tails straight up. Charlie sat on the floor of Jake's bathroom and watched them.

Her family had never had a cat or dog in quarters. Once Sarah found out about these kittens, the colonel might find himself with five house cats.

Jake pulled himself up on the edge of the bathtub and rubbed his knee.

"I don't know about you," he said, "but I'm hungry."

"This giving birth is hard work. Is there anything downstairs to eat?"

Charlie grinned at him. The man was making decisions left and right. "I'll make you an omelet. We can raid Vittorio's larder in the big house."

"Can you cook, too?"

"I beg your pardon? You think because the

colonel has Vittorio, I had a Vittorio of my own? I was a starving army wife. If it got done, I did it."

"Sorry."

He followed her downstairs and across to the kitchen in the farmhouse.

She pulled a packet of shredded sharp cheddar cheese and a carton of eggs from the refrigerator, split and slipped a couple of sesame bagels into the toaster.

"As a matter of fact, my getting it done ultimately broke up my marriage, not that Steve ever would have admitted it." She pulled out a stick of butter, took a copper-bottomed pan down from the rack over the island and dropped a couple of spoonfuls into it.

"How so?" Jake edged a hip onto one of the bar stools on the far side of the island and watched her.

"When Steve came home the last time, he'd been gone fifteen months. His choice — he extended. That should have set off alarm bells." She opened the refrigerator again and began hunting through the vegetable cooler. "I know we have some fresh mushrooms in here someplace. Vittorio usually has some portobellos."

"They're too big to hide," Jake said.

"Right. Ah, here they are." She pulled out

193

a covered container. "Chop up a couple of these, would you? They're already washed." She pointed to the knife block. Jake selected the correct knife, took the cutting board she offered and began to slice and dice the fat brown mushrooms.

He was as competent at that as with everything else he did — no wasted movement and no sliced fingers. "What changed?" he asked without slowing down his chopping.

"While he was gone I took a teaching job at the base school that evolved into full time." She shrugged. "We badly needed the money. Sarah needed a good computer and soccer equipment. I was shuttling her back and forth to practices and play dates with her friends. Half the time we ate on the run at the kitchen table.

"Steve walked into a household that functioned beautifully without him. He'd left an adoring little girl and a housewife who deferred to his every wish. He came home to a busy teacher with her own interests and her own friends. The baby daughter had turned into a smart-mouthed teenager who understood a bunch more about technology than he did. When she refused to go on one of their special fishing trips — I wasn't asked along — he threatened to drag her out of the house and toss her in the boat. When I explained to him that teenagers don't want to waste a whole Saturday sitting in a johnboat with a parent, he called me a bad mother and a lousy wife."

She broke half a dozen eggs into a bowl and dropped the shells down the garbage disposal. "Sarah says we should compost, but I can't convince Vittorio garbage is worth saving. I hope to start with the fall leaves, the few we actually rake and don't leave to rot. In a way, that counts as compost."

At her direction, Jake set china and glasses on the island. Charlie added two tablespoons of water to the eggs.

"My mother always added water," Jake said. "She told my sisters that adding milk made the eggs rubbery."

"Your mother's a wise woman," Charlie said, and began to beat the eggs with a whisk. "If you'd like wine, there's some white in the fridge. Otherwise there's iced tea."

"Which do you want?"

"Tea."

"Me, too." He set about fixing two glasses.

Charlie glanced up at him. Did he really prefer wine but couldn't ask for it? "I'm sorry, Jake. I didn't mean to be flip about your mother."

"No problem. So your husband couldn't reassimilate," Jake said. "Now, where have I heard that before."

"He wanted me to do *all* the assimilation," Charlie said. She stripped several green onions, cut them with the kitchen scissors and folded them and the cheese into the eggs. Jake added the mushrooms and watched as she poured the mixture into the hot skillet and swirled it around.

Charlie said, "Steve could always reduce me to tears with his criticism, but that time I didn't cave. He decided he had to 'bring his family to heel.' "

"Surely he didn't actually say that."

"Want to bet?" She folded the omelet and turned it carefully so that it didn't break apart. "I was sorry that I threatened Steve's manhood, and that his daughter no longer idolized him, but I couldn't fix it."

"Counseling?"

"Ha. As if. My father may be a psychologist, but Steve believed the same thing a lot of military people do. Seeing a counselor means you can't control your family. He kept accusing me of being out of control. He was right — only it was his control I was out of. Even his darling Sarah couldn't do anything to please him. He hated her clothes, her language, the way she decorated her room, her music, her friends. He even resented her computer skills." She raised her eyebrows. "Plates?"

He set them on the counter beside the eggs and found silverware in a drawer in the island.

"I hope you don't like your omelet runny."

"Nope. Looks perfect," he said. "Smells good, too."

Working together as smoothly as though they'd done it all their lives, they assembled the meal and ate together at the kitchen counter. Big breakthrough. Now she had ammunition to convince him to join the others at meals.

Charlie knew she'd been running her mouth, but Jake was having the same effect on her that he had on the animals — she trusted him.

"But you were still married when he . . ."

"Was killed? I couldn't say the words for weeks after they notified me. We'd agreed to divorce when he came back from his tour. My mother told me before she died that if a man falls out of love with you, he never falls back in."

"Who could possibly fall out of love with you?" The words sounded like a simple request for information, not a come-on.

She said with studied casualness, "The real question is, why did he fall in love with me in the first place? Want another bagel?" One look at Jake's face, with his narrowed eyes and tight jaw, and she knew she wasn't fooling him one little bit. She hadn't even revealed the depth of her hurt to her father, and here she'd spilled her guts to a man she barely knew. She might as well be made of plastic wrap.

"No, the question is, why did you fall in love with *him* in the first place."

She busied herself rinsing the plates and putting them in the dishwasher. "My mother was dead, my father was a zombie and I was seventeen. On my way off to college in the fall. I met him that summer at the pool on post. He was everything my father loathed, so of course I fell madly in love with him. Soldiers were what I knew. I got pregnant so we got married. My father paid for me to attend the local college. They had child care, and I could go to school while Steve did his job, so I could still keep house and be there when he wanted me to be. The first few years were great. We were poor, but we were really happy."

"What changed that?"

"He discovered that shooting at live targets that shot back was the ultimate high. He'd already started to change when he came back the first time."

"So had you," Jake said quietly.

"We'd had such different experiences while he was gone. Then he was deployed again when we'd barely had a chance to get to know one another again. When he came home the second time, it was the beginning of the end for us.

"Nothing measured up to that high for him. Not me, not Sarah, not barbecues in the backyard or swims at the pool. Most of my friends' husbands never wanted to go back in-country or leave their families again. A number of them got out of the army rather than take the chance, but Steve couldn't wait to go back. I make him sound like an unfeeling monster. He wasn't. He was funny and clever, and I think he loved Sarah and me as much as he could, but his eyes were always on the horizon."

"Men like that defuse bombs, or cave dive, or fight bulls."

"And most of them leave their families eventually," Charlie said, "Or don't marry and procreate in the first place." She caught her breath and studiously avoided looking at Jake. Everything about him said that he wasn't a fear junkie like Steve, but he'd been a soldier by choice, and he'd never married or had children. Was she missing the same signals she should have picked up on with Steve? She didn't think so, but how could she trust her instincts?

"Most of them don't ride bucking broncos, either," Jake said.

"I don't think Hank's a fear junkie. He's a glory hound. He wants to win, to shine, to be in the spotlight. If he can find something else that feeds his ego, he'll glom on to it and be happy again."

"Your Steve sounds like a war lover. They are a very rare breed. I've only known two. They were as dangerous to us as to the enemy."

She watched Jake slide the two place mats back into the drawer under the island, but his eyes were on her. "We should check on the kittens, and then off to bed."

She wasn't ready to take the next step with Jake. All she wanted was her farm and her life with her daughter. Now, she knew the smallest gesture could breach the dam and send her into his arms. Either he'd respond, or he wouldn't. Whichever, their trainer-student relationship would not recover.

He held out his hand.

What had she just said about dam-breaching? She took a deep breath and took it.

■ ■ ■ ■

Jake had not been near a woman — except hospital and rehab staff — since he'd been air evacced to Ramstein. Physical pain, loss, guilt and anger didn't leave room for testosterone. He'd planned to spend what remained of his life alone without dreams, hope, or direction. If he could have managed suspended animation, he'd have given it a shot.

This entire carriage-driving expedition was a last throw of the dice before he settled back into walking the city streets. For months he had felt himself grow dimmer, as though whatever light animated him — call it soul — was blinking out.

Then Charlie walked into his life. He'd been nearly blinded by the sunshine. She glowed with energy and drive. One part of him resented her for pushing him back into life. The other part wanted to grab her and hold on. He wanted to taste her lips, feel her body yield against his, look into those gray-green eyes and see that she wanted him as much as he knew he wanted her. Not gonna happen. She wouldn't make the first move, and he couldn't.

She'd opened up to him tonight, and

would undoubtedly regret the things she'd told him tomorrow.

He'd known the life stories of all his men. Made losing them worse. They'd made him a gift of their hopes and dreams. Dreams that had died with them. Could he lean on her strength to pull him back to the world?

CHAPTER THIRTEEN

"Weather report says thunderstorms again tonight," Sean said over breakfast. "What's on the agenda, Charlie?"

"Colin Campbell called this morning. They're logging about twenty miles from here, and he asked if we wanted to join them. Give you a chance to see what they do and decide if you'd like to try it."

"I want to come, too," Mickey said. "I can't cut down trees yet, but maybe one day . . ."

"Like that'll happen." Hank sneered. "How we gonna manage you? Wheel you in a wheelbarrow and dump you in the poison ivy?"

"If we have to," Charlie said quietly. She threw Hank a look.

"Let's see *you* climb a tree," Mickey said. "Get high enough so the limb'll break off, why don't you? Break both legs in the poison ivy and see how well you walk with steel pins holding them together."

"Knock it off, you two," Sean said.

"Mickey, we'll park your wheelchair up on the road by the truck and the flatbed," Charlie said. "You can watch the horses bring up the logs and load them. They barely need any supervision. They know their jobs."

"Do I have to go?" Mary Anne asked. "It's not like I'm going to do any logging."

"It's not just logging," Charlie said. "It's setting up the horses and hitching them to the logs. And, yes, you have to come along. This is a good time for one of your long-sleeved shirts, your scarf, a wide-brimmed hat, work gloves, boots and plenty of sun screen and fly spray. There'll lots of chiggers."

"Will there be snakes?" Sean asked. "I do not do snakes."

"Probably. But snakes don't like horses. The feeling is mutual."

Charlie stopped Jake on his way upstairs and whispered, "How are the you-know-whats? If I tell the others about the kittens now, what are the odds we'll be late for our appointment. You up to an open house when we get back? Is Mama Cat freaking out?"

"No so far. She has food she doesn't have

to hunt for, fresh water, a comfortable bed and her little family."

"I'll check with our vet when we get back from the logging and ask her how soon we can have her spayed."

He turned to start up the stairs. "That big tom has already been serenading her from outside the window. So far she's not interested."

"Wish we could have him neutered, too," Charlie said. "We tried one of the humane traps. He took the meat and managed not to spring the trap."

The group reconvened in the big metal equipment shed that served as a garage for the trucks and a workshop for the tractors and heavy farm equipment.

"Watch out for the grease pit," Charlie warned.

"My kinda place," Mary Anne said.

Since part of the appeal of horse logging meant that it was unnecessary to clear a road broad enough for trucks and flatbeds, they found the Campbell equipment pulled into a pasture beside a thick stand of trees.

The two black shire mares tied to the side of the Campbells' red stock trailer were bigger than any horse the colonel owned except the stallion. Already harnessed for the day's work, they were contentedly munching hay from nets tied to the side of the trailer.

"Hey, Charlie." Colin Campbell came around the end of the trailer, wiped his hands down his bib overalls and took hers. "Hey, folks. Come to do some loggin'?" He grinned at Mary Anne, who shrank behind Charlie. "Young lady, you look like you'd make a fine logger." He turned to Mickey. "Woods we're in today might be a tad rough for your chair, son, but you can help my brother Miles keep track of the load up here by the road."

"Yessir," Mickey said.

"You'll be by yourself until we bring the first log up to load. Keep well away once we start it rollin' onto the flatbed. Stay up in front of the truck. If one of the logs gets loose, no chair in the world can outrun it."

"I'll be careful."

Colin nodded and turned to the group. "Miles and Ian're already down in the woods. Hear that?" The growl of a chain saw set Charlie's teeth on edge. "Brought down a fine red oak yesterday evening. Have to cut it into sections the length of the flatbed and load it today." He patted the nearest mare's broad rump. "This here's Ellie and that's Nellie. They're good old girls. Any of you ever do any logging?"

Sean and Jake both raised their hands.

"Good. Then y'all got some idea what we're doing. Well, folks, let's drive Ellie and Nellie on down the hill. Charlie, you want to do the honors?"

"No, indeed. They're your horses, it's your business and I have no idea where we're going."

"They've been down there once today. They know where we're headed better 'n I do. Give it a shot."

Hank and Sean untied the mares and backed them away from their hay. They didn't complain. They knew they'd be well taken care of when the day's work was done.

"Here you go," Colin said, and handed the two sets of reins to Charlie. "We already took the chains down to hook up the log. Ground driving 'em down to the log's the easy part."

"I have a better idea," Charlie said. "Jake, how about you take them down? Colin and I will be right with you."

He looked hard at her and at the reins she held out to him. "No," he said.

"You've plowed behind horses," Charlie said. "I haven't. This isn't much different. Here." She handed him the reins once more.

He sighed, nodded and took them. She'd made the decision for him. She caught the query in Sean's expression and gave him a nod and a smile of reassurance. She moved up to the shoulder of the nearside mare. Colin moved to the mare on the far side.

"Come around," Jake said quietly, and tightened the right rein a fraction. Both mares stepped to the right as neatly as soldiers executing a turn on the parade ground.

Colin raised his eyebrows at Charlie, who winked at him.

Then Jake whistled a single note. The mares walked off side by side down the narrow trail.

"You done this before?" Colin asked.

"Once or twice," Jake said. "Not recently."

"You don't forget how to whistle like that. I can do it. My brother Ian can't, no matter how hard he tries."

"How about Miles?" Charlie asked.

"He tries, but he can't get the language right. He whistles, those ol' girls is like to go left when he means right. Hangs 'em up in the trees."

The heavy clay soil had been soaked by the last rain and remained as slippery as glare ice in spots, but the horses didn't put a foot wrong.

The people, however, slipped and slid their way toward the growl of the chain saw.

Once he had accepted the task of driving

the mares, Jake slipped into his role as though he'd not spent a single day off his father's farm. The horses responded to him the same way every animal Charlie had seen him with responded.

"Hey, y'all," came a voice from above their heads. Shading her eyes from the sun, Charlie looked up. The horses stopped.

"Up there's my baby brother Ian," Colin said.

The head poking out between the leaves of a big maple looked like the reincarnation of the Green Man. His skin seemed to have been made from the same leather as the harness. He hadn't taken nearly as much care of his face, however. He had way too many teeth for his mouth, resulting in an overbite that would have benefited greatly from braces when he was a child. His teeth might be bucked, but his grin was extra broad and his voice cheerful.

"Come down outta there," Colin said, "before you break your fool neck."

"Got to lop off some of these limbs. We fell this sucker the way she stands, we're gonna wind up with a deadfall widow maker."

"You fall, you'll make your Lucille a widow, and she'll blame me and make me support your children. Come on down and meet the company."

Ian lowered his chain saw on a line until Colin could take it, then started down after it. Hearing the disturbance over their heads, the mares huffed and sidled away from the noise. Jake cooed to them to calm them.

When he was fifteen feet from the ground, Ian suddenly shouted, "Oh, shoot!"

The branch he was standing on broke and crashed. He dropped along with it.

Both branch and man landed across the backs of the mares.

Given a choice of fight or flight, they chose flight.

Ian slid sideways to crash onto the ground beside Colin while the branch slid off to the other side.

Charlie dived out of the way. It missed her head by a hair. She rolled toward the safety of the trees as the mares exploded past her.

Jake leaned back against the reins like a water-skier while he and Colin yelled to the horses to whoa. Twenty feet down the trail Jake had the mares nearly under control again when they came to a narrow fork. Before Colin could tell him which path to take, Ellie went left and Nellie went right. In the middle stood a tall sapling.

The trunk hit the chains anchoring the

horses to the center pole with a crash that rocked both mares off their front feet and onto their rear ends.

Colin grabbed Nellie's bridle while Charlie ran down the trail and grabbed Ellie.

"We got 'em," Colin shouted. "Whoa, you fool horses!"

From Ellie's shoulder Charlie saw Jake toss the reins to Sean. In a second he was at her side with his arms around her. "Are you hurt?" he asked.

"A few bruises. Thanks, Jake."

He held her longer than necessary. She was shaking and leaned against him while he ran his hands down her back. "You could have been killed," he said.

"You're one heck of a drover, young man, to be able to handle that," Colin said. "And my brother is an ignoramus who nearly got us all killed. Ian, get your sorry self down this trail and help us back up these mares."

"I'm sorry," Jake said, looking at the two mares, who now stood quietly waiting to be rescued.

"Sorry? You did great. Shoot, I'll hire you anytime," Colin said, then glared at Ian. "You ever pull a stunt like that again, baby brother, and I am going to be a man short on this crew as of that moment, do I make myself clear?"

"Uh-huh. Y'all, I'm sorry. I thought sure that branch would hold me." Even bigger than Aidan, Colin Campbell's "baby brother" stood six foot seven and managed to stuff well over three hundred pounds of muscle and fat into his dirty bib overalls. He ducked his head and grinned sheepishly. "Nobody got hurt, though."

"Except for the scrapes on the mares and me and Charlie's hide," Colin said. "Might have busted her head and their backs. Back 'em up, Jake."

"Won't you take over?" Jake asked.

"Heck no. Go on." The mares obligingly backed away from the tree, and Jake headed them down the hill again.

At that point a small man trudged up toward them. "What the Sam Hill happened up here? The first log's chained up and ready to pull."

After explanations and introductions, Miles led them to the waiting log.

The oak they had harvested was still solid and healthy, but from the radius of the trunk, it would only have had a few more good years before it was claimed by disease or weather. As it was, the price of the timber would be a windfall for the farmer who owned the land without hurting the forest in which it had stood.

Miles Campbell was completely unlike either Colin or Ian, both of whom were big men. He was no taller than Charlie, whip thin and moved like a panther among the branches.

"Jake, how about you turn the girls around and back 'em up to the log so we can attach the chains," Colin said.

Jake handled the mares well and had them facing up the hill with less effort than Charlie required to turn Pindar.

"Said you'd done some logging?" Colin asked Sean. "Know how to chain a log?"

"Not to a horse, I don't."

"Come on, I'll show you. This'll take a minute," he said to the others. "Why don't y'all find a log to rest on. Don't sit on a copperhead or a fire ant nest."

Ian guffawed and leaned his bulk against a smaller oak.

The chains were attached to the horses in fewer than two minutes. At Colin's signal, Jake moved the horses forward until the chains tightened.

"They know the way to the road. Send 'em on," Colin said.

Jake nodded and flicked the reins against their broad backs.

They hunkered down, drove forward with their shoulders and dropped their rear ends.

For a second the log didn't move, then it began to slide up the trail behind them as if it were on rails.

"Don't get behind that log now," Colin said. "Sometimes it'll come loose and slide backward or bounce over to the side. Roll right over you." Mary Anne squeaked and slipped behind Sean.

"That is something to see," Hank said. "How come Jake gets to handle the mares?"

"He already knows how," Charlie said. "He used to plow with horses when he was growing up. I assumed you knew that."

"Don't know a thing about him except he's weird," Hank said. "Heard some rumors that he got a bunch of guys killed in-country."

"Watch your mouth," Sean said. "There were some men killed, but it wasn't his fault. Drop it."

"All right, all right." Hank held up his hands. "I'm just sayin . . ."

"Well, don't. Mary Anne, what say we follow that log to the road, watch 'em load and drink a soda out of the cooler."

Mary Anne nodded and followed. Sean held her hand to steady her when her feet slid in the mud.

Charlie followed Hank and Colin.

"I'd hire Jake tomorrow," Colin whispered

to Charlie. "Miles wants to get out of the woods and into the office to handle the paperwork. I said he could as soon as we found somebody to take his place."

Charlie felt her breath catch in her throat. Wasn't this what she and the colonel wanted? Good jobs for their students? But not Jake. Not yet. She couldn't face the hole he'd leave in her life.

Wouldn't it be better to lose him now before she cared too much? Or was it already too late. "Jake's not ready. I have no idea whether he can handle a chain saw."

"Fine, but I got first dibs."

The operation of loading the giant log onto the flatbed required pulling it alongside, unhitching the mares, moving them to the far side and rehitching them so that they could roll the log up the ramps set along the side of the flatbed. Jake stood back and let Colin and Ian handle that part. Colin used the long metal peavey hook to lever the log straight, then the mares took over. Again, they needed no instruction. They hauled until the log slid onto the flatbed, then relaxed so that the chains went slack and they could be unhooked.

"Now, we go back down and do it all over," Colin said.

"That is way, way cool," Mickey said.

Hank nodded. "True that."

It was the first time Charlie could remember that the two men had agreed on anything.

"It is way, way dangerous," said Sean. "You ever fell a tree?"

Both men shook their heads.

"You'll get your chance." Colin clapped Hank on the back. "Right, Charlie?"

She nodded and said to the others, "They're coming to our place for your next lesson. We've got some dead trees we need to take down before they fall down. You'll have the chance to fell 'em and load 'em."

"When?" Hank asked.

"We should finish here this afternoon if the rain holds off," Ian said. "Probably bring the equipment over tomorrow or the next day and sneak in y'all's little job the first break we get where it's dry. Most likely a week to ten days."

"Great!"

Hank was actually enthusiastic. It wouldn't last, Charlie thought. There were no buckle bunnies lusting after axmen. Cutting and hauling logs would not feed his ego.

Maybe their next expedition would.

CHAPTER FOURTEEN

"Tell Charlie what happened in-country," Sean said to Jake as they hosed down the big tractor outside the equipment shed. "Charlie likes you and you're crazy about her."

"Which is the best reason not to tell her," Jake said. "Actually, it's a good reason for me to go before I do any more harm."

"You've done some actual decision-making since you've been here. The world hasn't blow up yet."

Jake managed a grin. "I've been careful."

"I'm fed up with that excuse."

"It's not an excuse. It's true."

"So tell her what you believe. Then if you walk out on this chance, on her, at least she'll know what an idiot you are."

"Don't push me, Sergeant."

"That's what sergeants do, Major. Push dumb officers into doing what they know is right." He turned the hose full force on Jake.

"Hey!" Jake's feet slipped from the sudden force of the high-powered nozzle, and he sat down hard on the concrete.

Sean didn't blink. He kept the spray playing full force while Jake ducked and covered.

"What on earth is going on out here?" came Charlie's voice.

"Ask *him,*" Sean said.

"He's trying to drown me," Jake choked. He struggled to his feet. Two strides of his long legs brought him to Sean. He yanked the hose out of Sean's hands and turned it back on him.

Sean took off at a dead run. Jake aimed the hose at his retreating back and limped after him. By the time they reached the gravel driveway outside the building, the others had seen the water fight and ran over to join in. Even Mickey threw his chair into high gear and threatened to flip over as he bumped across the grass.

Jake was an equal-opportunity sprayer until Hank grabbed the hose and turned it on Mary Anne, who chased him, took it and turned it on Mickey and Charlie. The water came straight from the well. Even in the summer it was ice-cold.

The chase deteriorated into shrieks of laughter as everyone tried — not too hard — to avoid getting drenched. Charlie raced around the corner of the barn and ran straight into her father.

"Uh-oh," she said.

"Having fun?"

"Not any longer."

Instantly everyone froze. Mickey, the current owner of the hose, dropped it. It flopped around in a last explosion of water and stretched out on the ground like a deflated snake. Sean picked it up and turned the screw on the nozzle to cut the stream entirely.

"Don't let me spoil your fun," the colonel said.

But of course he had, even if he hadn't meant to. If she'd had the hose at the time, Charlie would have sprayed her father first and thought about it later, but the moment passed, and his dignity survived intact.

"It's hot," she said. "We needed cooling off as much as the horses."

"Agreed."

"I guess everybody should get dry clothes on," Charlie said.

"Who started it?" the colonel asked. He wasn't angry. As a matter of fact, he no doubt regretted interrupting their fun. Still, he might as well carry a sign that read, "Authority Figure, Take Care."

"No idea," Charlie said blandly.

The colonel's gaze swept across all the innocent faces. "Right. I came down to tell you that the permits have come through to ride along with the carriages in downtown Memphis."

"Dad, I haven't told them yet."

"Oh, sorry. Not my afternoon, obviously." He stepped back and gave her a sweep of his palm.

"Okay," Charlie said. "We've received permission for you all to ride along with the carriage drivers who take tourists around downtown Memphis. Happy, Hank?"

"Yeah! When?"

"We're setting the schedule now."

"I couldn't," Mary Anne said.

"You won't be doing the driving, honey bunch," Hank said.

"People will stare."

"Once you get all your finery on," Sean told her, "the only kind of stares you'll get will come from guys who want to hit on you."

"That's worse."

"You're driving with an experienced woman driver who's six-four and can handle any rowdies without even getting off her box," Charlie told her.

"Who're you driving with, Charlie?" Sean asked.

"I'll be back at base camp handling radio communication," Charlie said. "This is for the students. I'm already a licensed driver."

She looked over at Mickey, sunk in his chair.

"I guess I'll be with you, right?" he grumbled.

"The carriages aren't set up for disabled drivers," Charlie said.

Mickey sighed. "I get it."

"If you're game, though, you can put on your leg braces, and we'll hoist you up on the box beside Walter, who's even bigger than Gail, Mary Anne's companion driver. We'll strap you on. You won't be able to get down without help, but you should be safe unless the carriage turns over, which is unlikely."

"How big is the carriage?" Mickey asked.

"Very big. It's a vis-à-vis that holds six comfortably and has a low center of gravity. The colonel will follow in the pickup with your wheelchair in case of an emergency."

Mickey sat up and smiled hugely. "Heck, yeah, I'm game. When do we leave?"

"We'll have a scrappy supper early, then head for Memphis."

She noticed Jake was quiet and hung back when she sent everyone inside to put on dry clothes.

"What is it?" she asked.

He shook his head. "I need to check the kittens."

She watched him as he limped up the stairs. Maybe tonight would be too much for him. She tended to forget his bad knee, but she doubted it allowed *him* to forget the injury for more than a few minutes at a time. They were all tired. She should have put off the arrangements for the drive for another night.

The thing was, this was a Wednesday night with no special events scheduled down on Beale Street, no baseball games or concerts to ramp up the crowds. It should be a slow night in the city for the carriages, perfect for her students. There was a chance of rain, but it should hold off until two or three in the morning according to the weather forecast.

She wanted them to have as many different experiences as possible.

Next week they'd go to the military cemetery to watch an interment.

They would probably hate that, but it was another way they could make a living driving horses.

Time for dry clothes, a hot shower and an hour's nap before Vittorio delivered the sandwiches to the common room.

Sarah refused to join them for this just as she had for the logging. She preferred to be on the net. Charlie knew she hadn't been monitoring her use as much as she should, but Sarah had a good head on her shoulders. She had always been trustworthy. No reason she should change now.

Actually, Sarah was busy plotting her escape. After their encounter in the sushi restaurant, Robbie Dillon had sent her dozens of emails.

They were all headed, Erase after reading. But she didn't. She saved them to her private password-protected file. Not that her mother would try to read them. "That's like opening someone else's mail," her mother told her. "We don't do that in this family. I trust you."

Sarah felt a little guilty not telling her mother about their correspondence, but Charlie would go ape if she knew.

If she had a cell phone she could text him, Sarah thought, but Marchbanks, her new school, didn't allow students to carry cell phones. Plus, according to her mother, "We can't afford another cell phone, and you certainly don't need one on the farm." Of course she *did* need one, but try to tell her mother that. Try to tell her mother *anything*.

Or even *find* her half the time.

Sarah sent Robbie a picture of her taken before they moved down here — not in a bathing suit or anything. Her friend Laura had sent her boyfriend a picture and found it a week later on the internet. Sarah might trust Robbie, but she didn't necessarily trust his friends, whom she hadn't even met.

Robbie was okay that she couldn't date until she was fifteen, and then only in a group. He said they had to keep their relationship secret, though. She definitely understood that. She'd never been part of the in crowd at any school, but with a boyfriend like Robbie, she might be.

She wished she could talk to Mary Anne, somebody close to her own age. All her friends back at post only wanted to talk about their friends and parties and problems. Now they didn't even answer half the time. They'd moved on. Sarah hadn't. Yet.

She knew her grandfather could be conned into giving her a car for her sixteenth birthday. Until then, she'd have to ride the school bus, which Robbie warned her was not cool. He also warned her not to bring her lunch from home. Much cooler to eat in the cafeteria. With him to guide her, she wouldn't make stupid kid mistakes.

Now here was his invitation to a pool

party at his house the Saturday afternoon before school started. So in a couple of weeks she'd have a chance to meet some of the crowd from March-banks. "Yes!" she said with an arm pump.

Then she slumped in pure misery. Her mother would never let her go. She already didn't like Robbie just because he was a couple of years older than she was and the other people at the party would probably be older, too.

Charlie would demand to meet Robbie and probably his parents and his uncles and aunts and cousins. Somehow Sarah had to find a way. Then she had an idea. She had seen Jake and her mother together. If he had the hots for her, she could use that.

She looked at her email, accepted Robbie's invitation and hit Send.

CHAPTER FIFTEEN

After an early dinner, everyone piled into the farm trucks and drove the beltway to the Memphis-Arkansas Bridge before turning north to the stable. The area didn't look as though there could be a horse for miles in any direction.

Urban blight? Plenty of that. But half-hidden in a restored building at the north end of Main Street, the stable housed horses, carriages, workshops, storage for hay and feed and draft horse harnesses in efficient comfort.

Charlie introduced everyone, and said, "Okay, people, we're expecting a slow night tonight. No concerts, no baseball or basketball games, nothing unusual downtown on Beale Street."

"We hope it's slow," said Gail, the head driver, "You never know. Still, it seemed a good time to have y'all drive with us."

Hank raised a hand. "Can I wear a top hat?"

Jerry, the law student with whom he was driving, made a face at him. "I don't have an extra and you are not borrowing mine."

"Yeah, I guess you need all the help you can get," Hank said with a broad grin. Jerry resembled a young Abraham Lincoln without the beard. "A top hat's not going to help you much, man."

Hank had gone today for the second shave he normally skipped when they were at the farm and he looked gorgeous. The lady customers would jockey for his carriage just to flirt with him.

"We drivers can refuse to take anyone we consider too drunk or too belligerent or weird or lustful," Gail said. "You'd be surprised what people try to get up to in the back of an open carriage."

"Do we get to watch?" Mickey asked.

"No way. If we limited ourselves to sober customers, we wouldn't work so often or get such good tips, although mostly we drive families that want to treat their kids. At some point some macho idiot is probably going to demand a race between two of our carriages. No racing and no betting."

"How come?" Hank asked. Charlie had warned Gail that Hank would be the one to push boundaries.

"Main Street down here looks quiet in the evening after the trolleys stop running and with no people on the sidewalks, doesn't it?" Jerry said. "But the trolley tracks are barely wider than the carriage wheels. You get a wheel trapped, and it may take all of us to lift it out, even if we don't break a shaft. And that's at a walk. These guys are well trained and quiet, but if they break into a gallop, all the carriage brakes in the world aren't going to stop them."

"And if you get caught in the turntable at this north end where the trolleys turn, you could flip the carriage," Gail said.

Mary Anne moaned.

"Won't happen tonight," Gail assured her. "We'll all be waiting for customers beside The Peabody Hotel and driving the same route. There's safety in numbers, even against macho idiots." Gail looked around the group. "Now, here's a copy of our pre-drive checklist."

"Look at all that stuff!" Hank said.

"We have to carry water for the horses," Gail continued, "and liquid solvent to clean up the street if they decide to piddle."

"What about the manure?" Sean asked.

"They all wear a 'bun bag' to catch that." She continued to check off the equipment the carriages required, from first-aid kits to buckets and scrub brushes. "See, it's not all fun and games," she told them when she finished. Mary Anne raised her hand. "We won't actually have to drive, will we?" She wore her makeup and wig, black slacks and a black silk shirt with sleeves that reached down to her brown driving gloves. In the illumination from the old-fashioned streetlamps, she looked totally scar-free.

"You're with me," Gail said. "You don't have to take the reins unless you want to, and only for a few minutes with an empty carriage. Maybe on our way back to the stable for the last time you can drive." She turned to Charlie and whispered, "You were right. They *will* hit on her. Don't worry. I'll handle it. How come I get her and not the gorgeous one?"

"Hank?"

Gail shook her head. "I meant the tall, thin one with the crazy blue eyes and the floppy hair. Him I could go for. The man positively exudes sex appeal. It's that Heathcliff thing."

While Charlie had never thought of Jake as Heathcliff, not one of her favorite heroes, Gail was right. He looked incredibly sexy. Tonight he'd dressed in black jeans and a black long-sleeved T-shirt. If his plan was to fade into the background, it hadn't worked. He hadn't wanted to come along any more than Mary Anne had, and now he gave Charlie an accusatory glance. She felt a jolt that had nothing to do with electricity and everything to do with hormones.

He stood silently beside his driver, a happy elf of a man named Darrell, while he finished his pre-drive checklist. She felt a stab of jealousy that she had no business feeling. Gail was younger, slimmer, had tighter abs and was better looking than she was.

Gail climbed up on her driver's box without bothering to use the mounting block. Sean had to lift Mary Anne into the left-hand seat.

"We're lead carriage tonight, so off we go," Gail said. Mary Anne made that whimpering noise as the gray Percheron, Sammie, walked south down Main Street.

It took some time to get Mickey securely fastened into the left-hand seat of the Cinderella carriage. "It's gloriously tacky," he crowed. "I love it."

Sean and Jake were the last of the students to climb into their seats and depart. Charlie crossed her fingers and settled beside the radio in the office to intercept their calls.

Five minutes later the receiver crackled.

"First client," Gail said. "Nice couple from Detroit."

"How's Mary Anne doing?" Charlie asked.

"Fine, so far. She's so scared she can't move or speak." Gail chuckled. "Come on, girl, say something."

"Urk," said Mary Anne.

"Good enough. Evening, folks. We're about to give you a taste of what it was like before cars, when travel had some class. First, we'll swing down Second Street and around Court Square. Let me tell you about . . ."

Charlie switched to another carriage.

Ten minutes after they reached the carriage stand at The Peabody, all the carriages had passengers and were on the move. The drivers knew the history of the area and could tell a bunch of stories about everything from the original settlement through the Civil War, known here as The War of Northern Aggression. That always tickled the Yankees. The drivers regaled their customers with ghost stories, tales of the yellow fever epidemic, Beale Street in its heyday, all the way up to the present. The passengers got a history lesson as well as a pleasant ride.

Since the drivers left their radios on while they had customers in case they needed to call for help, Charlie listened in.

She'd been right about Hank. Jerry, the second-year law student who normally talked nonstop, had turned over the patter to Hank. If there were such a thing as "carriage bunnies," Hank would have a coterie by closing time.

Sean concentrated on finding out about the customers and talking to the children.

Jake, on the other hand, left the talking to his driver. Since Darrell's store of funny stories about Memphis was never ending, that worked fine.

Mickey's first customers were an elderly man and his small wife.

"Son, I just realized you're wearing leg braces. You a veteran?" the man asked.

Charlie heard Mickey's soft groan. "Yessir. Iraq."

The man wanted the entire history of Mickey's army career and his background, where and how he'd been wounded.

"Now, Carl, you leave the nice young man alone," his dumpling wife said.

"I was in 'Nam in sixty-eight," Carl said. "Now that was a screwed-up mess, let me tell you . . ." And the war stories flowed.

Back at the office Charlie wanted to interrupt, but there was no effective way to shut the guy up. The customer might not always be right, but he was always the customer.

Mickey managed well. He kept up a running patter of *gee, how about that, must have really been bad.* After the couple were deposited back at The Peabody, Mickey leaned over and whispered into the mike, "Hey, Charlie, I just picked up a hundred-dollar tip. Pays to be a crip, am I right?"

"He's splitting it with me, aren't you, Mickey?" Walter, his driver, said. "That is, if you don't want to stay in that seat for the next twenty-four hours without a potty break."

Still not a word out of Jake. Darrell kept up his patter, too, but Jake might as well not have been on the box with him.

"Hey, man, if it ain't ol' Jake! Can I take a ride? You done come up in the world."

Big guffaw.

"Evening, Rotgut," Jake said amiably. He shouldn't have been surprised to run into someone he knew from the shelter. "Sorry, this isn't my carriage. Can't offer you a ride."

The man gave another rough burst of laughter. "You gonna get a job with these folks? We'll all come down and take a ride with you." His speech was slurred, his voice high and his accent placed him from somewhere in Louisiana.

"Ain't seen you down to the shelter long time. You gonna buy ole Rotgut a drink, you bein' so high-and-mighty?" His tone dropped to whiny.

"Buzz off, buddy," Darrell didn't sound so happy now. "Jake, you know this guy?"

"He knows me, all right," Rotgut said.

"Don't give him any money, Jake," Darrell whispered. "He'll tell every bum on the street we're an easy touch."

"Hey, I don't beg!" Rotgut was getting belligerent. "I'm asking to borrow some money from my old friend Jake here."

Jake reached into his hip pocket, pulled out a twenty and handed it down to Rotgut. "Nobody else, Rotgut."

"Yeah, we'll call the cops on you all in a heartbeat," Darrell said. "Walk on, Ranger."

"Good to see ya, Jake, and thanks for the loan." Rotgut faded back into the shadows in Court Square.

"Why'd you do that?" Darrell demanded. "You know he'll go drink it up.".

"He's got a steel plate in his head and a Bronze Star to go with his Purple Heart. His wife left him and he can't hold a job. So I know."

"Oh," Darrell said.

The night was busier than they'd expected. Several times customers had to wait in line until another group was through with their tour. Jake and Darrell took their turns in the rotation without meeting Rotgut or any of his buddies on the lookout for them.

"Looks like we can wind things up by ten o'clock," Gail said at nine-thirty, as the group lined up outside The Peabody.

"Thank the Lord for an early night occasionally," said Walter, "Although I'd drive with Sean anytime. The kids love him."

"Uh-oh, I spoke too soon," Gail said. "Here we go, people. Look sharp."

"Those bridesmaids should have shot the bride for making them wear those dresses," Walter whispered to Mickey.

Mickey snickered. "Vomit-green with ruffles. Ew!"

"Mickey, hush."

Jake watched as the entire wedding party, a dozen ruffled green bridesmaids and their tuxedoed groomsmen, erupted from the Union Avenue door of The Peabody, rushed the carriages and demanded rides for everyone.

"Leave the champagne with the doorman," Gail said, "and you're on."

After the fee was negotiated and the bottles and glasses turned over to the doorman for safe-keeping, the crowd swarmed

235

noisily into the carriages.

They switched seats and carriages and jockeyed for position for ten minutes before they finally settled who would sit where and with whom.

Jake shook his head. This definitely wasn't the job for him.

One man called, "Home, James."

Gail's voice carried over the noisy group. "Everyone, for safety's sake, once you sit, stay seated in the same spot. You can get hurt if you don't. Okay?"

She carried sufficient authority to earn a chorus of *uh-huh* and *yes, ma'am.*

Jerry whispered, "Please don't let anyone throw up in the carriage."

The drive began calmly enough. The passengers were noisy, but happy noisy.

Five minutes into the drive after they had turned down Main Street, empty now that the trolleys had stopped running, one of the men in Darrell's vis-à-vis shouted, "Hey, you cowards! I got fifty bucks says our horse can beat y'all's horses!"

Jake tensed and glanced back at the young man, who'd obviously had too much to drink.

"No way!" The cry rose up from the folks in Gail's victoria. "Fifty bucks says you can't!"

"No bets allowed and no racing, either," called Darrell. "Y'all sit down and behave now."

Fortunately, Jake thought, it took a lot to get the horses to move faster than a slow trot. They preferred to amble.

They could, however, gallop like oversize racehorses if provoked enough.

The young man who had started the betting stood up behind Jake, uttered a piercing rebel yell and grabbed Darrell's long buggy whip.

"Hey, you," Darrell shouted, "Sit down and give me back my whip!"

"Yee-ha! Catch us if you can!" The man leaned across the front seat of the carriage, raised his arm high over his head and cracked the whip hard against the big Belgian's rump.

Ranger's explosive leap forward threw the man into the lap of one of the bridesmaids and Jake lurched sideways. Just in time he managed to grip the side of his seat and brace himself.

The girls shrieked, the man yelled and the carriage rocketed down the center of Main Street behind the galloping Belgian, who was determined to reach the stable as fast as possible.

Gail shouted. "The rest of you, hang on

to your horses! Darrell's got a runaway."

"I'm standing on the brakes," Darrell shouted. "Whoa! Ranger, walk!"

"Whoa!" Jake's baritone rose above the muddle of sound as though he had a bullhorn. "Ranger, Whoa. Now!"

The Belgian reacted to the command and stopped. The shouting had ended and the only sounds now were the sobs of one of the bridesmaids.

"Aw, man!" said a very drunken voice from the floor of Jake's carriage.

Darrell pointed at the man and snarled, "You! Off!"

"Man, you can't do that. I paid for this —"

"You heard the man," Jake said gently. "Off."

Something in Jake's tone penetrated the idiot's fogged brain. He was assisted to the street by the young women, who had progressed from terror to rage at the instigator.

Standing beside the carriage, he whined, "How 'm I gonna get back to the hotel?"

"Walk!" came a chorus of drivers and riders alike.

"Ranger, walk on," Darrell said. The passengers had sobered up fast and sat without speaking for the remainder of the ride. Back at the hotel they piled out in silence, very subdued. Not too subdued, however, to remember to take possession of their remaining glasses and bottles of champagne.

"Sorry about that," one of the passengers said to Darrell. "Guy's a jerk. Here, hope this'll make up for the trouble." He handed up a sheaf of bills. Darrell saw the denomination on the top bill and raised his eyebrows. "Thanks for taking care of us," the man said, and shook Jake's hand. "You got some voice on you."

On the way back to the stable, Darrell said, "Thanks, Jake. Ranger's a good horse, but he's young. Hasn't driven his share of idiots yet. When that guy grabbed my whip and whacked Ranger, I knew we were in trouble. Ranger's never been lashed in his life."

"The carriage brakes would have stopped him eventually."

"Not before we hit the trolley turntable up at the north end of Main. Catch a wheel at a gallop, and we'd sure as shootin' turn over." He began to laugh from relief. "Ranger sure listened to you. Talk about the voice of authority."

Back at the office, Charlie heard Darrell's words and nodded.

Jake. Even animals trusted him to look after them. He must have been an incredible commander.

She wondered, though, what had happened to his team when they followed him?

CHAPTER SIXTEEN

Thursday after the carriage drive was spent dissecting the evening's events. Mary Anne had hated the experience, while Hank and Mickey loved it. Both Sean and Jake were noncommittal.

"I could get used to that," Hank said. "Pay's not bad, the tips are great and it's not hard work."

"And you can hit on the pretty girls," Mary Anne said. He gave her a sharp glance but didn't respond otherwise.

"I couldn't do it alone," Mickey said. "Not until I was secure on my pins. But I could sure drive weddings in the Cinderella carriage with somebody along to ride shotgun."

"As in shotgun weddings?" Sean said. "Not too many of those any longer."

When Jake brought his dishes back into the common room and added them to the trolley, Sarah, who had come over for lunch, touched his arm. "Jake, can I talk to you?"

"Sure. What's up?" He was surprised that Sarah had approached him. She hadn't seemed to pay much attention to him. Only Mickey and Hank appealed to her. He led her down to the tack room.

Sarah sat down behind the rein board and began to play with the reins attached to the wrought-iron horse's head. "Mom said you left home when you were my age."

"Not by choice."

Sarah's eyes widened. "They kicked you out? Mom said you ran away. I figured you couldn't stand it at home any longer."

"You aren't considering doing the same thing, are you?"

Sarah avoided his eyes. "I knew a couple of girls on post who ran away, but they both had drug problems. The cops eventually found Patsy and brought her home. Her parents tossed her into rehab, but we had to leave before she came out, so I don't know whether it took or not. Nobody knows what happened to my other friend Shelley."

"You didn't answer my question. Are you considering running away?"

Sarah avoided his eyes.

"This may sound like a stupid question, but what would you be running from."

"I hate this place!" She yanked on the reins so hard the iron horse head bounced.

"I don't know anybody, I never go anywhere, there's nothing to do. I haven't been to the mall except with Mary Anne to get her wig. I don't even have anybody to go to the movies with. All I do is sit in my room all day and play video games and talk to people who are miles away doing stuff that I used to do. This is the only vacation I'll get this year, and I haven't even had my bathing suit on."

"Have you considered visiting some of your friends from the base?"

Sarah rolled her eyes. "They don't want me. I'm like — who's the guy who got swallowed by the shark?"

"Do you mean Jonah? I think it was a whale."

"Whatever. They pitched him overboard because he was bad luck. That's me. After Daddy got killed everybody was so *supportive.*" She made a face. "Right. That lasted about a week. Then I could tell every time they saw me, they thought about how the same thing could happen to their dads. Or moms. A couple of my friends' mothers are on their second or third deployment. The father of one of my best friends is deployed for the fifth time, would you believe?"

Now that she'd started, Sarah couldn't

seem to stop talking. She paced the tack room, pulling steel bits off their hooks and putting them back, batting the iron heads of the horses on the rein boards so that they bobbled like dolls.

Jake was honored that she'd pick him to unload on, but she should have been saying these things to her mother. What could he do? He couldn't make anything better for himself, much less for Sarah.

"The wives didn't want to be around my mother, either. The first week we got so many casseroles we couldn't fit them in the fridge. Then zip. And the minute school was over, we got kicked off base and had to move down here. If it wasn't for Granddaddy, we'd be living in the truck and eating out of garbage cans."

"I don't imagine it would have gotten that bad."

She rounded on him. He'd expected tears, but her face was set and angry. This was a soldier's child. She'd already learned to keep her emotions in check, but at fourteen she shouldn't have to.

"We're supposed to get some kind of a pension, but it takes like forever to process the paperwork, and it's not nearly what Daddy was making, which wasn't much in the first place."

"I know adults are always telling teenagers that things will get better. Like most clichés, it has an element of truth in it."

"So are you glad you ran away?"

Jake leaned back. How should he answer that? "I had to leave. Sarah, after that day, I never saw my family or the friends I grew up with again."

"Never? But you talked on the phone and wrote, right?"

"Nope. No phone, no emails. No photographs, no wedding or birth announcements."

"But didn't you try to make up with them?"

He nodded. "I tried. It didn't work. My mother wouldn't speak to me."

"Do they know you were wounded?"

"I have no idea."

Sarah stared at him, aghast. "That's terrible. Are you sorry you left?"

"I hurt my family, all the people I loved the most. But I thought I had no choice. You do have a choice. You're surrounded by people who love you. . . ."

Sarah snorted. "My mother has to know everything I do. I'm sick of it."

"You have a good life. Be a little patient."

"My mother's as big a control freak as Granddad, but she won't admit it. That day in the common room — I know you like my mom. Maybe you could talk to her, tell her to lighten up."

Ah. So that was why she'd come to him. She'd paid attention when she'd walked into the common room and discovered him and Charlie.

"I'll see what I can do."

"Thanks." She slid off the rein board bench, leaned over and kissed him on the cheek. A moment later she was gone. He touched his cheek. He should never have agreed to speak to Charlie. What did he know about parenting? When would he ever learn? If he spoke to Charlie and she did give Sarah more freedom, and things went bad, it would be another disaster that could be laid at his doorstep.

Sarah was counting on him to help. She shouldn't.

His father died younger than he should have because Jake had abandoned him. He'd tried hard to be the kind of son Micah wanted, but his father did not want the person Jake was.

He'd known he'd cause his family pain, but he figured they'd accept his choice after a while. He'd tried again and again to convince his father to let him go. Micah didn't believe in *rumspringa,* the year that

Amish teenagers were allowed to leave their farms and live among the English.

He was certain that once Jake left, he wouldn't come back. Most Amish kids did return to the Amish community after *rumspringa*, but they made the choice of their own free will.

Jake was miserable his senior year. First finding out that he would not be able to accept the partial scholarship to college, then being told he couldn't participate in graduation ceremonies or the parties afterward. The only person who ever argued with Micah Thompson was Jake's mother, Gudrun. Because of her, Jake was allowed to remain in school through high school instead of returning to work on the farm full-time after the eighth grade.

But even she couldn't buy Jake's freedom. He'd never considered joining the army until he lost the scholarship. He'd planned to go to college. If he joined the army, the government would pay for college, let him work on credits while he was on duty. He'd make enough money to do some traveling at least in the States. It wasn't the perfect solution, but it was what remained open to him.

He saw himself bringing gifts home at Christmas and sending postcards from the places he went.

Never happened. The first of his decisions that tore hearts out.

Had his father told the truth about his defection? Surely his sisters had told the men they married.

Maybe not.

He had to talk to Charlie. He understood that after losing her husband, she might be holding on to Sarah too hard. But could that be worse than not holding on hard enough? Jake didn't think so.

Late the following afternoon Ian Campbell brought two sets of harness and logging chains and dropped them off in the big equipment shed where the tractors and other farm equipment were stored.

"Y'all need to learn to ground drive a team before you hitch 'em to a log," he told the group assembled around him. He turned to look directly at Jake. "Shoot, you already know more about ground driving a team than I do. What Charlie can't teach 'em, you sure can."

Jake ducked his head and avoided Ian's eyes.

"Won't you need this stuff yourselves?" Hank asked as he fingered the heavy logging chains. He had a gleam in his eye that said he was going to enjoy this.

"This is our old stuff. We got new. Well — newer than this. It's not real heavy-duty, but Charlie says y'all plan to cut some of the locust trees out by the pond. You can handle that without us supervising. Good practice and good riddance." Ian shivered. "I hate those things. Thorns long as my hand. Y'all be careful ground driving, ya hear? We'll be back next week sometime, and we'll give everybody a lesson on loading."

He climbed back into his truck and waved out the window. "I got to get back to the site. Them brothers of mine can't load a log by themselves for spit."

"As I recall," Sean said with a grin as they watched him drive off, "Ian is the one who fell out of the tree."

"Let's get this harness cleaned, oiled and hung up," Charlie said.

They finished an hour later and wandered down to the common room for what had become the afternoon ritual. Pitchers of iced tea and accompanying nibbles before everyone showered and changed their sweaty clothes for dinner.

Charlie left them to it. As she walked out from under the shadows of the barn and into the start of a glorious sunset, a large maroon rental sedan pulled off the road and into the driveway. It stopped at the front door of the main house, and a thin woman wearing a bright red linen pantsuit and the biggest wraparound sunglasses Charlie had seen in years climbed out.

Charlie prided herself on her height. This woman stood an intimidating six-two at least. Then Charlie spotted the red leather platform sandals with the six-inch heels. Actually, the woman was probably an inch or two shorter than Charlie, and as thin as Sarah. On a girl as young and coltish as Sarah it looked good. This woman looked anorexic.

From time to time people drove up to the house seeking directions, or were interested in seeing the horses.

Charlie pulled off her work gloves and came across from the stable. "May I help you?" she asked.

The woman's expression was difficult to read behind the sunglasses, but the arrogant turn of her head said she considered she was speaking to a servant. "I am here to see Master Sergeant Sean O'Riley."

"Sean? He's around somewhere." Charlie glanced at the woman's sandals. How did she walk in those things without falling on her nose? "I'll see if I can find him for you.

Whom shall I say is calling?" Charlie didn't quite fake the British accent, but she came as close as she dared. She didn't often dislike people, but she had "taken agin' " this woman instantly.

"I am Brittany Galloway, and I will wait here." A moment's pause. "Thank you."

Charlie nodded, turned on her heel and trotted toward the barn. When she was only six feet away from the car, she yelled at the top of her lungs, "Hey Sean, some woman's here to see you." She met him at the barn door.

"Woman? What woman?" He glanced over Charlie's shoulder. "Oh, great. Just what I need."

Charlie had the impression that given the option, he would have run the other way. As it was, the woman had seen him and was mincing gingerly toward them across the lawn.

"I'll handle this," he whispered to Charlie, then took a deep breath and strode forward. "Hello, Brie." He opened his arms as if to hug her.

Today he hadn't bothered with the fancy latex covering for his hand. Sean said it was simpler to control without it, didn't make him sweat and gave him a more precise feel. The prosthesis did look rather like an articulated skeleton, though.

Charlie could tell the moment the woman saw his hand and stopped dead. Just as with Mary Anne's bald head, they'd all gotten so used to Sean's hand that they didn't even notice whether he was wearing his covering or not.

This Brie person sure did, however. She stepped back as though he were coming at her with a pitchfork.

"How'd you find me?" he asked, dropping his hands. "I asked Lizzie not to tell you."

Charlie had no reason to stick around, so she walked back into the barn. And into the first stall.

"I cannot believe you told Liz where you were and not me," she overheard Brie Galloway say. "No, she did not tell me, but it's not difficult to locate a retiree from the military. It was, however, embarrassing to find you'd been in a halfway house." She waved a hand. "What is this place? What on earth are you doing here?"

Sean's voice hardened. "Learning a trade."

"I beg your pardon? You do not have to work. You have your pension. Douglas and I have offered you a home." She narrowed her eyes. "What sort of trade?"

"You've seen that TV show about the loggers? Well, I'm learning to log with draft horses."

"Nonsense! It's bad enough that you retired as a noncom when you could have been an officer, but how can I possibly tell my friends that my father is a lumberjack? Pack your things and tell whoever is in charge that you're leaving."

Charlie froze. His daughter? Couldn't be the one who was becoming an engineer in St. Louis. She'd assumed the other one — the one who was trouble — was younger and an alcoholic or drug dealer or kleptomaniac or something. This woman was rich, chic and not much younger than Charlie. Or older than Charlie, but with more expensive skin treatments.

And a juggernaut. Charlie wanted to go support Sean but couldn't figure a way to do it.

"Who's that?" Mary Anne whispered.

Charlie jumped.

"His daughter. I hate her already."

"Oh, good grief. He's told me about her. She makes the wicked witch look like an archangel. He's been hiding from her."

"You knew?"

"Well, sure. I know all about his family."

I don't. "What do we do? We can't let him leave with her."

Mary Anne laughed. "He won't."

"I flew down from Cleveland the minute I found out where you are," the woman was saying. "As the elder sister, it's my responsibility to —"

"No, it's not your responsibility and neither am I," Sean said easily. "As long as you're here," he said to Brie, "come on into the common room and meet the others."

"Uh-oh." Mary Anne and Charlie sped to the common room, slipped in and sank onto the nearest couch as though they'd been there all along.

Hank looked over at them. "What's happening?"

"Shh, here they are."

"Folks," Sean said, "I'd like you to meet my eldest daughter, Brittany Galloway. Brie, this is Hank, and Charlie, who teaches us and runs the place."

Hank stood up and held out his hand. Brie gave it a quick glance to be certain it wasn't mechanical or filthy and touched his fingers. Charlie didn't offer her hand.

"And this is Mary Anne."

Mary Anne came into the light. She was in her working garb of sweaty sleeveless muscle shirt and bald head.

Charlie heard Brie's intake of breath. A week ago Mary Anne would have fled.

Today she grinned at Sean and stuck her burned hand out for Brie to shake.

Brie looked down at it as though it were a rattlesnake. "Uh . . ." she said.

"I guess it's too dirty," Mary Anne said, and winked at Sean. "Here's Mickey."

He wheeled into the room from the back hall followed by Jake, who took one look, turned on his heel and left the way he'd come. Charlie heard his limp on the stairs.

Mickey was his usual charming self. "Hi," he said with a wide grin and a proffered hand. "Nice to meet Sean's family."

"Father, might I speak to you alone?" Brie asked. She looked at Mickey's wheelchair as though it were an alien spacecraft and Mickey the resident alien.

"Oh, we're all friends here. Let's see. Mickey's a computer geek who's learning to walk, Hank's a rodeo rider missing half his foot, Mary Anne's a truck mechanic with burn scars and I'm a one-armed bandit."

"Don't forget Jake," Mickey said. "He's got a bum knee and can't make a decision. Other than that, man, he's great."

"Don't forget me," Charlie said. "I'm an army widow with no money and a teenage daughter. We're quite a crew, aren't we, Sean?"

"We sure are. And I'm going to continue

to be a part of it."

"Now, Father . . ."

"Don't call me Father. I was Dad before you married Dr. Galloway and got rich and uppity. I'm sorry if I embarrass you. I suggest you tell people I died a war hero."

"Don't be ridiculous."

"Tell them the truth, then. I didn't go to OCS because I couldn't pass the test and didn't have any college credits at that point. I was a doggone good noncom, and I'm going to be a doggone good logger."

"You can't ignore your family."

"Brittany, this *is* my family."

Nobody coached them, but everyone except Mickey stood and moved behind Sean. Mickey wheeled in beside him.

Charlie felt certain she was going to cry. Either that or she was going to coldcock the woman. On the whole, she preferred the cold-cocking alternative.

"I'll walk you to your car," Sean said.

"Don't bother. Wait until I tell Liz about this."

"She already knows."

Charlie had read about characters in books "storming out," but she'd never seen anyone actually do it until now.

Trailed by the others, Sean followed his daughter as she strode across the lawn. At one point she twisted her ankle and nearly went down, but she recovered and limped to the rental car.

As she roared past them on her way to the road, Mary Anne waved. "Y'all come back, ya hear?"

"Sorry about that," Sean said after they watched Brittany roar off down the road. He sounded normal, but he was shaking.

Mary Anne linked her arm through his and hugged him. "I divorced my jerk. You're stuck with yours."

"She's always wanted to be rich and social. She hated being a noncom's kid, so she got herself a job managing a doctor's office and managed to convince her boss to divorce his wife and marry her."

"Grandchildren?" Charlie asked.

"Not yet and I suspect not ever. I regret that if she has any I'll never get to see them, but I am not about to move to Cleveland and live over their garage."

"Good for you," Hank said. "How about an actual beer to celebrate?"

"First, we have to find Jake, the stinker," Mary Anne said.

Mickey leaped to his defense. "You know Jake. He hates that kind of thing."

"I'll get him," Sean said.

They let him go. Easy to see he needed

time to calm down and process what had just happened.

The beer drinkers were only halfway through their second beers when Sean burst into the room. "That sucker!" He grabbed the beer Hank handed him and collapsed on the sofa beside Mary Anne. "The man has got a damned menagerie in his bathroom!"

At his heels, Jake said, "Sorry, I meant to tell everybody. I forgot. Sean, I figured you could hear them from your room anyway."

Charlie shrugged and gave Jake a wry grin. Everyone started talking at once.

Jake held up his hands. "People, Mama Cat had her kittens in my room."

"Kittens!" Mary Anne gushed. "Can we see? How many? What colors? Boys or girls?"

Charlie shook a finger at her. "If Mama Cat moves the kittens, you're going to wind up driving Pindar solo."

"All but one are yellow tabbies, one is gray. Two boys, three girls."

"Can't see 'em unless you bring 'em downstairs," Mickey said. "I'm getting tired of being earthbound. How come I don't get a jet pack instead of a wheelchair?"

"Government corruption," Hank said. "Don't complain. You got robolegs. Cats don't turn me on. I'll wait."

Mary Anne was still raving about the kittens ten minutes later when Sarah slipped in to snitch extra dessert.

"Kittens?" she squealed. "What kittens? Where?"

Charlie bowed her head. Great. She doubted the colonel wanted to adopt five small cats, but she suspected he'd wind up with at least a couple of them.

"Mother," Sarah whined, "you knew and didn't tell me?"

"With everything else we've had to do, I forgot." She really had, and Sarah was absolutely justified in being angry. "I'm sorry, sweetheart." She dropped an arm over Sarah's shoulders, but Sarah shrugged her off.

"Jake, can I see them? Mama Cat won't even know I'm there."

"I doubt that," Jake said. "Come on."

Ten minutes later she clattered back down the stairs. "They are so cute! I've got to go tell Vittorio and Granddaddy." She flew out the patio door.

"How's Mama dealing with the attention?" Charlie asked.

"Seems to enjoy it. If we're careful, she may even learn to like human beings, although I wouldn't count on it."

"So long as the babies do," Mary Anne said.

Sarah was back in fewer than five minutes. "Granddaddy says I can have one." She tossed her hair. "I bet I can keep all five. Can I go see them again?"

"Jake," Charlie said, "you don't have to do this."

"Yeah, I do. You're right that if they're going to be socialized, they have to start having human interaction sometime. Might as well be when they're too young to get away." He followed Sarah.

Mama had shoved and clawed the counterpane into precisely the shape she wanted for her nest. A couple of the kittens had managed to make their way over one of the mountain peaks she'd created and were mewing plaintively, unable to get back to her.

"I want them all," Sarah whispered.

He used the side of the bathtub to pull himself to his feet and Sarah followed him out the bathroom door. As soon as they were in the hall, she said, "I've wanted a kitten my whole life, but my daddy was allergic. Please, please, please say I can have these."

"Sarah, your mother and grandfather may not like the idea of five small cats in the house. Do you have any idea how much damage those little guys can do with their claws and teeth?"

She tossed her head. "I'll keep them in my room, and we can buy a big tower scratching post. I'll clean their litter box twice a day."

Like that would last. "You may have to pick *one.* Two at the most. Your family can certainly find good homes for the others."

She smiled at him coyly, but she didn't answer.

Jake realized with a jolt that she knew she was being seductive. She was fourteen and perfectly willing and able to use her feminine wiles to get her way with a fortysomething male.

"You are such an old sweetie," she said as she started down the stairs. "I used to think you were scary, but you're not. I'll bet you can persuade my mother to let me go to the swim party this weekend."

He stopped three steps from the bottom. "What party?"

"Oh, it's just a little get-together with some of the kids in my new school. No biggie." She flitted into the common room and was instantly immersed in chatter about the kittens.

Jake stared after her. He had been soundly

bushwhacked by a fourteen-year-old girl, and he had no idea what to do about it.

CHAPTER SEVENTEEN

Finally a cool front came through and dropped the temperature and humidity to something approaching bearable. The morning was fresh and the breeze pleasant.

"Everybody, pair up," Charlie said. "This morning we're going to drive in tandem, then this afternoon, we're going to hitch up Pindar and Aries and practice driving a pair. I'll take Sean with me. Jake, you take Mickey. That leaves Mary Anne and Hank."

"Can't we drive Terror instead of one of the draft horses?" Mary Anne asked.

"Not this morning. You can drive Terror after lunch when the others are working the team."

"Who'll drive with me?"

"Time for your solo run, I think."

Mary Anne's eyes widened. "I can't."

"You can't drive that little pipsqueak?" Sean said. "He gives you any trouble, pick him up and toss him on his little pony tush."

"Can't Sean come with me this afternoon?" she begged.

"Okay, either he will or I will." Charlie pointed at her. "Promise you'll do all the driving."

Mary Anne nodded. She didn't look happy.

After the horses were harnessed, Charlie said, "This morning we're going to play follow the leader. Sean and I will lead. We're going way into the back of the property past the lake. There are some little hills and copses back there. We don't keep it cut, because we don't need it at the moment for the horses. We'll drive slowly, but you'll have to pay attention. There are a couple of streams to ford and some obstacles requiring tight turns and good reinsmanship."

"Could we have a picnic?" Mary Anne asked. "Since it's so pretty."

"Sure, why not? I'll ask Vittorio to fix us some sandwiches and sodas to take with us. Jake and Sean, get a couple of the big tarpaulins off the marathon carts. We can sit on those. Hop to it, people." She clapped her hands.

"I'm sorry about yesterday," Charlie said to Sean when at last they were under way.

"Me, too."

"I wasn't very friendly to your daughter."

Sean laughed. "Neither was I. Not easy to be friendly to Brie."

"From what you said earlier, I thought your younger daughter was the problem."

"Nope. Lizzy's pretty levelheaded, but Brie was our first, and my wife tried to make her into a princess. I mean, what normal middle-class family names a child Brittany?"

"I guess she agreed with her mother. She still looks princessy. Turn right at the bottom of the hill by that sycamore tree. There's a path that goes up over the levee and back into the woods. Hard to see until you're right up on it, but it's a nice drive. There's a great open space for the picnic by the stream."

Sean's reinsmanship had improved, although he hadn't been bad to start with. Pindar seemed to turn without any signal from him.

Charlie looked behind her. The others were following in excellent order. Jake relaxed by Mickey, who seemed at ease driving Ariel. Mary Anne sat forward in her seat, but Hank was driving Annie one-handed with his foot up on the dashboard.

"I wasn't around much when Brie was little," Sean continued. "Betsy, my wife, decided early on she was going to be the next Little Miss America, or some such. She

265

signed her up for her first contest when she was three."

"Really? I've seen those shows on TV — the kids in fancy dresses and false eyelashes and makeup?"

"Brie loved it. Betsy made the costumes, but even so, entry fees and travel — they eat up a bunch of money. You know those kids have bridges made to fit in their mouths when they start losing baby teeth?"

"Yuck."

"By the time I realized the whole shootin' match was out of hand, they were gone two or three weekends a month, staying in motels — inexpensive motels, but still."

"I cannot see you as one of those pageant fathers with the video cameras."

"That's cause I wasn't," Sean said drily. "Betsy hid as much as she could from me, and I didn't want to know. Still, it seemed like all we did was fight over Brie's career — that's what Betsy called the pageants. The thing that slowed it down was Betsy got pregnant with Lizzy — the one who's finishing up her engineering degree at Washington U. in St. Louis. Real bad pregnancy. Gestational diabetes, preeclampsia. Then she had a bout of postpartum depression. As usual, I was off on a temporary duty assignment and no help. Betsy's mother had to come and take over."

"That must have been a terrible shock for Brie."

"She never forgave Betsy, Lizzie or me. According to her, we ruined her life. Betsy had to give all that pageant stuff up. Too hard on her nerves. Brie was a really beautiful little girl, but when she entered a couple of pageants in high school on her own, she never won. First runner-up a lot, but not the crown. Everybody seemed to realize she cared too much for the wrong reasons."

"Her mother couldn't help at all?"

"Betsy died when Brie was a freshman in high school. Heart attack. That's when Brie tried to get back into pageants."

"Oh, Sean, I'm so sorry."

"Brie's still trying to be the winner she was when she was three years old. Isn't that the saddest thing you ever heard?"

"It's right up there in the top ten, Sean." Charlie leaned against his shoulder and slipped her arm around him. Calm, easygoing Sean. Everybody had a story. She should have discovered Sean's history earlier. But he wasn't a squeaky wheel like the others. He seemed to be completely whole, even if he was missing a hand.

What had she missed about the others?

CHAPTER EIGHTEEN

Charlie never knew whether Jake would come to the patio to join her or not. She felt like a teenager waiting for a telephone call from the boy she had a crush on. But this was worse than any crush. She stayed at high alert until either he showed up or she gave up.

When he did come out, they usually talked about the horses or the farm. She told him stories about growing up an army brat, about living in Germany and Greece, about her mother, even about Sarah.

Not, however, about Steve.

She was eager to learn about Jake's life in an Amish community, but every time she asked him a question about it, he changed the subject.

They'd become friends. That was all they should ever be — at least so long as he was her student. But friendship wasn't all she wanted.

Now, when she had rediscovered passion, she'd fallen for a man who didn't feel passion for her in return.

She still hadn't even convinced him to join the others at the dining table.

She'd pretty much given up that fight. Maybe one day she'd find out why he stayed away at meals.

Tonight Charlie gave up waiting for him on the patio. She was so tired she left after only thirty minutes. If he showed up, he could wait for her for a change. She expected to fall asleep instantly.

Instead, she felt too tired to sleep. She tried all the usual techniques, then tried tossing and turning, but that didn't do much good, either. She put a pillow between her knees to straighten her back. Still nothing.

Her mind flipped around like a ball in a pinball machine, never hitting the bell.

But she knew what the problem was. Jake. Might as well admit it. Gail, the carriage driver, recognized that he was great looking and sexy. As if Charlie needed another woman to point that out to her. He was also kind, caring and competent, but monumentally screwed up with a hair-trigger temper that seemed to go off when he felt somebody he cared about needed protection.

She truly believed that under his layers of outward control lurked a lava lake of passion ready to blow the top off the volcano. With Jake she felt as though she were poking at a humongous fire ant nest with a very short stick. Any minute the ants would swarm out and bite her. And it would hurt big-time.

What did she want from him? She was in a position of authority with vulnerable survivors. Any kind of relationship with Jake would be unprofessional and would compromise not only her future and the program's, but his recovery, as well.

How would it play with Sarah and the colonel? She felt certain Sarah already guessed.

At the patter of raindrops on her window, she rolled over and tried to ignore the sound.

Not more rain! The weather was supposed to be fine for the remainder of the week.

The sound came again. Then nothing. Then more showers. She sat up and looked at her window just as a handful of gravel hit the glass.

She was out of bed and had the window raised in an instant.

"Charlie! Wake up!"

She leaned out. "Jake? What on earth?"

This didn't sound like seduction.

"Get your clothes on and come down. You're having a baby."

"Molly's not due for another week. Her udder hasn't begun to swell yet."

"Tell Molly that when you get down here. I'll see you in the barn."

He was wrong. Mares foaled late if anything, never early.

She pulled on the jeans she'd worn all day and a clean T-shirt without a bra. She ran barefoot down the stairs and stopped by the patio door to slip on her barn muckers. She hadn't washed her face or combed her hair.

The foaling stall, as far from the stallion stall as possible, was fitted with soft lights that were always burning when a mare was inside. The door was wire mesh to the floor so that anyone outside could see the entire space.

It was already bedded deep with straw. Always better for a mare to foal in than shavings. She expected to find Molly munching at her hay net or snoring in the corner. She did not expect to find Jake in the stall beside her.

"Get out of there," she said.

"Take a look."

Charlie slipped in quietly beside him.

The mare had been exhibiting the signs of

late pregnancy for a couple of weeks, but no more than normal. The muscles at her tail head had relaxed, and her belly had distended and dropped. Charlie ran her hand down Molly's flank, felt sweat and received a snort and an irritated cow kick in return.

A moment later she received a handful of yellow colostrum from an udder that would have made a Jersey cow proud.

"Good grief, you're right. She's in labor. It's too early."

"Not that early. She could take hours."

"She never has in the past. This is her third foal. How did you guess?" Charlie asked.

"I came down to check on her," he said.

"At three in the morning?"

"I don't sleep all that well."

"I thought we were bringing her inside too early, but now . . ."

"Happens that way sometimes."

Inside the stall the mare walked in a circle. She'd worn the hay down in her path and was really sweating now. Her black pelt showed in the overhead light. From time to time she stared at her belly in annoyance, and several times kicked at it.

"Getting close," Jake said. He grabbed Charlie's hand and held it hard.

Fluid gushed onto the hay.

"This is the scary part," Charlie whispered. "She's starting."

The mare gave a groan and sank onto her chest and then her side, straining with her whole body, her legs stretched behind her.

Jake and Charlie prepared to help if necessary.

"Please," Charlie whispered, "give us two front feet and a nose." That was the optimum presentation for a foal.

The foal sac broke as the foal began to emerge. "Yes!" Charlie said. Before the baby slid onto the hay, its head was already free of membrane. It blinked at them with wide, baby eyes.

"Welcome to the world, little one," Charlie said. She went down on her knees to help Molly give one final push so that the baby's hind legs were clear of Molly's body. "Jake, go to the wash rack and bring some towels, please."

He nodded and a moment later knelt beside her. Charlie rubbed the baby's wet face and nostrils with one of the towels he handed her.

"What's wrong with Molly?" Charlie said. "She's still straining."

"Charlie, move the baby out of the way. Now!"

Charlie stared at him. He'd never used that tone with her before. The baby was already struggling to stand. Charlie grabbed it around the waist and hauled it forward, away from Molly's hind legs. Was Molly bleeding? If she hemorrhaged, there was no way to stop the blood in time to save her life.

Charlie expected to see a gout of blood. Instead, she saw two more feet and another nose. Twins! No! Twins seldom survived.

Jake grabbed the second foal in both arms as it emerged and lifted it like a puppy. It gazed up at him with wide, trusting eyes.

"It's tiny," Charlie said.

"It's breathing," Jake replied. "Hello, little guy."

Molly struggled to her feet and looked at once for her foal. She saw the baby in Jake's arms first and reached over to nibble its wet coat.

"Hey, Molly, over here," Charlie said, and turned the mare's head to the fine big foal already wobbling on its feet. A little confused, Molly reached across and nibbled this baby, as well.

"This place is getting crowded," Jake said. "How do we keep her from stepping on the little one?"

"Put the foal down. Let's see what Molly

does. She could reject it totally, or its sibling could decide not to share. I've only seen a couple of pairs of twins born, and none where one was so much bigger than the other. I left my cell phone upstairs. You have yours with you? I need to call our vet. She doesn't usually come out until morning with a normal birth."

"No way is this normal," Jake said, and handed her his cell phone.

While she talked to the vet, who agreed to come out to the farm at once, Jake brought two cushions from the sofa in the common room and propped them against the outside of the stall on the dirt floor.

When Charlie realized what he was doing, she raised her eyebrows.

"This floor is as clean as the common room floor," he said with a shrug. "And a lot more comfortable to sleep on than wet hay."

"You have a point." Another decision. They seemed to come easier for Jake these days — at least the small ones that had to do with animals. People, not so much.

For a while they stood shoulder to shoulder against the stall door, ready to jump inside to protect the little foal. Molly nuzzled it toward her rear legs. Unlike the firstborn, the little one was able to stand under Molly's belly and grab a teat on the first try.

The big one was too tall to reach under its mother's belly without hunkering down and bending its neck. Molly kept shoving it toward her back end, and eventually, it latched on.

"Yes!" Jake and Charlie threw their arms around each other. He pulled her off her feet and swung her around in the aisle. The geldings hung their heads over their stalls to see what all the excitement was about. The other horses began to whicker softly as they caught the scent of the foals.

Jake set Charlie on her feet, held her face in both hands and kissed her fiercely.

She kissed him back. After a few moments the kiss deepened, and she opened to him, tasting him as he tasted her. Their bodies fit as seamlessly as she'd known they would. Her last conscious thought before she gave in to the pleasure of holding and kissing him was, *Fire ants.*

He broke the kiss first, leaving her hungering for more.

"We can't leave them," he whispered into her hair. "I'll stay."

"We'll stay," she said. "Together."

The veterinarian, Kathy Waldran, drove in twenty minutes later. She found Jake sitting on one of the cushions in the aisle while Charlie, sound asleep, lay curled on the other with her head in his lap. He put his finger to his lips.

Kathy's footsteps were enough to wake Charlie, who looked up into Jake's face and realized with a start where she was. "Hey, Kathy," she said, scrambling to her feet. "I'm sorry to call you out at three in the morning, but . . ." She stood aside. "I thought you'd want to come."

"Oh, my goodness," Kathy whispered. "Well, hello, mama. You got your hooves full, haven't you?"

Mickey was the first to hear the commotion and come out to see what was happening. His whoops roused the others.

"Kittens and now twins?" Hank said. "You ladies live in fertile territory. Must be something in the water. I'd be careful if I was you."

Mary Anne slugged his shoulder. "Won't be yours, at any rate."

"Ow. I sure hope not."

Sarah brought over the breakfast trolley at seven, ecstatic about the twins.

Finally, over a cup of coffee and one of Vittorio's cinnamon rolls, Kathy pronounced both mama and babies healthy and happy. "Somebody needs to keep close watch on 'em," she said. "They'll have to stay in the foaling stall for a few days until we're sure they're both strong and suckling."

"I don't dare put them out with the other mares and foals," Charlie said. "Who knows how they'd react?"

"How fast can you build them a paddock?" Kathy asked. "You should have a few days anyway. Doesn't have to be big. The same size as the stallion's paddock outside his stall would work fine. Depending on how well they get along by themselves, you can eventually start them in the pasture with one of the quieter mares that already has a foal at foot. The barren mare is bound to want to steal one of those babies, so you'd best move her to the back pasture for a couple of weeks."

"I'll watch them," Mary Anne said.

Everyone looked at her in astonishment. She blushed.

"Mary Anne, that is a shire mare," Hank said. "She's bigger than Annie."

"I know, but the babies are my size. Charlie, what would I have to do?"

"Yell for help if you think there might be trouble brewing."

"What kind of trouble?" Now Mary Anne looked worried.

"If someone got kicked or sat on or driven away from the milk spigots."

"But I couldn't protect them from that."

"You can yell."

Charlie and Kathy walked out to the foaling stall with Mary Anne and left the others drinking coffee and eating cinnamon buns.

"She said that to get out of driving Terror again tomorrow," Mickey concluded.

Hank drained his coffee cup and set it on the counter with the other dirty dishes. "I'll bet she wishes now she'd kept her mouth shut."

"She's game, I'll give her that," Sean said. "Let's hope she can stick it out."

"Let's hope Molly doesn't have any problems that require fast action," Jake said.

Because the day was already hot, they set up fans to keep the babies cool. To her credit, Mary Anne took up residence on the cushions Jake had brought out, although Hank fussed because the sofa was now uncomfortable.

Charlie managed to put in a full slate of driving lessons with everyone except Mary Anne, who widened her eyes and said she couldn't possibly leave *her* babies.

"The big one's a filly, the little one's a stud colt," Jake said. "Took a while, but I finally got a good view."

"So they are fraternal twins," Charlie said. "That's really unusual. Thank you, Jake. I wouldn't have known about them until morning if you hadn't wakened me. By then it might have been too late."

Chapter Nineteen

An hour before dinner, Charlie barged into the colonel's study. "I have to talk to you."

"Sure, what's up?"

"Your granddaughter just told me — told me, didn't ask me — that she's going to a swim party next Saturday afternoon with a boy named Robbie Dillon." Charlie ran her hands through her hair. She stopped in front of the antique mahogany table he used for a desk and glared at him before she began to stride up and down the room.

"What did you tell her?" the colonel asked. He put the book he was reading facedown on the table and leaned back in his leather desk chair.

"That it sounded lovely, but I needed to know who she was going with, when and how she was going and getting home again, where the party was, whether there would be parents chaperoning, who had invited her and that I needed to meet him ahead of time."

"And?"

"Can you say 'ballistic?' She'd mentioned a swim party before, but apparently it's been moved up. Turns out the kid who invited her is that boy she met *once* when everyone went to Collierville for sushi. According to her, this Robbie person is gorgeous and smart and everything a Prince Charming should be, plus he's an upperclassman at Marchwood Academy. Dad, he drives his own truck." She raked her hands through her hair again and stalked up and down the colonel's study before dropping into the wing chair across from his desk. "He could be Jack the Ripper for all I know."

"Surely this didn't all come about after one meeting at the sushi house," the colonel said.

"Hardly." Charlie jammed her hands in the pockets of her jeans. "I knew I should be paying more attention to what she was doing on the net. Seems they've been emailing one another and talking on the phone while nobody's around to listen. No wonder she's been agitating for her own cell phone."

"So why hasn't he driven over here to meet you and me like any well-brought-up Southern gentleman caller?"

"According to Sarah, nobody does that anymore, like nobody dates. The whole teen scene works like a culture of germs. His excuse is that he's working as many hours as he can at the sushi house this summer to make enough money to pay his truck insurance."

"That sounds responsible of him. Where is this party?"

"At his house, apparently. She didn't know the address, can you believe? She says it's a big mansion in Collierville. He sent her a picture of it on his phone. He says it'll be about ten kids from Marchwood that she ought to meet before school starts."

"How late will it go on?"

"According to Sarah, afternoon after lunch for three or four hours, then he'll bring her home. He swears his parents will be there to supervise. No booze, no drugs."

"Why are you so worried?" The colonel leaned back and tented his fingers in front of his face. Charlie remembered that expression and called it his psychologist face. It had made her mad when she was Sarah's age and it made her mad now.

"She's only fourteen," Charlie said. "Whatever she thinks, she's lived a sheltered life on base where nothing much bad could happen to her, and if it did, there was always someone handy to rescue her. She's asking me to send her off with a boy I have never met to a house full of people I don't know to meet other people who may or may not even exist. I don't care what she tells me about what is or is not done these days."

"What did you tell her?"

"That until I meet Robbie and his parents to check them out, she's not going anywhere with him. Period."

"She'll pitch a fit."

"She already has. I am ruining her life. She'll never be able to show her face at Marchwood. No boy will look at her after this. I tried to tell her I'm careful because I love her. . . ."

"Didn't work, did it? In other words, same ol', same ol'. You said the same things."

"And you never backed down for a minute."

"Was I right?"

That brought Charlie up short. "Not always. After Mom died, you came down on me like a ton of bricks, when you bothered to notice me at all. Which was seldom."

"Charlie, we were living in the District of Columbia. It's dangerous. I had just lost my wife. . . ."

She leaned toward him and put her elbows on his desktop. "And I had just lost my mother! That never seemed to occur to you. I never knew what to expect from you. You'd wander around for days barely acknowledging my existence, then you'd wake up to the fact that you had a daughter and order me around like one of your clerks."

"I'm sorry, I —"

"Except you never order your clerks around, do you?"

"So I can assume she won't be at my dinner table tonight?"

"I doubt it. She's sulking."

"And emailing that Dillon boy about what a monster her mother is." He chuckled. "Sound familiar?"

"I didn't have a computer." Charlie reached out to her father. "How do I know I'm doing the right thing? I can't bear that she's miserable, but I can't let her take chances, either. She's all I have left."

He raised his eyebrows. "Thank you so much."

"Oh, Daddy, You know I'm not excluding you, but I didn't give birth to you. You know how it is."

"Unfortunately, I do."

"My gut tells me I'm right, but am I?"

"Probably. But it'll cost you."

"Doesn't it always?" She strode out the French doors and headed for the stable to check on the twins. Why couldn't human children be as uncomplicated?

After she saw that both babies and Molly were curled up together, she knocked on Mickey's door. She heard the clomp of his leg braces and, when he opened the door, found him standing in front of her.

"Caught me," he said. "Come on in. I'm doing my laps around the bedroom."

"Why not do them up and down the barn aisle?"

"I don't want Hank to see me fall on my nose."

"Then go walk around in the equipment shed. As long as you don't fall in the grease pit, you ought to be okay. The floor's smooth concrete and you can grab ahold of the tractors if you wobble. Jake and Sean can check on you if you do it while Hank's off driving with me. I can keep him far away from the barn."

"Yeah, maybe," Mickey said. " 'Scuse me. Standing still wears me out worse than walking." He sank into his wheelchair. "You threw me when you asked today what I wanted to do," he said. "I know I can't support myself just driving a carriage for funerals and weddings."

"So what else?"

"One thing the army did was train me.

I'm a programmer. I don't have to ride a desk in an office with a hundred other geeks to do that. There are plenty of jobs out there for really good geeks. And I am." He shrugged. "I can still drive a horse-drawn hearse to supplement my income."

Charlie sat on the bed. "You've done some thinking about this."

"Heck, yeah. I'm twenty-one years old and a gimp. What else do I have to do but worry about the rest of my life?"

"Not worry."

He shrugged. "So what's up?"

Charlie gave him a look of wide-eyed innocence. "Why should anything be up?"

"Come on, Charlie, you haven't been in this room since you showed it to me the day we got here. Am I on report for something?"

"Just the opposite. I want you to do some data mining as a personal favor."

"Spying? Who? Sean's witch of a daughter?"

"Not this time. Oh, shoot, Sean, I want you to spy on Sarah."

"Huh?"

"We're the kind of family that wouldn't dream of opening somebody else's mail. I've always trusted Sarah, maybe too much. She never had to hide her diary or her Facebook page."

"But . . . ?"

"I'm not proud of it, but I need your skills. Here's my problem." She outlined the situation with Sarah and Robbie Dillon. "He is probably a perfectly nice boy. He's probably telling the truth about his house, his parents, his friends. The point is, I don't know. And Sarah is so angry at what she considers my lack of trust in her judgment that she won't speak to me, and certainly won't ask him for clarification. I've told her she can't go to the party, but maybe if I were certain the whole thing was on the up-and-up, I might relent enough to drive her there myself, drop her off and pick her up a couple of hours later."

"She'd be mortified."

"Robbie Dillon's parents would understand, if they're the sort of people she assures me they are. But if they were the sort of people she says, wouldn't they already have called me to introduce themselves? Wouldn't this Dillon boy have come by to meet us even if he *is* working? I don't think I'm wrong to worry about sending my daughter off with a total stranger. Can you help?"

"Piece of cake," Mickey said. "Can I do it

tonight?"

"Sooner the better. Tonight would be great." She patted his shoulder. "Thank you, Mickey."

"And I will walk around the shed tomorrow when Hank's having his lesson."

The following morning as soon as breakfast was cleared away, Mickey nodded toward his room. Charlie followed him. Once they were inside, he shut the door behind him.

"Charlie, we got a problem."

Charlie caught her breath. "What kind and how big?"

"Pretty bad and pretty big," he said.

"Lay it out."

"I should have laid that Dillon creep out the night Sarah met him," Mickey said grimly. "Better yet, I should have let Sean lay him out. That fake hand of his is a killer."

"Mickey, tell me right now."

"Okay, but you better sit down. Use the bed. His name really is Robert Dillon, and he did go to Marchwood."

She frowned. "Did?"

"He got kicked out a year ago."

"What for?"

"I haven't broken the school firewall yet to get all his records, but he was questioned by the police about an assault on one of the students. A freshman girl."

"Like Sarah. Oh, Mickey. Was he arrested?" Instead of sitting, she began to pace the same circuit that Mickey took with his exercise. "Juvenile records are sealed, aren't they?"

"No charges were filed because the girl clammed up. Dillon's father probably paid her tuition to Harvard for four years. The Collierville paper had a squib about the incident and mentioned Robbie was being questioned. But he wasn't a juvenile. He was over eighteen then."

"He's *nineteen*?"

"Living at home over his parents' three-car garage. I found a picture of the house from some garden club tour. It's a McMansion all right. He got his GED this spring. Since he was kicked out of Marchwood, he's been picked up for DUI twice. Both times he got off with a slap on the wrist, some community service and a fine, which his father, an orthopedic surgeon, happily paid."

"Why would he be working at the sushi place?"

"My guess is his family's trying to make him shape up."

"This is awful." Now she did sit on the bed and drop her forehead into her hand.

"It gets worse. I did some digging in old social network stuff. I found a posting where he says he goes for young virgins with long hair."

Charlie closed her eyes. "Has Sarah gone crazy?"

"Take a look at his yearbook picture," Mickey said. He turned his laptop around so she could see.

Charlie blinked at the photo. "He *is* gorgeous."

"He's a rich thug," Mickey said. "I grew up with them. It's why I joined the army instead of going to college. Boy, was I stupid."

"How can I tell Sarah? She'll never forgive me for snooping. But I can't *not* tell her."

"She won't believe you."

"She'll believe *you,* Mickey, won't she?"

"Yeah. If I show her what I found. I can keep you out of it. I can tell her I was the one concerned about the jerk. I was feeling like her big brother, and checking stuff out is what I do. I'll catch her when she comes over to play with the kittens."

"Thank you, Mickey." She kissed the top of his head.

They left Mickey's room together and ran into Sarah coming downstairs from visiting the kittens. Apparently they were worth getting up early for. She said hello to Mickey but ignored her mother. Charlie nodded to Mickey and went to start her morning's lessons.

She expected an explosion from Sarah after she talked to Mickey. An hour later she got it. Mary Anne had just climbed out of the driver's seat while Charlie headed Terror. Sarah erupted out of the common room, pulled her mother into the tack room and slammed the door behind her. The rage in her face stunned Charlie. Steve's furious eyes, Steve's clenched teeth and fists.

"How could you?" Sarah snarled. "Mickey wouldn't do that on his own. You told him to. I know you did!"

"Sarah, calm down, so we can discuss this sensibly." She took a step toward her daughter with her arms open, offering a hug, but dropped them when Sarah backed away. She'd always had a temper, but Charlie had never seen her this angry.

"I am *dead* at that school! They'll all laugh at me! You always ruin *everything.* I hate you. Why didn't you die instead of Daddy?" She threw the door open wide, stormed out and slammed it behind her.

Charlie folded as though she'd been punched in the stomach, but she couldn't just let her go. "Sarah, come back in here."

"Make me!"

Charlie charged into the house and up the stairs after her. She knew Sarah's door would be locked, so she banged on it. "We're going to talk about this, whether you like it or not." Did all parents speak in clichés? She heard her father's words in her mother's voice. "This boy lied to you, Sarah. He's been convicted of driving drunk. He was expelled because he assaulted a girl. . . ."

"He never assaulted anybody. That girl is the liar. She got him expelled because he wouldn't date her."

"You knew about that?" Charlie leaned back against the wall beside Sarah's door. "Did you know he was nineteen?"

Pause. "Of course." Charlie felt certain Sarah had not known, but she'd never admit that now. "I knew you'd never let me go with him if you knew he was that old."

"You got that right, Sarah, please open the door." Charlie tried to sound reasonable, even cajoling. She was discovering that the Sarah she thought she knew no longer existed.

Oh, Steve, why did you have to go and leave me with this mess? I don't know what the heck I'm doing.

All at once she imagined Jake's face. She

wanted to leave Sarah locked in her room — preferably for the next twenty years — run to Jake, throw herself into his arms and ask him to take over. She needed his strength, his wisdom, his gentleness.

His unwillingness to make decisions annoyed her, but here she was longing to turn her problems over to someone else. Sarah was her responsibility, not Jake's. Not the colonel's, either, come to that.

"I am never opening this door again and I am never speaking to you, or Mickey, either."

"I'll tell Vittorio you won't be at lunch, then." Charlie thought her voice sounded pretty good considering she was a nanosecond away from morphing into Hulk-Mom and tearing the door off its hinges. "Sarah, I love you. Please believe me, I'm doing this to protect you."

"Yeah. From life." The heavy thud of a book hitting the door made Charlie jump.

Her adrenaline exploded. "That's enough of that, young lady. And you can forget about the swimming party — if it exists."

Holding the morning newspaper open to the crossword puzzle, her father waited for her at the foot of the stairs. Charlie was in no mood. If he did an "I told you so" or "She's just like you". . . .

She pushed past her father and out the door, across the short distance into the common room. "Where's Jake?"

The others were clearing up after breakfast. "What's wrong?" Mary Anne asked.

"Don't ask!" Charlie ran into the barn and down to Molly's stall. Of course that's where Jake would be, so Mary Anne could take a break. He'd be in with Flopsy and Mopsy, Mary Anne's names for the babies.

His back was propped against the stall while Molly nibbled hay. Both foals nursed happily from opposite sides of their mother's belly. Flopsy, the big filly, had learned to duck under to nurse, while Mopsy, the little stud colt, could still reach straight up.

"They don't seem to mind sharing," Jake said with a broad grin. His eyes widened. "Charlie?" He was out the door in an instant and caught her hand.

Now the tears came. Great, just great.

"Tell me."

She did. The entire stupid, ridiculous, dangerous story. "She hates me, and I don't blame her," Charlie said. Sarah was not Jake's problem, but at the moment, she'd be willing to take parenting advice from Molly who seemed to be a whole lot better at it than Sarah.

Jake dropped his arms and turned away.

"You're asking the wrong person. I give bad advice."

Maybe she was still angry from her confrontation with Sarah. Whatever it was, she exploded. "Jake, stop it! Get over it! People need you. I need you."

His face went blank.

She took a step toward him. She knew she sounded whiny, but she couldn't seem to help it. "I mean it. Somebody has to tell me what to do."

"Not me." He brushed past her and out the barn door. "I killed eleven men. I don't do advice."

Her adrenaline flared up again without ever having settled. She ran after him and grabbed his arm. "Not another single person is running from me today, Jake Thompson. You come back here right now." She hauled him around to face her. "How did you kill them? Did you stand them up against a wall and machine-gun them?"

"Of course not."

"Daddy told me the bare bones, but I want to hear it from you."

"Not now."

"Yes, now." She felt certain he'd pull away from her again.

Instead, he sat on Mickey's bench beside the door and dropped his head in his hands.

She sank onto the bench beside him and said softly, "It's okay. I'm scared and I took it out on you. You don't owe me an explanation."

After a long moment, he lifted his head but didn't turn to look at her. When at last he spoke, he sounded almost casual. "You never act on a single source of intelligence. It's like the old newspaper saying, 'Your mother says she loves you, but check it out.' Theoretically, my twelve-man team served in a strictly humanitarian capacity, but we also kept our eyes and ears open for valuable intel. We'd had a pretty good rep in the villages for bringing medicine, water trucks, food. We weren't dumb enough to think they liked us, but they tolerated us.

"Then a new colonel was assigned who didn't think we were getting enough intel fast enough. He'd met some headman for the first time at a conference and promised him medical supplies. We hadn't gotten to know the power structure that ran the village, but Colonel — never mind his name — gave me a direct order to take my team out for what he called a 'shake and howdy' visit. I didn't like it. He'd received a direct request from the elders for medicine. That never happened. Usually word was passed along until eventually it got to us. Everybody in the team thought it sounded hinky. I tried to tell the colonel that, but he refused to listen.

"It was a direct order. We had to go, but I told the guys we'd be on our guard, go in fast and be ready to leave faster."

"And it wasn't all right?"

"We took two trucks — five men in each plus a driver up front. Went okay at the start. We turned the trucks around in the square so we were already headed out. Made it easier to unload, too. We stacked the supplies in the headman's house. He seemed glad to see us, offered us tea, which we declined. Usually in the villages a few kids would run out to cadge chocolate while their mothers watched. This village was nearly deserted except for some old men drinking tea on the far side of the square. They looked to be unarmed.

"I told my men to load up nice and easy while I kept chatting with the headman. Some were climbing into the truck in the middle of the square, and the others were heading for the first in line that was headed out.

"That's when the square was hit by a handheld from one of the rooftops and blew up. It's not like a television explosion. Hot metal, burning canvas, parts of tires fly off.

If I hadn't been across the square, I'd have been blown up or cut to pieces. That's where shrapnel from the truck messed up my knee, not that I realized at the time I'd been hit. Somehow I made it to the driver's door of the other truck. I had to get it out of there before they blew it up, too.

"The driver was dead, and my sergeant was lying on the other seat with blood . . ."

She winced.

"You don't want to hear this next part," he said.

She braced herself. "I want all of it."

He hesitated before saying, "Fine. I yanked the dead man from behind the wheel, hauled my sergeant up and shoved him far enough out of my way so I could get behind the wheel. I prayed some of the guys made it into the back of the truck alive, so I floored it. A second handheld barely missed and blew up in the square. I planned to put my sergeant down out of range and go back to get the others."

"You must have known they were dead."

He hit his knee with his fist. "You never *know,* Charlie, until you see the bodies. You pray. Maybe they'd taken cover and returned fire. If my sergeant and I were still alive, somebody back there might be alive, too.

"Rule number one, never leave a man behind, alive or dead. A hundred yards down the hill we ran into a half-dozen of our trucks. The colonel had received new intel that we were driving into a trap and sent out a rescue mission. I tried to go back to the village with them, but I passed out. My sergeant died on the plane to Ramstein. According to the report afterward, the others were dead before I drove away."

There was silence.

"None of that was your fault," she began.

"If I hadn't led them in, if we'd pulled out earlier . . ."

"You couldn't disobey a direct order."

"I should have gone over his head."

"On a gut feeling? They'd have replaced you and sent out the mission just the same, wouldn't they?"

"Instead, I dropped them all straight into it."

"What happened to that village?"

"It no longer exists."

"Oh, Jake, those poor people!"

"They swore they got noncombatants out before they leveled the place, but nobody knows for sure. If not, that's on me, too."

"No, it is not. You tried to save your men."

"Tried and failed. I left them the way I left my family. I make decisions and people suffer. Everybody's safer if I don't make any."

"You've been making decisions since you've been here."

"Yeah, it's harder than I thought *not* to."

"If you can make little ones, you can make the big ones, too."

"How do *you* keep it together, Charlie?" he asked.

She laughed. "I don't."

"Yes, you do. What drives you?"

"That's easy. I want Sarah to be happy and I want this farm. Never, ever to move again. You must want something, Jake. What would you choose to fight for? What do you desire so fervently that you'll do anything to get it?"

"To go back to the beginning and make things right."

She shrugged. "Not gonna happen for any of us. The time machine's thrown a cog. You guard your pain as carefully as you'd guard one of the kittens. You poke at it like an aching tooth. If you start to walk away from it, you drag yourself back."

"I don't deserve to be free of it."

"When will you have paid enough? Today? Tomorrow? The last breath you take?"

"There is no enough. I'm trying to limit future damage."

"Everybody makes decisions that harm themselves and other people. I can't begin to list the things I've done that come under the heading of stupid and hurtful. You could say I was such a lousy wife that I sent my husband off to be killed and deprived Sarah of her father."

"You didn't kill him. You weren't there. I was. I killed eleven good young men with their whole lives ahead of them. What kept me alive when they died?"

"You obeyed an order and walked into an ambush and everybody died but you. You didn't run from your men, you tried to save them. If you'd refused to go on that mission, you'd have been court-martialed and someone else would have led them into that ambush."

"Then it would have been on his head. As it is, it's on mine."

She threw up her hands. "Have it your way. You killed them. You deprived those eleven good young men who trusted you of their lives. You made their wives widows, their children orphans, their relatives and their friends grieve for them. Maybe one of them would have found a cure for cancer if he'd lived. Does that make you responsible for everyone who dies of cancer?"

"Of course not. You don't understand the

nature of command."

"The heck I don't. I've been around it all my life. I've eaten at my father's table with more generals than you'll meet in a lifetime."

"They died. I lived. Why?"

"If it were anyone else in the same situation, you'd say it was the luck of the draw. Your decision to go into that village didn't cause their deaths any more than I killed Steve. Fulfilling your dreams, being happy, living life, loving someone, having a family, working at something you want to do — that's the way to pay for their deaths and your life. To make their lives count, yours has to count, doesn't it? You can't do that by opting out of life, not taking a stand."

She could tell by his face that he was angry. He'd never forgive her, but she had to try. "Everybody here likes you and looks up to you. Why would we waste time on a man who is so dumb he'd walk away from that?"

She turned on her heel and left him gaping.

She could barely breathe. She had no right to tear into him that way. What was that old story about the mule that wouldn't move? The farmer hit him between the eyes with a two-by-four. When the donkey began to trot, he told his friend, "First, you have to get his attention." At least she had Jake's attention. Being sweet and supportive would not have worked. For her it never did

"Charlie, wait!" Jake caught up with her, took her arm and swung her around.

Her face was blazing and her hair was soaked with sweat. She seldom got angry, but when she did, she went all the way to fury. The only people who could make her angry were the people she loved. Jake made her furious, and guess what that meant.

He wrapped her in his arms.

"Let go of me!" She put her hands flat against his chest and shoved. He held her fast until she stopped struggling.

"Not now, not ever. Calm down." He propped his chin on her head. "Your father told me the same thing. I refused to hear him."

She shoved him so hard he released her and stumbled backward. "You better hear *me.*"

He took both her hands and held her at arm's length. "I asked you once who could *not* love you? I came out to this farm and this course as my last chance to find something to care about. When I got off that bus, I found you standing in the sun blazing like a homing beacon."

He pulled her into his arms, and this time she didn't fight him. "Dearest Charlie," he whispered into her hair. "I can't change overnight. I keep sliding back into guilt, but with your help maybe I can keep going forward."

She lifted her face, and he kissed her. When she opened her eyes, he was smiling down at her with that smile she'd longed to see since she found him in Picard's stall.

"You said yourself, I'm making decisions I couldn't have made when I arrived here. I'm not copping out, but I can't help you with Sarah. I simply don't know how."

CHAPTER TWENTY

Sean knocked on Jake's door at midnight. "Jake, open up."

"Don't let the cats out," Jake said sleepily as he pulled Sean inside and shut the door after him. Mama Cat and all five kittens were curled on the foot of Jake's bed. Mama Cat didn't move.

"We got a problem. I just saw Sarah climbing out her bedroom window."

"What?" Jake grabbed for his shoes. He was still wearing his jeans.

"I think she's running away."

"Get the others," Jake said. "We have to stop her."

"Meet you by the stallion stall," Sean said.

When they convened, Mickey said, "She's meeting that thug. Bound to be."

"She's not that dumb, is she?" Hank asked.

"Of course she is," Mary Anne said. "She has to prove we're all wrong and he's Lancelot and St. Francis rolled up in one."

Mickey watched the yard from the stable door. "I don't see any movement. You sure you saw her, Sean?"

"Yeah. I been thinking for a while that dormer over the front porch would make for an easy shinny down. Didn't think Sarah would try it. She could fall and get herself killed."

"Maybe she's stuck up there where we can't see her," Hank said.

"I watched her climb down the drainpipe," Sean said. "Then I lost her in the trees."

"Maybe she's already out of sight down the road," Mickey suggested.

"Not time enough," Sean said.

"More likely she's waiting for that boy to pick her up," Mary Anne said.

Jake frowned. "He's no boy. He's betting that if anything happens to her, she'll never tell on him."

"She'd die before she'd let Charlie and the colonel know they were right," Mickey said.

Mary Anne pointed. "Hey, look, isn't that headlights?"

"Sean," Jake snapped, "start the truck, but don't turn on the lights."

"Where's Hank?" Mary Anne asked. They looked around, but he wasn't there.

"Let me know if you can't stop them," Mickey said and held up his cell phone. "She's young enough for an Amber Alert. I'll call the cops and have his truck stopped."

"It's turning in," Mary Anne whispered. "He's cut his headlights." A moment later the passenger-side door opened. The overhead light came on briefly. A dark figure slipped into the seat, the door slammed, but the truck didn't start.

"Maybe they're just talking," Mary Anne said. The other truck roared to life. "Maybe not," Jake said. "We have to cut them off."

He jumped behind the wheel and put the farm truck into gear while Mary Anne and Sean piled in the back and opened the window into the cab. "Where is Hank?" Mary Anne said. "Did he bail?"

"I don't think so," Sean said. "There he is."

Annie galloped across the mare's pasture toward the road. The moonlight glinted off her red coat and Hank's dark hair.

"He's bareback!" Sean shouted. "He'll never stay on!"

"He's going to beat them to the road if he does," Mary Anne said. "Come on, Hank!"

Dillon's truck — or the truck they assumed was Dillon's — headed for the end of the driveway.

"They're going to make it out to the road." Sean sounded frantic. "Jake, faster!"

"I'm going as fast as I dare without lights."

"Then turn them on," Mary Anne said. "They must know by now we're back here."

Dillon's brake lights came on. The truck skidded sideways and stopped with its left front wheel hanging out over the culvert under the farm's driveway. He tried to back up but the wheels spun, then caught. The truck rolled backward.

Jake turned on his headlights as he stopped inches short of Dillon's rear bumper.

Past Dillon's truck, Jake's headlights showed Annie standing foursquare across the gateway, effectively blocking the exit onto the road. Hank stood beside her with his hands on the reins, a big grin on his face.

A second later, the passenger-side door opened. Sarah stumbled out and bolted toward Jake and the others.

"Hey, girl, get back here!" came a voice from inside the truck.

Jake and Sean were in a dead heat for the driver's door when the passenger door snicked shut.

Mary Anne intercepted Sarah, who was sobbing.

"Out!" Jake pulled on the door handle.

Dillon tried to inch the truck forward as though he planned to drive over the mare. He must have realized that in a collision between his baby truck and a two-thousand-pound mare, the truck could be totaled.

"Let him go!" Sarah cried. "Please, please, just make him leave!"

"I don't think so," Sean said as he cracked his knuckles.

"Jake, please, let him go."

Jake leaned over and tapped on the driver's-side glass. "I won't hit you, young man," he said, "if you roll down your window."

Nothing happened.

"If you don't, I'm going to loose my friend here on you and your truck. He's pretty good at mixed martial arts, and I suspect he'd like to remove a few useful parts of your anatomy. Now!"

Slowly Robbie's window slid down. Sarah gasped.

Jake leaned on the door so that his face was even with Dillon's. "If you had managed to leave this property tonight with Sarah in your car, not even your father's money and a team of lawyers would have protected you. If anything bad had happened to Sarah, however, none of that would have mattered to you, because you would have been dead. Now, you are probably too stupid and too mean to take this to heart the next time you decide to go quail hunting, but I assure you that this particular group will be tracking your every move."

"You threatening me, old man?" Dillon said. He'd recovered a trace of truculence.

"Absolutely. Even the lady over there knows ways to kill you so that nobody ever looks for your body, much less finds it. Say 'yessir.' "

A minute, then a sulky "yessir" came from the truck.

"Good. Now, if you'll wait a moment until we remove our equine gate, you can be on your way."

Jake popped the side of the truck with the flat of his hand, and stepped away. Annie obligingly moved out of the driveway. The truck gunned its way through, fishtailed as it made the turn onto the roadway and flashed off toward Collierville.

"Nice ride," Jake said to Hank.

"Give me a leg up," Hank said. "I'll ride Annie back to the pasture. I guess I can ride so long as I don't use stirrups."

Sean climbed into the bed of the truck while Mary Anne bundled Sarah into the bench seat beside Jake.

"Please don't take me home," Sarah sniffled. "Take me back with you."

Jake patted her knee and drove the truck down the driveway without its lights.

Once they were in the common room, Mary Anne made a mug of cocoa for Sarah, who hunched small on the sofa, hiccuping and shaking. Mickey brought her his comforter and wrapped it around her shoulders.

"Want to talk about it?" Sean asked.

She shook her head. "How did you know?"

"Saw you climbing out of your room," Sean said. "You coulda broken your fool neck, girl."

"But . . ."

"Figured you were meetin' that boy," he continued. "Both my girls have pulled stunts like that."

"What were you thinking?" Mickey snapped. "I showed you everything . . ."

"But I had to give him a chance to explain, don't you see? He wasn't anything like what you told me. It had to be a mistake. . . ."

"Because, if it was true, then you'd made a fool of yourself in front of the adults," Mary Anne said gently. "Been there, done that. Got the T-shirt. Mine says Big Fool right across the chest." She looked down. "What little there is of my chest."

Sarah gave a tiny smile.

"I called him and said I had to see him. He said he'd leave work and drive right out. I mean, that proved he cared about me, you know?" She began to sniffle again. "He said we were just going to sit and talk, not *go* anywhere." Her voice rose.

"Then when I started asking him about the stuff Mickey found out, he got mad." She hunkered down in the comforter. "He called me a trailer-trash army brat who ought to be grateful he even looked at me." She dropped her head. "He said some other stuff, too, about what he was going to teach me. Do I *have* to tell you?"

"I'm going to kill him," Sean said matter-of-factly.

"No, please don't! I just want to forget it."

"He deserves an old-fashioned horsewhipping," Hank said. "And we've got plenty of horsewhips."

"Please, please, just let me sneak back into the house. I'm so grateful to you all, but please don't tell my mother. She'd never trust me again."

"Not for a while, at any rate," Mary Anne said.

"He should be punished," Jake said. "But since he never left the property, I don't think there's anything he can be charged

313

with. Did he touch you, Sarah?"

"No, Jake. Not even when he yelled at me."

"He was planning to," Mickey said.

Sarah turned wide eyes on him. "Oh."

"He's going to try it again with someone else," Sean said. "The next girl may not be as lucky."

"The colonel can alert the sheriff he's got a possible predator in his jurisdiction," Jake said. "I don't see there's much else we can do officially."

"Don't tell Granddaddy, either!" Sarah wailed. "He's worse than my mother."

"Sarah, we have to," Jake said.

"Please, Jake. Please, no. I'll never do anything like that again. I've learned my lesson, I promise. Nothing happened except I got scared."

"Sarah . . ."

"Okay, how's this? Let *me* tell her. It's too late tonight. Tomorrow morning I'll apologize for shouting at her, and right after she's calmed down, I'll tell her what happened tonight in my own way."

Putting as good a face on it as possible, Jake thought. "Everyone?" Nods of agreement.

"I'll bet we've all done worse, even Mary Anne," Hank said.

314

"Jake?" Mickey asked. "Sounds fair to me."

"All right, Sarah, if you promise to tell her yourself first thing tomorrow morning."

"I promise. Thank you, thank you, Jake, everyone." She grabbed Mickey in his wheelchair and hugged him, then hugged each of them in turn, finishing with Jake. She clung to him. After a moment's hesitation, he hugged her back.

"How on earth am I going to get back in the house without getting caught?"

"How did you plan to do it on your own?" Hank asked.

"I figured I could climb up the drainpipe again, but I don't think I'm strong enough really. I planned to sneak in the back door, but between the colonel and my mother. If I couldn't climb in, I was going to sleep on the couch in the common room and tell everyone I'd come out to see Molly and Mama and all the babies."

"That might have worked," Jake said. "If Sean hadn't noticed you."

"If *Sean* hadn't noticed you," Sean said, "getting back in the house could have been the least of your worries."

In the end, Hank and Sean lifted her to the porch roof. From there she climbed back into her window, waved at them all and disappeared.

"It's after midnight," Sean said when they had reconvened in the common room.

"We did good tonight, didn't we?" Mary Anne said. "If I can handle *this,* I can certainly handle a teensy Welsh pony by myself."

CHAPTER TWENTY-ONE

Mary Anne was scheduled to drive Terror after lunch the next day. Charlie was surprised that she actually seemed to be looking forward to her lesson.

Once they were settled and walking figure eights in the arena, Mary Anne said almost tentatively, "Don't be too hard on Sarah. Not like we haven't all done that stuff or worse. I mean, who doesn't fall for one real loser, right?"

"You can say that again," Charlie said. "Unfortunately, I married mine."

"Yeah, me, too. Charlie, can Terror and I try a slow trot? Will you take over if he tries to run away?"

"Yes! What made you change your mind?"

Mary Anne shrugged. "The twins. Molly is so gentle with both of them, and I think the foals really like each other. Just like me and my brother."

"I didn't know you had a brother."

"Yep. He's stationed in Germany at the moment, so he's not under fire. My mom and dad are both gone, and he raised me. I always liked gears and axles better than I did books, so the army seemed a good fit. I have to find a way to make a living, and I don't think I'll be driving carriages. Husband and kids don't seem to be in my future."

"I don't see why not. You're a lovely woman."

Mary Anne snorted. "Yeah, right."

"Any man worth being married to won't care about the scars, and the colonel says after your surgeries they won't be noticeable."

"I'll believe that when I see it. Terror, trot on. OMEGA!"

When they finished washing Terror down, Charlie said, "You may not be able to make a good living driving carriages, but you can make an excellent one working on carriages and farm equipment. A good tractor mechanic can make a fortune."

"Nobody'll hire me."

"Anyone with good sense would."

"Thanks, Charlie."

"Hey, ladies, it's beer time," Mickey called from the common room.

He handed Charlie her favorite diet soda

as she sank onto the sofa, cushions back in place.

"Jake's out by the foaling stall watching the twins," Mickey said. "The rest of us quit early. After last night I could sleep for a week."

"You didn't stay up with Mary Anne last night to babysit them, did you?" Charlie asked.

"We were otherwise occupied, weren't we, guys?"

Mary Anne glared at him.

"What? Sarah's already told her, right? I mean it's after lunch. What'd you do to her, Charlie? Ground her till school starts?"

"Put bars on her window, more like," Hank said. "Good thing she's skinny. She could have brought down that trellis and broken her neck."

Charlie had no clue what they were talking about. Hank and Mickey were smirking into their beer bottles. Sean, on the other hand, was watching her as if she were going to explode any second. "Okay, guys, what am I missing?"

Hank and Mickey sobered instantly and refused to meet her eyes.

"She didn't tell you, did she?" Sean said quietly.

"Sean," Mary Anne said, and grabbed his

arm. "Don't."

"She broke her promise, Mary Anne. It's three in the afternoon. That's a long time after breakfast. Charlie has a right to know."

Charlie felt her heart lurch into her throat. "Know what? Sean, what has Sarah done? I saw her at breakfast, and she seemed a little quiet . . ."

"You brought it up, Sean," Hank said. "You tell her."

"I think you better sit down, Charlie," Sean urged her.

Two minutes into Sean's speech, Charlie surged to her feet and began to pace. Mary Anne cringed behind the kitchen counter. Hank tried to leave, but Charlie stopped him. Mickey didn't even attempt escape.

Charlie went from being worried to horrified to enraged to terrified in the short space of five minutes.

After Sean finished, she glared at them.

"What possible excuse could you have for keeping this from me? All of you?"

"Jake said . . ." Sean started.

"Jake said?" And all her emotions fell away except for rage. How dare he?

She'd trusted him. Just like everyone else. He'd finally made a decision, and it was a doozy.

"We'd all jump off a cliff if Jake said to,

wouldn't we?" she snarled. "That's his thing. What he's good at. What he *does*! What gives any of you the right to decide to keep something this — momentous — from me. I'm Sarah's mother! This isn't some little prank! She could have been kidnapped, raped. Robbie Dillon could have killed her!"

"But we stopped him. He didn't even get to the road," Mary Anne said, her hands held up in front of her. "And she swore she was going to tell you herself. She promised Jake . . ."

"She promised Jake? And he made the unilateral decision to let her do it on her own time?"

"We all agreed. She was supposed to tell you first thing this morning."

Charlie pointedly looked at her watch. "Gee, it's nearly three. Little late, isn't it? Actually, we've had lunch, haven't we? I guess she's not going to keep her promise. Big surprise. You think any kid would willingly tell her mother something like this? Would any of you when you were fourteen? When were you — or should I say Jake — going to decide she'd broken her promise and tell me yourselves?" She glared at each face in turn. They all looked down. "Never? If Mickey and Hank hadn't let the cat out of the bag?"

She ran her hand across her forehead. "Oh, heck, I shouldn't blame *you*. You saved her, while her mother and her grandfather slept the night away in blissful ignorance. After that stunt she pulled last night, how on earth could you trust her to tell me? She knew I'd freak."

"Jake said . . ."

"She's not his kid. Not yours, either."

"Charlie, that's not fair."

"I have reached my limit of being fair and understanding. I want to rant and rave and tear my hair out. I want to love somebody who loves me back." Where had that come from? They all stared at her as though she'd begun to speak in tongues. Which, in a way, she had.

All right, she loved Jake. So much for keeping a professional distance.

And she was going to kill him.

"You're right," came a voice from the doorway. "I warned you I didn't know anything about teenage girls. It's not their fault, it's mine. I took her at her word. Obviously, I was wrong again. I hurt you, Charlie. I won't chance doing it a second time."

He turned on his heel and was gone. Charlie stared after him. Would she never learn? It wasn't his fault. It was Sarah's. And she'd taken it out on these people she cared about and on Jake, whom she loved.

They all heard the farm truck start up and drive away.

"Jake!" Charlie called and ran after him. "I'm sorry!"

The others followed him in time to see Jake slide around the corner and head toward Collierville.

"We have to stop him," Mary Anne said.

"We can't," Sean said. "Too big a head start."

"Will he come back?" Mickey asked. "He was pretty upset."

"Of course he will, once he's over being angry," Charlie said. "He has to come back." *Because I can't bear it if he doesn't.* She tried to believe her words, but they came out phony because *she* didn't believe them. Worse, he might have lost himself all over again. That was her fault.

"He didn't leave because you got angry, Charlie," Sean said to her. "He took a chance, and in his mind, he's made a mess of things again."

"I didn't mean to blame . . ."

"Doesn't matter. He thinks you did." Sean walked out. A moment later they heard Sean's door slam.

"Oh, who'll look after the kittens?" Mary Anne said, and ran up the stairs.

Hank and Mickey left Charlie standing there. She sank onto the sofa and buried her face in her hands.

"Mom?"

She looked up as Sarah came haltingly through the door. "I listened. Jake trusted me to tell you this morning. I promised, but I was scared to. Please don't blame Jake."

She already had. "You shouldn't have put any of them in that position, Sarah. And you should have kept your promise." She was too wrung out to be angry.

"I knew you'd go ballistic when you found out, so I kept putting it off. I've been hanging around outside trying to get up my nerve. You must hate me."

"Oh, Sarah, I love you, baby. I never learned how to show you enough or tell you enough, but I do." She took both Sarah's hands. "Always believe that, even if I don't say the words."

"Where's Jake? I have to apologize to him."

"He took one of the trucks and left."

Sarah pulled her hands away and her eyes grew wide and frightened. "He's coming back, right?"

"I don't know." Charlie's eyes were overflowing, but she didn't wipe the tears away. "I drove him away, Sarah."

"But you love him. *We* love him!" Sarah began to cry little-girl tears that screwed up her face until she looked five years old. "He can't leave us the way Daddy did."

Charlie wrapped her arms around Sarah. "I'm sorry, Sarah. Maybe I did drive your father away. I drive away all the people I care about."

"No, Mom, that's not how it was with Daddy. But this is Jake. He's not like that. We have to go after him, make him come back."

"If he does come back, it has to be his decision, his choice. Maybe if he loves us enough he will. All we can do is wait and pray."

CHAPTER TWENTY-TWO

He'd done it again, only this time he would not run from his responsibility.

Charlie had asked him what he wanted bad enough to fight for.

He hadn't had the nerve to tell her the truth. He wanted Charlie. But only if and when he could offer her a whole man.

Only one way to do that. He couldn't go back in time and change anything, but he could go back to the beginning and try to fix what he'd screwed up.

Charlie was right. He needed to give meaning to his life if he were to pay for his survival.

If he couldn't do that, he would disappear so deep not even the colonel would find him.

He slammed on his brakes and slid into a gas station parking lot so suddenly that the truck behind honked and made a rude gesture.

He sat behind the wheel of the old farm truck — the stolen truck — and took deep breaths until he settled down. No more running. Even if this pilgrimage turned out badly, he would never go back to the streets. Time to fight himself to become the man she needed. Only then could he tell her how much he loved her.

The colonel knocked on Charlie's door and came in without waiting for an answer. She lay facedown on her bed, arms wrapped around her pillow.

He sat on the edge of the bed and rubbed her back. "Jake's gone?

"I ran him off."

She rolled over and brushed the remains of the tears from beneath her eyes. "He thinks *he* makes bad decisions. Hah! I'm world-class."

He put his arms around her, and she huddled against him.

"First, I fall in love with him almost at first sight, then when he says he loves me back, I yell at him and chase him away."

"You could report the truck stolen."

She sat up. "Daddy! I will not, and don't you dare. He has to come back on his own or not at all." She caught his small grin and rolled her eyes. "Don't kid. I'm not in the mood."

"Coming back is his decision solely. Is taking him back yours alone?"

She scooted back against the pillows at the head of the bed. "If he asks me to take him back, I will. After I apologize. How come I never get mad except at the people I love?"

"Because the people you love matter to you." He stood up and said, "I bought a loft on South Main Street by the river this afternoon."

"I beg your pardon?" She sat up straight. "What?"

He walked to the door. "I've been looking and negotiating for a while. I finally found a great place. I'm closing at the end of the month."

"You didn't think to mention that?"

"I apologize for the timing, but I'm doing what you asked. You're right. You no longer need me looking over your shoulder."

"Now? You can't leave! I *do* need you. Sarah needs you."

"Where is she? I expected the two of you to be commiserating or working out strategy."

Charlie shook her head. "She shut herself in her room. I've talked to her through the door, but she told me she wants some time alone. I figured I'd give her some space."

"You didn't yell at her?"

"No, Daddy, I didn't yell. Jake's leaving put all that in perspective. I only got mad because I was so scared." She felt more tears leak down her cheeks. "When I think of what could have happened to Sarah . . ."

"But nothing did."

"Now you're leaving, too. First Steve, then Sarah, then Jake, now you. Hey, want to learn how to drive the people you love away? Charlie Nicholson at your service. Group rates apply."

"You're not losing me. I'm as close as your phone, and I can drive out here from downtown Memphis in forty-five minutes. Now, wash your face and try to get some rest."

"Rest?"

"I'm going to go talk to Sarah, if she'll let me." He pulled the comforter over her shoulders, opened the bedroom door and closed it softly behind him.

Sleep? In what century? What else could go wrong? Just when they were finally getting to know one another, the colonel — her father — bailed out? For her own good? She shouted after him, "I wish people would stop doing things for my own good!"

■ ■ ■ ■

Across the hall, the colonel tapped on Sarah's door. "Sarah, it's your grandfather. May I come in?"

No answer. He took that as a yes. The door wasn't locked. Sarah slumped against the head of her bed, legs drawn up to her chest. Her eyes were red rimmed, and she gave a little hiccup. She refused to meet his eyes.

He sat down on the bed and wrapped his arms around her. He was prepared for her to shake him off, but she held on to him and sobbed. He whispered, "It's okay."

"It's never going to be okay! I can't show up at that school like nothing happened. Everybody'll be laughing at me."

"I doubt if he'll talk about his experience, Sarah. But if he does, you're the victim."

"Granddaddy, I was so scared! And then I lied to Jake. It's my fault he left, just like Daddy."

"You're not responsible for your father's death."

She wrenched away from him, slid off the bed and went to stare out the window. "The last time he came home he was really weird. All they did was fight. He hated me, too.

He told her that one night when he came home drunk from the club. I heard him." She turned to look at her grandfather, and now her eyes were dry. "I didn't want them to get a divorce. My friends with divorced parents hardly ever see their dads. Who would I be if they got a divorce? I mean, until now I've never lived anywhere but on post."

"Could that be why you trusted the Dillon boy? Because he could show you how to fit in?"

"Maybe . . ." She sat beside her grandfather on the bed and leaned against his shoulder. "I was so mad when Daddy left, I yelled at him and told him he didn't have to go. He *wanted* to — anything to get away from Mom and me."

The colonel had no idea what to say to that because it was undoubtedly true.

"Everybody in post housing knows what it means when that black staff car rolls up the street. Everybody stops breathing until it stops at somebody else's house."

"I know."

"Since it was Saturday morning, Mom was vacuuming the living room. She couldn't hear the doorbell, and it rang over and over until I got royally P.O.'d. I ran down the stairs and yanked the front door open.

"When I saw them — the two guys in dress blues — I remember they had on white gloves — I slammed the door in their faces, ran up to my room and locked myself in. Like if I didn't see them or hear them, it wouldn't be real, you know?"

The colonel nodded. "I know."

"I wouldn't let Mom tell me, either. I cranked up the music so high the windows shook. She finally had to yell it at me through the door."

"Sooner or later you had to hear," he said quietly.

"I couldn't cry. I wanted to, but I felt like I had a fever and chills at the same time. And then I started screaming at her. I couldn't let it be *my* fault. It had to be hers."

"It was nobody's fault, Sarah."

"I said some awful things, Granddad. At the funeral . . ."

"I remember. I was there."

"I wouldn't go in the hearse with her or sit with her at the service. Then you two went off by yourselves, and when you came back, you said we were moving down here. I couldn't believe it. I wanted to stay there. His grave is there."

"He's not in his grave, Sarah."

"That night after you left, I found her on her knees in the living room looking at our photo albums and really sobbing. That's when I started to cry, too. I woke up at dawn in her lap. I know it's not her fault. It's not like we have anybody but each other."

The colonel drew in a deep breath. Sarah did not include him in the equation. Not that he deserved to be there after his years of benign neglect — or what he'd thought was benign.

"Now Jake's gone. I couldn't bear it if anything happened to him, too."

"He's not going to a war zone, Sarah. If he loves you both, and I think he does, he'll find his way back to you." He stroked her lovely long hair. "You're going to be fine. I promise you." He stayed until Sarah stopped sniffling, then went downstairs to his study to see if he could figure out how to find Jake.

Ten minutes later, Sarah put her head around Charlie's door and asked, "Mommy? Are you okay?"

Charlie opened her arms, and this time Sarah catapulted into them.

"I'm so sorry," she said.

"Me, too." Charlie rocked her big child in her arms as she had when she was a baby.

She was sorry about plenty in her life, but not about having Sarah. Charlie was getting the farm, the only thing she thought she wanted, but it didn't matter any longer.

What mattered was Sarah snuggled against her. What mattered was having Jake come back. She'd thought how great it would be to be the sole boss, the decision maker.

In a lonely house with no one to share the burdens and the joys with, no one to love. How sad to grow old with only the horses.

Better to lose the place she'd longed for than to lose Jake. Somehow, she'd find him and tell him that.

She realized Sarah was asleep. Charlie eased her down and snuggled her under the comforter, then lay beside her until, finally, she too slept.

CHAPTER TWENTY-THREE

The first thing Jake noticed was how much bigger the oak trees were than he remembered. And how much smaller the cattle barn and house looked. The place was still immaculate, however. His father believed in buying enough white paint at one time to fill his buggy. His sister Helga was keeping up the tradition.

He didn't know whether his mother lived with Helga or had her own place, but someone here had his mother's green thumb. The blue hydrangea still threatened to bury the eastern corner of the house unless kept ruthlessly pruned, and the old Blaze roses wrapped the posts on the front porch so thickly the white paint was barely visible through the blooms. He never smelled a rose without remembering his mother cutting bouquets for the kitchen table.

He sat in his rental car with the air conditioner on high until he could quiet his breathing and slow his pulse. He felt as though he were looking into a parallel universe. Everything was familiar but slightly off.

He finally turned off the ignition, squared his shoulders and took a deep breath. He climbed out from behind the wheel and strode up the brick path before he lost his nerve.

The top porch step no longer creaked when he stepped on it. He'd promised his father to fix it, but he'd never gotten around to it. Somebody had.

He stood in front of the screen door to the house, breathing as though he'd run a marathon. Who would open it? Would they slam it in his face? Time to take his punishment. He rapped on the wood frame and waited.

Nothing happened. No footsteps from inside, no voice calling out to him. His friend from town said Helga and her husband Johann Yoder lived in the house and ran the farm — the farm that would have come to Jake if his father had not disinherited him.

On a late August afternoon Helga might well be in the fields with her husband baling the last of the timothy hay for winter, but he'd be surprised if she were. This time of day she and the other women should all be at home preparing dinner for their families. Amish women always seemed to be cooking or cleaning when they weren't feeding stock or having babies. His mother had fitted in mending and quilting after the kitchen was clean and before the lanterns were turned off, but many women simply collapsed into bed after sixteen-hour days.

He'd prepared himself to be tossed out on his ear. He hadn't anticipated no one being there. The wait was harder than he'd imagined any confrontation would be.

He rapped harder. He couldn't call Helga and tell her he was coming because she had no telephone.

He'd climbed on the first plane to Columbia, Missouri, that had a seat free and left Charlie's truck in short-term parking. Charlie had a second set of keys at the farm. Should he decide not to return, he could call Sean. He and Hank could pick up the truck.

Money was not a problem. He had credit cards and got cash from the ATM at the airport. He wondered whether he should buy presents. They'd probably refuse to accept them.

So he'd rented a car in Columbia, bought

himself clothing, toiletries and a duffel to put them in, took a room in the mom-and-pop motel five miles away from the farm on which he had grown up and driven out here.

Again no response. He pulled the screen door open and let it close again softly. Unhooked. If he opened it, then let it go, it would bang like a rifle shot.

In the summer his mother would threaten not to feed any of them unless the children quit running in and out, banging the screen door. He smiled at the memory of her charging after them with that big wooden spoon she used to beat batter. She never connected, but they'd run and scream and giggle until they were far enough away to feel safe. Did Helga use that old spoon now or was it lost forever?

When he was growing up, no one in the community ever locked a door. Most didn't know where their keys were and had to search for them if they were required. Now, he wouldn't be surprised to find every door dead bolted when the family was away.

A sound. A light footstep inside. Someone was moving, coming closer. He fought a desire to run. Instead he rapped again and called out.

The footsteps stopped. A moment later the big front door swung open.

Behind the screen door stood a boy dressed in a white shirt and black pants. He was a tall eight or a short ten-year-old, blond, with wide blue eyes so like Jake's mother's that Jake caught his breath.

He cleared his throat. "Good afternoon. Might I speak to your mother?"

"She's not here." The boy stayed behind the screen door, a little wary now.

So Helga was out, but her son was too young to stay by himself. "Then may I speak to the person who is looking after you."

The boy thought for a moment, then without turning his back on Jake yelled, "Nana, there's an English wants to see you!"

"An English? Zebulon, you know better. That's rude. Who is it?"

The woman who came out of the shadows couldn't be Jake's mother, though she looked exactly the way he remembered her from when he was seventeen.

She patted her hands together and sent a small cloud of flour into the air, then wiped her palms down her white apron to remove the last remnants of the dough she must be kneading. The scent of yeast and baking bread rolled out the door toward him and made his stomach rumble. He'd been too nervous to eat since he got on the plane last night.

"Yes?" the woman said. Not his mother's voice. Deeper. His mother would have been more likely to say *Yah*? English was her primary language, but she maintained remnants of the Amish dialect she'd learned as a toddler.

"Helga?" he asked.

"Can I help you, mister? You got car trouble?" Her forehead wrinkled as she leaned forward to scrutinize him more closely. "Do I know you?"

"You did, once."

She narrowed her eyes at him. "I cannot think . . . oh." She sank to the floor, her legs crumpling under her.

"Nana!" the child screeched.

Why did he spring it on her that way? Jake pulled the screen door open and dropped beside her, propping her up against his chest. "Helga, breathe. I've got you."

He wasn't certain she had enough breath left in her lungs to speak. She lifted one hand and stroked his jaw as tears rolled down her sun-damaged cheek. "You got so *old*!"

"A foolish thing to say." She flashed a smile at Jake. "We *all* got so old."

He'd walked her into the kitchen and sat her down at the same kitchen table that had been there before he was born, then sat across from her. "Zebulon, bring the cookies and pour yourself a glass of milk. Jacob, in a minute when I can breathe we can have lemonade."

"I can't believe Zebulon is your grandson."

"The eldest of three I have from my Marthe."

"Where are they?"

"At day care. We have Amish day care now just like the English."

"I'm too old for day care," Zebulon said from his grandma's shoulder. He hadn't strayed more than a foot away from her since Jake helped her to her feet. "After school the bus drops me here."

Helga had introduced him to Zebulon as Mr. Thompson, not Uncle Jake.

"Marthe's boss drives her home from the village," Helga said.

"He's English, so he has a big car," Zebulon added. "He picks me up and takes us both home. Mama must not drive the car herself, but we can both ride."

"Where does your mother work?" Jake asked. When he left, Amish women almost never worked outside the home. Now that land taxes and farming were more expensive than ever, even the Plain People might require two incomes to survive.

"We have an Amish co-op to sell produce and cheese and Amish arts and crafts," Helga said proudly. "Not cheap tourist things that are made in China. Marthe works there." She poured Jake some lemonade without ice and handed it across the table to him. Without looking at him, she asked, "So, you have seen China?"

"I took a vacation there several years ago."

"I want to go to China!" Zebulon said. He leaned across his grandmother, picked up a ginger cookie — his fourth since they'd sat down — and tried to stuff all of it into his mouth at one time.

"Zebulon! You know better."

About wolfing the cookie or wanting to go to China?

Zebulon finished the cookie and drank half of his milk. "I want to see the ocean, too. I want to climb Mount Everest."

Helga spoke to him sternly. "Go finish your homework for tomorrow."

"But Nana, I want . . ."

"Go, your mother will be here soon."

He didn't quite stomp out of the room, but he came close. Helga watched while he climbed the stairs and slammed a door, then turned back to Jake with a sigh. She poured herself some lemonade and sipped at it. "He is too much like you. It is the schools that make them discontent with the plain way and hungry for English ways."

"Like me."

"Yes, Jacob Zedediah Thompson!" She shook her finger at him. "Exactly like you, but he has also computers at school and television and cell phones and bomb boxes—"

"Boom boxes," Jake said automatically. "And nobody carries those any longer."

"You see? Nothing is permanent for them. They are never still, never quiet. The cars race up and down on the road with the radios so loud the house shakes. Some of the children driving them look no older than Zebulon, although I know they must be. How can they think with all that noise all the time?"

"Many of them can't."

"And you? Can you think when you are a soldier with a gun and booms going off all around?" She held up her hand. "I know it is booms. Do not correct me."

"You think of staying alive and in one piece and keeping your men alive and in one piece, too."

"You must be good at it. They made you a major."

She had to have kept up with his life if

she knew his rank. "A *retired* major. I tore up my knee in Afghanistan. I'll always limp."

Both her hands flew to her mouth. "Oh, Jake, I am so sorry. I didn't know. Are you in much pain?"

"Not from my leg."

The back door slammed. Helga jumped and her eyes widened.

"Helga, who is from the car outside on the road?"

Jake recognized Johann when he stomped into the kitchen. He'd been five years older than Jake and powerful even then. He was just under Jake's height, and had swelled over the years to twice Jake's width. Except for his burgeoning belly, his weight looked to be pure muscle.

Without the hat he would wear out of doors, his hair was still thick and black, but streaks of white ran from the corners of his mouth to where his beard stopped at midchest. His sleeves were rolled to the elbow, and his black pants were held up by black suspenders. He looked like the Amish farmer he was, who had spent a hot day working his farm.

Johann recognized Jake, as well. He crossed his arms and glared. "I feared when I saw the car it was you come back," he said. "You must leave."

Helga came out of her chair and grabbed his arm. "No, Johann," she pleaded.

"It was not proper to feed him, Helga." His eyes never left Jake's face.

Helga gave Johann a shove that set him back two steps. "No! No man will enter this house and not be fed."

Jake got to his feet. No way would he make trouble between Johann and Helga. It was no more than he deserved. What he'd expected, but not what he'd hoped.

"Sit, Jacob," Helga said in a voice that cut like ice. Johann backed up another step. "And you, Johann, sit down at the table. I will bring lemonade."

"No, Helga . . ."

"Sit! This is nonsense. Jacob is here. I am going to send Zebulon to tell the others to come. Mama must be fetched. She may not see him again."

"She won't recognize him *now.*" Johann had come down from commanding to plaintive. "I am sorry, Jacob. The doctors say your mother has Alzheimer's."

"Don't look like that," Helga said to Jake. "Of *course,* we took her to the doctors." She turned to the doorway and called up the stairs. "Zebulon, I have an errand for you. Right now."

Helga shooed the men into the living

room while she bustled about to get refreshments ready for whoever would come after Zebulon notified them about Jake.

He stared at the fat Hereford cattle in the paddock outside and thought about his mother, lost to them all while she was still alive. Would she know him? How could he bear seeing her if she couldn't recognize him?

Johann didn't speak, but Jake could hear him huffing into his beard.

"I didn't come to make trouble," Jake said.

"Huh. You always made trouble. Helga refused to marry me for a year after you ran away. She said if you came back, she would welcome you whatever the bishop said and it should not be my problem. And now she has."

"Will they shun her, too?"

"I doubt it. Such things are not done any longer for running away or for giving aid to those who do. We save shunning for people who commit crimes or heresy. But you will cause scandal and gossip again and all the family will have to live with that."

"Johann, I want to see my mother and my sisters. Surely you can understand that."

"Sure I can. I cannot understand running away and staying gone for over twenty years.

Why do you come back *now*? Are you dying?"

"Not that I am aware of." How could he explain his timing? Because he had to try to apologize for the hurt he had caused? Because the farm in Tennessee made him remember what it was like to be at peace? To have a family? To love and be loved without reservation? Because he missed them all?

Because he had to start somewhere?

Or because he could only offer Charlie his love if he became a whole man again.

His relatives began to arrive as soon as they could hitch their buggies and drive up. Helga said that they all lived close. They pulled their Standardbreds and Morgan horses under the shade of the big oaks, set their brakes and left the horses untethered.

Rebecca, his second sister, lived closest and came first with a teenage daughter she did not introduce. "The boys will come with Samuel," she said as she climbed down from the buggy. He remembered her as slim as a nymph with long brown hair that she plaited in a single braid and wrapped under her cap. Now she outweighed him, but like Johann, she looked muscular. Her eyes were stern. "So, you show up from nowhere, ain't?"

Marthe arrived with her boss in his automobile. Before she was even allowed to greet Jake she had to listen to Zeb's tale about the newfound English who his grandmother said was some kind of relative, and about China. She gave Jake a cool nod and went straight to her mother in the kitchen.

Finally, Joan, his baby sister, came with her husband and young daughters. Joan had not changed so much as Rebecca and Helga. She was still slim, with blue eyes that reminded him of his mother's. He reached out a hand to her, but she didn't speak to him. She barely glanced at him before she went to the kitchen.

He followed her and asked, "Is my mother coming?"

Becca turned her head. "She comes with Roger in the big buggy where she is more comfortable. Helga said we must bring her. I would not have."

The unair-conditioned house seemed ready to burst at the seams and explode into flames, as well. Jake wiped sweat off the back of his neck with his handkerchief, uncertain what to say.

"Move to the yard," Helga shouted. "All of you! Zebulon, you organize games for the children in the back out of everyone's way. Johann, go get ice from the icehouse. Marthe, watch after the children. Joan will make the lemonade. She makes it better than you."

No one argued. They moved. Jake had known a dozen generals who couldn't command an entire division of troops nearly as well. Helga must have learned it from Pappa. Mama was never much of an organizer.

"Put the food on the tables in the backyard in the shade," Becca called. She followed Jake to the porch and said, "When Zeb showed up and said you were here, we picked up dinner and came." She walked out of sight around the house.

"Remind you of old times?" asked Samuel, Joan's husband. Helga said he was a farrier and a good one.

"We never had parties," Jake said. "My father thought parties were borderline sinful, and my mother usually went along with him. She's twelve years younger."

"Joan told me his first wife died of pneumonia."

Jake nodded. "We worked, went to school as long as the state forced us to and to church on Sunday. My mother conned Pappa into letting me stay until I had the credits to graduate a year early. I did my reading in the school library and worked with the horses at home."

"Do you ever regret it?"

"I miss my family all the time. Do you mean was I wrong to leave? No. I was right to leave. I only wish I had not hurt my family so badly when I did."

"Did you have *rumspringa*?"

"Never."

"I had *rumspringa,*" Samuel said. "I went away to farriery school in Colorado. I didn't plan to come back." He smiled over at his wife. "Then, I met Joan on a visit. That's all she wrote."

"Are you content?"

"Yes. I belong here. You left because you did not. I don't blame you."

Becca came around the corner of the house and pointed down the drive. "Roger is here with the boys and Mama." She crossed her arms and scowled at Jake. This time his heart did just about jump out of his body.

Roger climbed from his buggy and handed down a tall, straight old lady whose snowy hair peeped out from under her cap. Jake recognized nothing about her except those still-bright eyes the color of a bluebird's wing. Then she smiled at everyone. The same smile he remembered and cherished without even the luxury of a photograph to cling to.

His father had not produced children with his first wife, nor in his first years with Jake's mother. Helga came along after they had given up the idea that they would ever have any. Then, as if Helga had unblocked the road to fertility, Rebecca came a year later, Jake eighteen months after Becca, then finally Joan two years later, definitely unplanned. His mother found herself with four young children and no family close by to help her take care of them.

She always smiled and never complained, although she must have been perpetually exhausted. He'd expected her to be bent and shrunken, but the disease that had attacked her mind had not yet wrecked her body. In a way it had preserved her.

Becca settled her in the white wicker rocker on the front porch. Jake dropped to his knees in front of her. "Mama?" he whispered, and took her hand. "Mama, it's me, Jacob." Her hand felt like twigs covered by raw silk.

She looked at him narrowly, then giggled and shoved him away. "You certainly are not my Jacob. You're an old gray-haired English." She pulled her hand from his grasp. "My Jacob is young and ran away to the English. Do you know him? Is that why you say you are him?"

Standing at her shoulder, Becca shrugged. "This is not one of her good days. Don't upset her."

He patted his mother's hand.

"One day my Jacob will come back to run the farm. If you see him, tell him I miss him." She nodded and covered his hand with hers.

He felt Becca tug on his shirt. "You saw. She does not know you. Now come away."

"Let me at least try . . ."

"Come away! Now!"

He sat back on his haunches. His knee hurt like blazes, but he managed to stand without hanging on to the rocker. His mother had already forgotten him. She lay back in the rocker with her eyes closed, humming tunelessly.

He jumped off the edge of the porch and walked away while he fought tears.

"I told you," Becca said. She followed close behind him.

"I doubt she'd recognize me on a *good* day. She's right. I'm an old gray-haired English." He looked back. "She looks remarkably good, Becca. Can't be easy taking care of her. Do you have plenty of help?"

"Don't go there, Jacob. We are not rich,

but we have all we need for us and her, too."

"I didn't mean . . ."

"Didn't you?"

"She's my mother, too. Surely I can contribute to her care?"

"I told you not to go there. You never did before."

"I tried every way I knew, but the money always came back in my face."

"So you walk in on us from nowhere and expect us to welcome you?"

"Not welcome, but at least see me, speak to me."

"Johann is afraid that you want to come home, to take back the farm."

"No way. Pappa disinherited me, remember?"

"English law works different. Or you could buy a farm where we would have to see you."

"Would that be so bad? All these people — children, grandchildren that I didn't realize existed . . ."

"Stay away from our children!"

For a moment he felt certain she was going to slap him. Her cheeks turned red, and her fingers flexed.

She took a breath so deep it was almost a sob.

"Becca, I'm sorry. I didn't mean to upset you."

"Upset me? I'm not upset. I wrote you off years ago when Pappa died and you didn't come."

"I didn't know, Becca. The army didn't receive a death notice and not one of you wrote to tell me. Would you even have let me into the funeral if I'd come?"

She waved him off. "You should have tried, since he died of the broken heart you gave him." She pointed to the barn. "Johann found him stretched in the aisle by the milk cows. Alone."

"That's not true!" They'd been so intent, neither had realized Helga had come up to them. She stepped in front of Becca.

"You know the doctors said Pappa had that weak blood vessel in his brain since he was a child, maybe."

"He might have lived with it for twenty more years they said. It was Jacob."

"Helga, Becca . . ."

"Hush!" Helga snapped. He shut up. "Pappa lived almost ten years after Jake left. You know it. Look into your heart that you cannot forgive."

"Jacob ran away in the middle of the night and hid!" Becca said. "He at least should have told Mama that he was leaving."

"I didn't want her to have to choose between me and Pappa."

She rounded on him. "Did you ask if we wanted to go, too?"

He recoiled. "Would you have left, Becca?"

"That is not the point. You didn't trust us."

"You'd have had to lie to Pappa. Surely you see that?"

"He was right to leave."

"What?" Becca sounded thunderstruck.

Quietly, Joan walked over and stood at Helga's shoulder like reinforcement. But she wasn't smiling. She looked, if anything, angrier than Becca.

"Pappa would never have let him go," she said. "He only wanted Jake to be happy the same way he was." She turned to look at Jake. "Jacob would have been miserable all his life. Mama knew it. I knew it. Helga knew it. You most of all knew it."

"We loved him and he left!"

"And now he has come back."

"He should have come when Pappa died."

"I was in Guam, Becca," Jake said. "I found out because I got a letter of condolence from one of my non-Amish friends, who thought I knew. The family didn't notify the army, so they didn't notify me."

Becca turned on her heel and strode up

the hill toward the buggies. Helga followed her and signaled him to stay with Joan.

"I wrote to all of you," he called after her. "You sent the letters back unopened, refused. My friend said I was still shunned, that you couldn't speak to me."

"You're here now," Joan said. "Why did you not at least tell me, Jake? All those nights you and me, we looked up at the stars and talked about the things we would see and do when we left. You should have asked if I wanted to go with you."

He lowered his head, unable to meet her eyes. "Pappa could throw me out and everyone would say I betrayed him, so good riddance. He would have sent the whole community to bring his baby girl back."

"You should have given me the chance, Jacob Thompson!"

"Would you have been happy away?"

"I have a good husband, beautiful children, a good life. I am happy here." She shoved him. "But you should have *asked*!"

As she turned away, he caught her arm. "Wait, please, Joan. I'm so sorry. I've regretted it ever since. I wrote again and again to tell you . . . ?"

"But Pappa and Johann sent the letters back."

He nodded.

"Oh, Jacob!" She had to reach up to put her arms around him. He hugged her back. "I forgive you."

"Joan?" came her husband's voice. "We need more lemonade."

She laughed. "Coming, Samuel." She touched Jake's cheek and ran to the house.

"Is that what you want? That we should all forgive you?" Becca stood by the hydrangea, watching him as though he were a rattler ready to strike. Helga stood behind her as if to head her off if she attacked. "You want to come home again? Be a good Amish man?"

He had worried over the answer to that from the moment he made his airline reservation. Now, he was amazed at the words that tumbled out of his mouth.

"I begged Pappa to let me leave with his blessing, not like a thief in the night. Becca, I was seventeen years old. I wasn't certain what I wanted, but I knew it wasn't the life I had. I hated leaving the people I loved, but I was more afraid of staying than I was of leaving. I made the only choice I could.

"I don't want the land. I *would* like your forgiveness whether I deserve it or not. But I can live without it if I must. I do not regret leaving, although I regret the way I had to do it. If you never want to see me again, I can live with that. But I would like to send you letters and have you answer if you can."

"You won't come back?" She sounded suspicious. "You are a bad influence on the children. You fill their heads with tales of guns and oceans."

"Becca," Helga said sadly. But she didn't disagree with the words.

He didn't blame any of them. This afternoon he'd tossed what Helga called "a boom" into the middle of their ordered lives. They'd settle down again after he left, although if he were lucky maybe either Helga or Joan would answer his letters. But he had learned what he needed to know. He'd had to leave *alone,* without even telling his mother he was going. And if that choice was right, maybe he could learn to live with the others he'd made.

"Becca, what if Pappa had refused you permission to marry your Roger?" he asked.

"He gave his permission."

"But what if he hadn't."

"We'd have married anyway."

"See?"

"It's not the same thing."

"Yes, Becca, it is."

"Come, everyone," Johann called from the porch. "We eat."

Jake started for his rental car, but Becca's

voice stopped him. "Where are you going, Jacob? Did you not hear? It is time to eat." She grabbed his arm and half dragged him toward the backyard.

"Becca, I don't want to intrude. . . ."

Suddenly she smiled at him. His mother's beautiful smile. "It's not a fatted calf, Jacob. Will sauerbraten do?"

That's when he lost it. Completely. He managed to hold his three sisters at once while they all sobbed. Becca was the first to break free. She slapped him on the chest. "You are a fool, Jacob Thompson." She sniffed. "But you are our brother. Come. Help Mama to the table."

He pulled into his little mom-and-pop motel twenty miles from the farm after dark and half stumbled into his room. It was far from plush, but he felt as though he could sleep on a concrete slab. His eyes burned from the fire that had grilled the bratwurst and heated the water for the sweet corn; his knee ached from getting up and down to speak to his mother, and his head ached from too much noise and too many people.

If the community tried to shun everyone who spoke to him, after today they'd wind up with a lot fewer members.

This night was as close as he might ever

come to reconciling with his family. Eating dinner with them might get them in trouble, even after all these years. Perhaps in time he might come back again, even though Becca was afraid of his influence on the children and steered them away from him even at the dinner table. Marthe interposed herself between him and Zebulon, much to Zeb's displeasure. If it were up to him, the boy would have appropriated Jake and picked his brain until he drove away.

He longed to call Charlie to tell her what had happened, but what he had to say, he needed to say face-to-face. She was probably still justly angry at him. He planned to use the drive to the airport and the plane ride to get his thoughts in order.

Wanting Charlie's respect had forced him to confront his demons. Wanting her love had forced him to beat them. This particular Saint George had his dragon on the ropes. Tomorrow he'd drop off his rental car in Columbia and fly home to Memphis.

Home to Charlie.

CHAPTER TWENTY-FOUR

"Charlie." Mickey stuck his head in the door. "We got a problem."

"Another one?" Charlie leaned back and began to laugh. She couldn't seem to stop. Every time she caught Mickey or Sarah's eyes, she laughed harder until tears streamed down her face. She knew she was on the edge of hysteria, but she couldn't stop. "The only thing worse is an earthquake."

"Close," Mickey said. "Would you buy tornado?"

Charlie sobered fast. "Tornado? There's no bad weather scheduled."

"According to NOAA the front was supposed to go north of us sometime tomorrow morning. It's changed direction and it's coming fast. Southhaven just got hit. Trees down, power lines on the ground. It's a big one, Charlie. It's headed straight for us. Look outside."

Just then the tornado sirens in Collierville sounded. A second later all the lights went off. The only illumination came from streaks of lightning followed much too closely by claps of thunder.

"Where's the colonel?" Charlie asked. She got to her feet and headed out the back door.

"He drove downtown to talk to his decorator," Sarah said with a sniff. "Imagine Granddad with a decorator. And Vittorio went home early."

"Look outside," Hank said from the hall. "It's black out there."

"Get Sean and Mary Anne. Everybody, go climb down into the grease pit." Charlie ran toward the equipment shed. "Sarah, show them how to get down there. Come on, people. Time's awastin'."

The afternoon had been windy with lots of clouds, but nothing like this. The wind whipped Charlie's hair into her eyes. One gust nearly knocked her off her feet. She could hear the others pelting behind her and the whir of Mickey's chair.

"There's a pipe ladder in the wall at the far end to climb down," she shouted. "You'll have to let Mickey down by his arms. We can't get his wheelchair below. Sarah, show them, you've done this before." She started the big tractor, backed it around and aimed it at the pit.

"Hey, you gonna run us down?" Hank shouted into the wind.

"Get down there, then I'll park it over the pit so the outside walls can't fall on you if the shed gets hit in the storm."

"We'll be able to climb out, won't we?" Mickey said.

"I'll leave room for you to crawl out between the tractor's rear tires. *Now,* people!"

Sarah and Mary Anne scrambled down the ladder. Hank and Sean lowered Mickey by his arms until his feet were on the floor and his body propped against the concrete wall with Mary Anne's arm around his waist. "What am I supposed to sit on?" he complained.

"Your rear end!" Hank said. "Here's the cushion out of your chair." He tossed the thick seat cushion down. Mary Anne caught it and lowered Mickey onto his backside.

Sean and Hank scrambled down, then Charlie drove the tractor so that the tires straddled the opening. "I'll park Mickey's chair on the downwind side," she called.

"Hurry!" Sarah said. "It's getting darker." A flash of lightning was followed almost at once by a crack of thunder that echoed in the metal building.

If the time between the lightning and the thunder could be measured at a mile per second, that last strike was much too close. "I'll be down in five minutes," Charlie called. "I've just got to turn the inside horses into the pasture."

"What?" Sean called from the pit. "Charlie, are you crazy? You don't have time."

"Sure I do," she said. "The rest of you stay put. You'll be safe." Over the din they couldn't hear her footsteps.

"We have to go help her," Sean said.

"No, we don't," Sarah said. "She said to stay put. If we all go out there, we'll get separated. I'm doing what she says."

"For once," whispered Mickey.

CHAPTER TWENTY-FIVE

As he drove through Collierville, Jake watched the clouds boil up behind him.

The flight from Missouri had been harrowing. They'd barely gotten airborne when the winds began to buffet them. The plane landed safely at Memphis, but he made a vow not to fly on a feeder airline in bad weather again anytime soon.

Charlie's truck sat in the airport parking garage where he'd left it. Rain drenched it as he drove out from under the roof. He should probably warn Sean he was on his way, but that would entail pulling off and stopping in a parking lot. Even if he believed in talking on cell phones while driving, in this weather he needed all his concentration and both hands on the wheel. The trucks whipping by threw up cascades of water that left him momentarily blinded.

He turned on the radio to hunt for a weather station, but all he found was static.

Great. When he finally pulled off 385 and onto the highway that led to the turnoff for the farm, he stopped under the overhang of a gas station and called.

No answer. Then he realized that the lights at the station were off and the pumps were not in use. No electricity. Not unusual in a storm. It might be off for ten minutes or ten hours. Nothing to do but keep driving and show up unannounced the way he had at Helga's. The storm seemed to be taking direct aim at the farm. He ran across the dial on the radio once more and found a single station announcing a tornado warning. A moment later the sirens went off.

Charlie and the others might not be able to hear the sirens from the farm. This was not merely another thunderstorm — he could smell the ozone. He knew that smell from his childhood. A tornado shelter was a necessity where Jake grew up, and Micah Thompson had built a strong one. Good thing. Jake and the others had hunkered in it often while funnel clouds raced across the sky around them. Their house had never experienced a direct hit, but over the years, they'd lost two run-in sheds and one double plow.

Chances were minimal Charlie's farm would take a direct hit, but he still wanted to be there, to be with Charlie and the others in case they needed him.

He wanted a life with Charlie and Sarah. Whatever it took to make it work, he'd do it. He didn't care where they lived or what they did, so long as they were together. Maybe he could find land close to Charlie's. They'd work it out somehow.

A branch blew by him. He swerved to miss it and momentarily lost control of the truck, before he wrested it back into the center of the road and turned off on the side road that led to the farm. When he turned into the driveway and parked, everything seemed normal. "Charlie," he shouted, leaping out of the truck. "Sean, Mary Anne — anybody!"

Jake ran into the near end of the stable and saw Charlie at the far end.

"Charlie!"

She turned, barely able to keep her feet in the wind coming in the side door. "You left. You took the truck and left." She had to shout. "Where did you go? What did you do?"

"No time for that now. There's a tornado coming. I had to warn you."

"We've got weather radio. I already got the others into the grease pit in the garage. That's the safest place to ride it out. Since you're here, you better go join them."

He grabbed her shoulders and held her at arm's length. "You know that's not the reason I came back."

"Do I?"

He couldn't tell whether the moisture on her cheeks came from the rain or tears.

"I left because I did it again. I made the wrong decision, and you got hurt. I chose not to tell you about Sarah. You trusted me, and I betrayed you just the way I've betrayed everyone else I love."

"Who said anything about love?" She dashed the rain from her cheeks.

"I did."

"You don't run out on people you love."

"I did."

"Well, stop it." She sounded furious. "People make bad decisions all the time. You do, I do, Sarah did. Love is risky. Deal with it."

A five-foot branch covered with leaves struck his shoulder. The sky had gone black. Around them the trees whipped and bent. Bits of gravel from the driveway flew up and struck their faces. He turned his back to the storm. "I did."

She touched his cheek. "You're bleeding." She turned and started walking away. "It's getting closer. We have to get the horses outside. I can't leave them trapped in their stalls."

"I'll turn them out. Get to the grease pit."

She flung her hair out of her eyes. "Too many horses for one person to move." The wind hurled the words back at him as he limped after her.

He heard the horses kicking their stalls. Storms normally didn't bother them, but they knew this one was different. They always knew. "Open the stall doors and turn them out," he said.

"They could run out onto the road and hit a car. We've got to move them into the pasture."

"I said *I'll* do it. Charlie, you go *now.*"

"We have ample time if we hurry." She grabbed the halter and lead line from Pindar's stall, slid the door open only wide enough to get in, haltered him, threw the door wide and pulled him forward. He fought her. He was terrified to stay where he was, but too scared to go outside into the wind. "Come on!" she yelled, wrapping the line across his nose and pulling. "Jake, we'll have to put the geldings in with the mares. No time to take them to the geldings' pasture."

Once in the aisle, Pindar seemed to realize the danger lay inside. He dragged her out the side door, across the gravel road to the pasture gate and tugged at his line while Jake held the gate open.

She barely had time to pull off the halter before the big horse galloped across the pasture to join the mares and foals. They were huddled together in the far corner, heads down, rumps to the rain. The mares formed a circle around the foals, shielding them with their bodies.

Jake brought Annie and Aries out.

As she ran back into the stable, Charlie was caught by a gust of straight-line winds that threw her to her knees.

"Charlie!" Jake pulled her to her feet.

"I'm okay. Come on." She ducked inside and away from the opening. She rubbed her shoulder and grimaced. "Leave me. I'm fine."

The wind blew small branches against the metal sides of the barn and rattled the metal roof like a giant hand playing a snare drum.

Charlie hauled Terror, the pony, to the pasture while Jake opened the stallion's stall. Picard reared and backed against the rear wall. The whites of his eyes showed and his nostrils flared in terror.

"Easy, big guy," Jake cajoled and grabbed a handful of mane. Picard lowered his head when he felt Jake's touch. In that instant of calm, Jake slid the halter on and snapped it under his jaw.

The stallion reared straight up, dragging Jake off his feet and narrowly missing his skull with his right front hoof. "Knock it off, big guy," Jake said. "We're trying to save your neck."

No way could they put him out with the other horses. He'd try to kill the babies and geldings and attempt to breed the mares, even in the middle of a tornado.

The only choice was to let him out into the stallion paddock attached to his stall. It wasn't large, but it would give him some freedom of movement. The fence was electrified, although with the power off, it wouldn't actually zap him. Jake hoped he wouldn't test it. He stood back out of the way as Picard thundered through the open door and into his paddock, then raced to the fence across from the mares' pasture and began to rear and scream for the other horses.

That left Molly in the foaling stall with Flopsy and Mopsy. He found Charlie putting a halter on Molly, who quaked with fear.

The wind had risen to a banshee scream, and the rain pelting on the metal roof made so much noise Jake couldn't hear what

Charlie said.

Jake put his mouth to her ear, and yelled, "We can't put them out."

"We have to!"

"Shut the outside doors, open their stall door and leave them in the aisle."

"What if the tornado hits?"

"Inside, they've got room to move. We put them out, the others could kill them. Come on, we have to shut the doors first."

It took both of them to pull the fifteen-foot-wide steel doors together and latch them from the inside. Jake felt the gravel from the driveway sting his face and arms. He tried to shield Charlie, but she pushed him away.

When they opened her door, Molly hunkered against the back wall. Mopsy was small enough to shelter under her belly, but Flopsy was already too tall to do more than lean against her. Their eyes were wide and frightened, but so long as Molly remained in the stall, they'd stay with her.

"Leave her," Jake said.

"What about us? We can't open the outside doors. She could run away."

"Out the common room door. Then we run along the back of the barn to the grease pit." He grabbed her hand. "No time to argue. Is there room for us with the others?"

"Barely. I parked the big tractor over the pit so the roof wouldn't fall into it." She ran with him.

As they opened the common room door, the giant oak on the far side of the patio leaned away from the barn and then toppled slowly, its roots tearing out of the sodden earth. It fell between the barn and garage and barely missed hitting the roof of the common room.

Even over the cacophony of the storm and the scream of the wind, the tree hit the ground like a bomb. At the far end, the heavy branches propped the trunk a couple of feet above the ground and surrounded it like a green cave.

"We have to go back!" Charlie shouted.

From one second to the next, the world went still. No wind, no rain — silence.

Charlie clutched Jake's hand and whispered, "It's coming. We can't reach the shed."

"Crawl under the tree. Now! Get as far under as you can." Jake thrust her toward the oak as the first blast of hail hit him. "Behind the branches," he said and shoved her to her knees. "Lie flat as you can. They'll stop the debris." Or some of it, he thought.

A direct hit from a level-five tornado could roll that tree across the pasture like a toothpick and the pair of them with it.

If they were lucky, the tornado was a category one or two and would stay up in the clouds — airborne until it passed them.

She dragged him down beside her. He slid under the tree, shoved her farther back against the trunk and covered her with his body. He felt the hail pound through the canopy above them and hoped the leaves would stop the worst of it.

The wind redoubled as it bore down on them. Then came a single scream and the thud of hooves. A second later the stallion vaulted through the branches over their heads and thundered off toward the back pasture.

Charlie buried her face against Jake's shoulder. He pulled her body farther beneath his and shoved them both deeper into the mud.

"I'm so scared," she whispered.

"Me, too." He wanted to live, to love Charlie for a lifetime. Life had never been so precious as it was this minute with Charlie in his arms. He wouldn't let it go . . . wouldn't let *her* go. Was this the reason he'd been saved before?

Any second they could be ripped away

from each other, or impaled by a branch or chopped in two by a piece of flying metal roof. The tree that protected them could roll and crush them. He offered a silent prayer. *Save Charlie. Take me if you have to. I can't live without her.*

If we survive this, he thought, *I'll embrace the heck out of the rest of my life. And it better be with Charlie.*

"I love you," he shouted at her.

"You wait to tell me until we're going to die?"

"We're not going to die. Do you love me?"

She hit him in the chest with the flat of her hand. "Of course I love you. Don't you dare die on me."

"I love you too much to lose you. Trust me." He wrapped his arms tighter around her.

He'd always heard a tornado sounded like a freight train. This one sounded like a dozen locomotives pulling a thousand freight cars straight for them.

"I trust you. I love you, Jake, hold me."

He held her face against his shoulder. Around them the world seethed. Branches scraped his back, one hit his head so hard he saw stars.

In seconds it was over. The locomotives lifted toward the clouds, taking the dirt and debris with them.

They clung together and listened to the retreating wind. "That was too darned close," Charlie said. "You can let me go now."

She turned her face away from him. She was trying to sound casual, but her voice shook. "You can take it back if you want to. Nobody's responsible for anything they say in the middle of a tornado."

"I can't take it back. I'm stuck with it. Unfortunately, so are you. Being loved by me has never worked out well for the lovee," he warned.

"I'm willing to take the risk," she said. The rain and mud cut swaths down her cheeks. "My lovers haven't been all that fortunate, either."

"This particular love is not a risk," he said. "I get to love you forever whether you love me or not."

"You know I do. I've loved you since I found you crooning to the stallion. I knew you were special."

"Specially screwed up."

"That, too. I'm sorry I blamed you about Sarah."

"I shouldn't have let her con me. I don't know much about teenage girls, but she knows I care about her."

Charlie chuckled. "Too right she knows. She played you good. Jake, Sarah and I are a package deal."

"I'm aware of that."

"It doesn't put you off?"

"Off loving you?" He shook his head. "I wouldn't be put off if you came with a pride of lions."

"Sometimes I think Sarah's worse. You are a good man, Jake Thompson." She caressed his cheek and left a streak of mud. Her eyes widened. "Oh, heaven! The others! The horses! The stallion!"

"Come on." He slithered backward in the mud beneath the tree.

"You're bleeding," she said.

"You're muddy."

They managed to scramble out from under the branches. He lifted her dirt-covered chin and kissed her softly.

"Not like that," Charlie said, "Like this." Nothing soft about her kiss. It was deep and open and painted with the heat of their bodies and their hearts.

"Okay," he said when they broke apart. "You want me, you got me."

"For how long?"

"Forever," he said.

"No doubts about your decision?"

"This is one decision my heart's making

for me. I love you, Charlie. I have nothing to offer you except that heart. It's too soon, I know, but at some point, maybe you'd consider marrying me."

"Who says it's too soon? Yes, yes, yes."

In the aftermath of the tornado the world had taken on a yellow-green glow. All that remained of the storm was a gentle rain that shimmered in the late-afternoon sky. In the west, the sun peeked out, promising a spectacular sunset.

"Look," he said, and pointed to the east. On the horizon, a double rainbow arched across the sky.

With their arms around each other, they turned in a slow circle. The other large trees seemed to have survived, only the giant oak — their savior — had fallen.

"From the back the stable looks okay," Jake said.

"The equipment shed doesn't." She slipped out of Jake's arms and ran toward the remains of what had been a large metal building only seconds before.

The roof and two walls had collapsed.

They picked their way carefully over the twisted metal.

"Hey, anybody!" Sean's voice. "Hey! Remember we're down here."

Charlie made her way to the lip of the

grease pit and peered between the wheels of the tractor. "Is everyone all right? Sarah?"

"We're okay, Mom. Where were you? I was so scared."

"I'm fine, baby."

"Drive the tractor out of the way so we can climb out," Hank said. "Got a little claustrophobia working here."

"I don't think I can move it," Charlie said. "Jake and I will have to pull you over the edge."

"Is Jake up there?" Sean asked. "Jake, my man, you came back."

"Where's my wheelchair?" Mickey asked.

"Where was it?" Jake asked.

"By the tractor. We couldn't get it down here, so I'm sitting on my rear in the grease."

"It's probably been blown to Bolivar," Charlie said.

"Hey, crip, now you'll *have* to walk," Hank said.

"That wheelchair cost twenty-five-thousand dollars, jerk."

"Mary Anne?" Charlie asked.

"I'm okay," Mary Anne said. "I don't ever want to do that again."

"Is that a horse up there?" Sean asked.

Charlie jumped as she felt warm breath on her neck. "Well, hello there, Picard." She locked her fingers through the stallion's halter. "That was some jump you made for a big ol' fat draft horse."

He snorted softly.

"Anybody got a belt I can borrow to use as a lead line?" she asked.

"Here," Sean said, and handed up his leather belt. "If my jeans fall down, cover your eyes."

Five minutes later everyone stood on the concrete floor of the garage amidst the debris.

"What a mess," Charlie said. "It'll take weeks to clear out and rebuild. In the meantime, we need to get tarpaulins to cover the equipment."

"You're insured, aren't you?" Sean asked.

"The structure is. I'm not sure it'll cover all the work that'll have to be done."

"Could have been the carriages," Mickey said. "Hey, is my carriage okay?"

"Didn't hit the carriage barn," Charlie said. "They should be all right. So's the stable."

The weather sirens still keened in the distance. "Is that another one?" Mary Anne whispered.

Charlie shook her head. "They'll go on for half an hour at least. Look at the sky. The worst is past."

While Jake led the stallion back into his paddock, Charlie searched inside the barn for Molly and the twins, only to find they'd never left the foaling stall. Both foals were suckling while Molly munched from her hay net. She gave Charlie a casual glance as if to say, *Tornado? What tornado?*

Charlie shut the door to the stallion's stall and went back to hand Sean his belt. "The stallion got a few little nicks and scrapes," she said. "Nothing we can't handle later. We need to check the others."

Sensing that the storm was past, all the horses gathered by the pasture gate.

"We really lucked out," Sean said from the common room door. "Mickey's wheelchair needs a good scrub, and it may not start without a new battery, but it slid under the front end loader where the wind couldn't blow it away. We probably lost a bunch of wrenches and tools in the pond or the back pasture, but that stuff can be replaced."

"Uh, Charlie."

Charlie's head whipped around to stare at Mickey, who leaned against the wall using both his canes. "Not all that lucky." He pointed out the front door.

A mature maple tree had fallen straight across the road in front of the farm.

"We have to move it," Jake said. "The neighbors may need help. Charlie, go get the tractor."

Charlie looked at him in astonishment. That was the voice of command.

"We can't get it out," Charlie said.

"Come on," Hank said. "We need to see if we can move the stupid tree without it."

Down by the road, Jake climbed across the limbs. The tree was neither as old nor as big as the oak, but it was taller and heftier, and long enough to span the road and ten feet on the far side. "The ditch on the other side is flooded," he said. "Even an ambulance couldn't get through." He looked at the others. "Hank, you and Sean get Pindar and Aries harnessed with the logging harness and put the chains on them."

"What about you and me?" Mickey asked. He'd reclaimed his chair, but kept his braces on.

"Find the peavey hooks and the chain saws if they're not buried under the debris." He turned to Sarah. "Does your computer have a battery backup?"

"Sure. I have to have a backup. Our power goes out if there's a cloud in the sky."

"Then go on the net and get word to Collierville that the road is closed in front of the farm."

"NOAA should know we've been hit, but not how badly," Charlie said. "Sarah, see if you can raise anyone down the road and tell them about the tree. Here, take my cell phone and call the colonel. He's probably frantic."

Sarah nodded and ran for the house.

Before Jake had time to do more than assess the fallen tree, Sean drove up on the four-wheeler. Two chain saws lay in the back on top of safety goggles, heavy gloves and a can of chain saw fuel.

"How do we cut up this tree?" Jake asked. "You're the expert."

"Expert twenty years ago, maybe. We don't have time now to take all the big limbs off. Once the horses are in draft, we'll have an idea of where the branches are going to dig into the ground or catch on the fence and hang up . . . We'll remove those limbs, but leave the others until later. Hank and I can handle the saws. You'll have to drive."

"Charlie . . ."

"I can't handle them the way you can," she said. "Driving a carriage is different from this. You're the only one of us that ever plowed behind a pair."

"Long time ago."

"It'll have to do. Here come the horses."

"Right."

"Good thing we borrowed this stuff to practice logging with," Mary Anne said. "How do we hook the horses up?"

"Wait for me," came Mickey's voice. His muddy chair bumped across the sodden lawn toward them. "You forgot the peavey hooks." The metal bars stuck out like lances on either side of his lap.

Jake and Charlie harnessed the horses and attached the chains. Sean fastened them around the tree.

"Everybody out of the way," Sean shouted. "Okay, Jake, give it a shot."

"I have no idea how this trunk's going to move."

"If it moves at all," Sean said.

"It'll move," Charlie said. "Jake can do it."

Jake felt his heart swell. This was one trust he would not betray if he had to drag the blasted tree out of the road single-handed. He grinned at her, clucked and gave that single earsplitting whistle he'd given at the logging site.

The two horses moved forward until the chains tightened and brought them to a sudden standstill.

"They've never been to a pulling contest where they dragged concrete blocks across an arena," Charlie said. "They're carriage horses. They don't know how to strain that way."

"It's in their blood," Jake said. "They'll pull." Both horses backed up a step and shifted sideways in an attempt to avoid the weight behind them. When they discovered they were harnessed together, they stopped straining and relaxed. "Walk on," Jake commanded, and gave that whistle once more.

This time they knew what to expect. Their rumps dropped and their shoulders strained forward as they felt the weight of the tree. "Walk on!" He clucked and snapped the lines against their rear ends.

For a moment he thought they wouldn't or couldn't exert enough power. The chains clinked, Pindar huffed, Aries snorted and both horses dropped four inches in height as they hunkered down against their harness and shoved their broad chests against their collars.

The log moved.

"Walk on!" Jake shouted.

"Keep going!" Sean called. "We don't have to cut the branches. She's going to ride up over the fence."

The mud helped. The tree slid forward a foot at a time while the others stood well out of the way, offering both applause and encouragement for both him and the horses

— mostly the horses.

Once the big branches slipped across the fence and off the road, the horses had an easier job pulling the smaller branches from the top of the tree out of the way.

"Got it!" Sean shouted. "You're clear."

Everyone cheered.

"Whoa!" Jake loosened the lines. His whole body trembled with the exertion. He hadn't yet dried out from the storm, so he couldn't tell how much was rain, but he suspected what drenched his shirt was mostly sweat. "Good boys," he whispered. "Good ol' boys." He leaned his forehead against Pindar's damp neck.

In the distance, he heard sirens coming fast.

A minute later two pumpers and an ambulance swept by on the road, which had been impassable only minutes earlier. The driver of the first pumper stopped and leaned out the window. "Anybody hurt?"

Sean shook his head. "Damage to the buildings, but no casualties. We don't know about farther down the road."

"We'll check." He waved and took off with his sirens blaring once more. The other vehicles followed.

"You did it," Sean said, and shook Jake's hand with his right one. In all the excitement, he'd apparently forgotten he could crush Jake's fingers.

"No, they did it." Jake slapped Pindar's shoulder. "Come on, let's get them unhooked and into the barn. They deserve some extra oats."

The rest of the day degenerated into chaos. Weather radio reported that the tornado had lifted after it took out the colonel's equipment shed, only to drop down and rip off their nearest neighbor's barn roof.

The colonel drove in unscathed an hour after the tornado passed. Relieved, Charlie and Sarah hugged him.

"I got hold of Dick Rigsby down the road," he said. "He lost four locust trees, which is no great loss, and one of his oaks had the top twisted off it as though it had been felled with a chain saw."

"How're his cows?" Sean asked.

"Fine. So are his family and hands. They have a storm shelter."

"Which we are going to put in as soon as possible," Charlie said. "I am not going through this again."

"Can't fit their Santa Gertrudis bull into a storm shelter," the colonel said.

Sarah ran out with the small battery-powered television. "They've lost some roofs on the McMansions in Collierville, but nobody's hurt that they know of."

The colonel looked around him at the branches, leaves and pieces of metal siding that cluttered the whole area. "Not going to be much carriage driving for the next few days."

"Sure there will," Mickey said. "Now that they've got the hang of it, the horses can pull all the debris out of the garage."

"And we've got to get the Campbells to cut up those trees and remove them," Sean said. "Jake and Hank and I can gain some experience helping them."

"You'd better plan on doing it yourselves," the colonel said. "I doubt the Campbells will have a free day before Christmas."

"Looks as if I'll have my hands full fixing the equipment so it'll run," Mary Anne said. "Mickey can clean the tools we recover."

Sean and Mary Anne heated canned tomato soup, spiced it up with basil and sour cream and made sandwiches, which they ate at the colonel's kitchen table.

The colonel disappeared to his office and joined them half an hour later. "Maurice and DeMarcus are both okay, so is Vittorio. They'll all come back tomorrow. We're going to need all hands."

Jake sat at the table with the others for the first time. Sarah was staring at him with adoration. Charlie hadn't seen that look of hero worship since Steve left for his third tour.

She walked out on the dark patio after she'd finished eating and sat in the glider. The others were having too good a time to miss her. Reaction had set in. She was so tired her hands shook.

Ten minutes later she heard him in the rustle of the leaves, but he didn't slide onto the glider beside her.

"Where did you go after you left?" she asked quietly. Back to the streets?

"I went home."

She caught her breath. Had he come back only to leave again forever? What if he asked her to go with him? *Would* he ask?

Her adrenaline went from normal to stroke zone in a nanosecond. She fought to keep her voice level. "You asked me to marry you."

"Not yet. I have nothing to offer you, not even a healthy mind, although I'm getting there. I can't support you and Sarah."

She turned around to stare into the darkness. "It's not that you can't marry me, it's that you don't want to."

She didn't see him move, but in the next

instant he was beside her, arms wrapped around her. "You asked me what I wanted, and I gave you garbage. I want you. With you the world is full of light and laughter. Before you, there was nothing but darkness and despair. During the tornado, I wanted to live, but only if I could live with you."

She sniffled. "Then what's all this bunk about not marrying me?"

"While I was gone, I figured out that I've had enough of the big wild world. I want to go back to my roots, the whole rural thing."

"You want to go back to Missouri and buy a farm?" The hair rose on her spine. Would she, could she uproot Sarah and her for Jake?

"I was thinking more of finding some acreage around here, if I can find any I can afford."

She laughed. "Jake, I *have* a farm."

"I can't . . ."

"What are we, Victorian? You want to buy in officially, that's fine. Pay for the tornado shelter. But none of that matters, Jake. I could hand you a bunch of stuff about needing your expertise to help run the place. I do, but I could get along without you or hire somebody. I thought running this farm alone would be exciting. But without you, it's no fun at all, it's lonely and miserable and I have visions of spending every night for the rest of my life alone in that big Lincoln bed."

"Will Sarah accept me?"

"She accepted you before I did. So, will you marry me or what? I warn you, I don't like long engagements."

He pulled her into his arms and kissed her thoroughly. When she could catch her breath, Charlie asked, "Is that a yes?"

"Definitely."

"Then get yourself down on one knee and propose properly."

"No way," he said.

"Oh, shoot, I forgot you *can't* get down on one knee."

"Not and get up again. Will you accept me sitting in the glider?"

"I'd accept you swinging from a trapeze."

"What if I come apart at the seams again?"

"You won't, but if you do, we'll handle it *together.* One day I may even be able to meet your family. Jake, when we needed a leader to get that tree off the road, you stepped up. When we needed decisions, you made them. It's in your blood. You can't help it. This, Jacob Zedediah Thompson, is not a bad decision."

"You're taking a big risk."

"So are you. Life's a risk, Jake. Whatever

we face, we'll face together."

"Then, Charlotte . . ." He slipped off the glider onto the floor. "Ow, I may never get up from here. Charlotte, will you marry me?"

"I'd add come hell or high water, but we did that already. Yes, Jake, love of my life, I will marry you forever and forever."

"About time!" The floodlights over the patio came on so bright that they had to shade their eyes. Mickey walked onto the patio using his braces and two canes, the others crowded after.

"You eavesdropped?" Charlie protested. "I cannot believe that! You all flunk the course."

"After today? Fuhgeddaboudit," Mickey said. "And remember, I get to drive the Cinderella carriage to the wedding."

ABOUT THE AUTHOR

Animals are important in all of **Carolyn McSparren**'s books. She has bred, birthed, trained, ridden and driven horses most of her life. At the moment she rides her dressage horse, a 17.2-hand half Clydesdale, and drives her carriage horse, a 16.2-hand half-Shire mare. A RITA® Award nominee and Maggie winner, Carolyn has lived in Germany, France, Italy and "too many cities in the U.S. to count." She teaches writing seminars to romance and mystery writers, and writes mystery and women's fiction, as well as romances. Carolyn lives in the country outside Memphis, Tennessee, in an old house with three indoor and half a dozen barn cats, three horses and one

husband, not necessarily in order of impor-
tance.